HESTER

HESTER

A NOVEL

Christopher Bigsby

VIKING

For Pam, with all my love

VIKING
Published by the Penguin Group
Penguin Books USA Inc., 375 Hudson Street, New York, New York 10014, U.S.A.
Penguin Books Ltd, 27 Wrights Lane, London W8 5TZ, England
Penguin Books Australia Ltd, Ringwood, Victoria, Australia
Penguin Books Canada Ltd, 10 Alcorn Avenue, Toronto, Ontario, Canada M4V 3B2
Penguin Books (N.Z.) Ltd, 182-190 Wairau Road, Auckland 10, New Zealand

Penguin Books Ltd, Registered Offices:
Harmondsworth, Middlesex, England

First American Edition
Published in 1994 by Viking Penguin, a division of Penguin Books USA Inc.

1 3 5 7 9 10 8 6 4 2

Copyright © Christopher Bigsby, 1994
All rights reserved

LIBRARY OF CONGRESS CATALOGING IN PUBLICATION DATA

Bigsby, C. W. E.
Hester / Christopher Bigsby.
p. cm.
ISBN 0-670-85588-X
I. Title.
PR6052.I35H47 1994
823´.914—dc20 94-18391

Printed in the United States of America

Nathaniel Hawthorne laid aside his pen, one January day, and went skating on the frozen lake below his home. The ice bore the marks for three days, a signature which glowed crimson at sunset. The ice melted. The signature remained. What once is written can never be erased.

Those who walk towards the sun are followed by a shadow. The future is the sun. The past is the shadow. Hester walked towards the sun.

I danced in the morning
When the world was begun,
And I danced in the moon
And the stars and the sun,
And I came down from heaven
And I danced on the earth
At Bethlehem I had my birth.

Dance, then, wherever you may be,
I am the Lord of the dance, said he
And I'll lead you all, wherever you may be,
And I'll lead you all in the dance, said he.

Dissent had floated down on England like dandelion seed. Walk abroad and you could feel the air heavy with threat, smell a summer lightning. Hard-faced men turned away from colour and warmth and sought the purity of black and white. Suddenly there was no softness. Everywhere was leather and steel, thud of hooves and jingle of harness closing about running figures. Strenuousness. God's name become a lash; beauty a monstrous affront.

There was a sound heard in village and town: the cold, sliding, metal scrape of a sword's withdrawing. Horses' flanks were churned with blood, and spittle flew. The kingdom was no longer a kingdom. Broken bodies, terror of the spirit. There were hessian sacks in tufted grass and never ask what might be found therein. Fear was as real as a table. Four square. Solid. A knife laid out to slice. A time had come. Something was being born, slimed and entangled but drawing a first terrible breath.

There are cliffs where each surging fold of water draws out the strength of compacted rock until a sudden sinking of land into sea washes out the past. Fossil creatures shine like bronze in the spray, burnished by the cold Atlantic swell. This is the past which they hoped to expose, flushed out from cover by the sea of their cold faith.

All nations have a purging time. Poisons and perversions are burned away. It is a time of leeches, poultices and heating cups. All codes and rules and practices and conventions and civilities and understandings are refused. All is in abeyance. The air is thin. Leaves stir in febrile spirals. The mad can pass as sane and the sane must doubt their sanity if they are to prove it real. Boys play truant without rebuke. Ink stains on fingers fade by riverbank and tidal pool. Shadows lengthen. The cool grey of church and cathedral is lit by sparks. Granite and marble shatter. A cry is heard that was never heard. Candles gutter as men listen for the sound of hope denied. In the name of change. In the name of resistance to change. In the name of purity. In the name of cleansing, like a sword in the thick clogged earth. In the name of God.

Yet the heart still races at a young girl's smile. Fruit is still preserved on the slate shelves of cool kitchen pantries. Fingers are still cut by twine so that the sinews shine white in the sun. Cattle still sway, heavy in narrow lanes. Lives continue to shape meaning out of mere event, though such shape be no more than that of a bubble turning slowly as it rises, like shining from a morning lake seen by one whose own disordered self exists in the space between faith and thwarted desire. A territory which is our own; the country in which we reside.

The times are always the best and the worst, while without pain is no knowledge nor recognition of content. Once there was a unity. A time without time. Time was born out of sin. What was connected was separated. From separation language was born. From separation came song to reconnect blood with earth. From separation came the division of what is from what appears to be. And without story there is nothing. For what else can connect the young girl's smile, the cut finger and the cattle? What else can send the present to the past so that we will know that we have lived before and will live again? This is a story from those times when a stitch was dropped and a thread began to unravel, this way, that way, until the pattern seemed quite undone and the world to unmake itself.

Everything died that year. Toads flattened into outline, as though pressed in a Bible. Rabbits panted in the sun, stretching their legs out until the moment of death. Fruit shrivelled. Old women stopped for breath, then stopped for ever, their breath never coming. Birds died on the wing and inscribed a lost meaning in their tangled fall. Water was brackish, the air thin, the ground cracked, the will defeated, the imagination enervated, the heart broken. The spine of history was snapped and time so many notes without stave.

At such a moment was born a child whose eyes were clouded for a day. The child was a girl; the clearing eyes a deep gentian. She was born in sin and the knowledge of that sin lay in her heart awaiting the fructifying moisture of self-contempt. She was born to change the world as we are all born to change the world, though she contained within her the mildewed seed of the past. She was the first, faint sound of a new pure instrument or one whose impurity would inspire a harmony in the hearts of those who thought the world a clock without hands, a sleeper denied his dreams.

Lacking a father, she looked only to the woman who held her and, though her infant arms flailed, her eyes seemed to focus with a cold abstraction long before she should have been able to rest her gaze on a single face. There was a fierceness in her from the first. She took the breast to her mouth and tore at the nipple as though desperate for the sustenance it offered. Her hand, the while, traced an abstract pattern on her mother's skin, raising a faintly patterned abrasion on the white of the flesh.

From time to time the mother would cry out in pain but her daughter seemed to take it for laughter or find in the stifled gasp an urging to greater efforts. Certainly at such a moment the dimpled fist would rake across her mother's nakedness as though this child of God and the devil wished to write its own epitaph on living tissue.

3

She knew nothing of her mother's ignominy, nothing of a heart once turned to ice by calculation, cruelty and a cold detachment from human need. She knew nothing, either, of the reckless passion which melted that ice, of the secret which time would decode or the man who transmuted love into sin and sin into a kind of living death. She was a pearl in a deep-sea oyster whose brilliance lay fathom deep awaiting the hour.

*

To the south and west of the city, up against the river Yare, which broadens towards Yarmouth but which here is no more than ten or fifteen feet across, is the hamlet of Colney. Like many a Norfolk village, no matter how small it may be, it has clung tenaciously to this flat land for centuries. The Romans were here and the Vikings, the name of nearby Norwich bearing their mark. 'Sweyn came with his fleet to Northwic and wasted and burned the burgh,' says the chronicle. This was the land of Guthrum, the Northman, whom Alfred turned to the one true church. Domesday speaks of Colney's landowner, his serfs and cattle, while the Saxons raised a church here before the Normans moved up from southern triumphs to take possession of the land, bringing with them their alien language and still more alien ways. Here, ploughs turn up golden torques, burnished bright in the dull soil. There are secrets buried a spade's length deep. The plague passed this way more than once, the carbon-blackened ruins of the houses, purged with fire, still visible on the valley side, like shattered teeth in a broken skull. The Black Death brought its pustulating boils and blackened flesh in 1349 and then again and again, like a returning winter, until 1665. Yet life still forced its way through the soil. Wheat was still harvested and ground for flour.

Alongside the church, where the river narrows to a ford, was and is a farm, though today its buildings have been reshaped into houses and the cattle-yard transformed into rough-cut lawns. Then, the farmhouse was two narrow cottages run together as one alongside two low buildings where cows were calved and pigs rooted in the mud and straw. Next to this was a gaunt rectory and beyond that a once great hall now faded and decayed.

Above its doorway an heraldic device but so grown about with ivy and wisteria, so webbed by spiders and stained by time, that it is impossible to make out the shapes emblazoned there.

Across the river on the high ground to the west is another hall, from which the cathedral's spire, some three miles distant, can be seen, sometimes, as it catches the evening sun, seeming to blaze like a torch held up against the darkening sky. At the time of which I speak there was living in that place a man whose ideas were not those of his contemporaries. Indeed, he had withdrawn himself precisely because he shared so little with them. Today we might call him a scientist. They had sharper words for those who saw things others did not. That isolation, however, had worked upon his mind so that he fancied himself made of some other material than those he encountered. From the unkempt gardens of his home he looked down on those in the hamlet below, and in the distant city, in more than a physical sense. Perhaps the air he breathed, suffused as it was with chemicals stored in yellow-white jars and thin transparent tubes, did something to his mind. And this was a time when every hedgerow possessed its secret. Purple berries, red-tinged leaves, pink-gilled toadstools all held the key to the cipher of life. Now they are playthings for those bored with life before they have lived it. This man had other motives. His own body was distorted, not grossly so but it was as if some force had seized him at birth and wrenched him quite about so that one shoulder was higher than the other. No Richard III, nonetheless he was doubtless sensitive enough to keep his own company and try what he might with the chemistry of nature.

For several years he had lived in Amsterdam where his adoptive father's business took him and it was his knowledge of the language which had broadened his researches. Indeed, he had a great facility with other tongues, adding German and French to the Latin and Greek he had acquired with the help of a private tutor. Nor was the only fascination of such languages the ease with which they gave him access to knowledge. He was drawn to language itself which encoded meaning in sound and writing as though the rituals of speech and calligraphy were in some sense the essence of that meaning. If he had any objective in his seemingly random reading, or even in the experiments with which he filled his hours, it was the search for a door through which he could pass to some other sphere. He was no simple alchemist desiring to transmute lead into gold, save in a symbolic sense, though he did not forbear to do as poets do, place together substances which never met in nature to see if they might breed meaning. The transformations which concerned him were those effected when thought is converted into words and words exchanged for others in such a way as to change thought itself. The chemical reagents with which he chose to experiment existed as a kind of parallel to this concern, for here, too, he suspected some hidden code which must govern the exchange of properties and offer explanation for the transformations which he witnessed as mere powder exhaled its properties as gas, and metal chose to flow like animated water in his crucible.

Nor was he so aberrant in his concerns. At that same time in Norwich there lived a man whose travels had taken him through Ireland, France and Italy and whose whole house and garden became a paradise and cabinet of varieties, with plants and natural objects gathered together. Part mystic, part physician, Sir Thomas Browne contemplated death and its habiliments. Yet while he was rewarded and in the public eye, others, like the man of whom I speak, pursued their ends in private, though he had seen Sir Thomas walk between the Popinjay Inn on King Street and the Maid's Head by Cook's Row, and on past Bishop's Gate where men had been burnt for their faith.

It was in Amsterdam, the City of Refuge for Nonconformists, that he had met those who had fled their native Norwich there to worship as they pleased, and though he was not one of them he saw in their Nonconformity an image of his own rebelliousness. No religious purist, indeed, for reasons of his own, uneasy in the presence of Christian piety, he nonetheless responded to the fierce cabals they formed against restraint. He cared nothing for their pieties, deriding the Reverend William Bridge expelled from St George's, Tombland, for refusing to read King James's *Book of Sports*, which urged athletic sports and dances after public worship, but admired the will which resisted all coercion and which had speeded a number on their way to the New World on board the *Mayflower*.

As was to be expected of such a man at such a moment, he was the focus of rumour and suspicion. It was suggested that he had abandoned his wife before coming to the village, a woman, it was hinted, horribly disfigured in one of his experiments. Others believed him to converse with the devil but since none wished to attract the attention of witch-finders, notorious for the randomness of their science, none spoke aloud and in public what they whispered in private.

For a time he employed a housekeeper, a woman whom no other would, her hare-lip branding her a sinner and perhaps more besides. The two co-existed, each wrapped up in their own privacies, walking around one another like animals with adjacent territories. She abjured the study, with its clutter of retorts and crucibles, he the kitchen, its copper saucepans hung side by side like a series of blank family portraits. Her lack of skill as a cook was matched by his indifference to food or any other pleasures, as it seemed. In some ways her mute resistance to him seemed part of the bargain he made in sacrificing his privacy. Hers was perhaps deeper than his own. Certainly she offered no companionship, if that is what he sought. He was content, or so it seemed, only with himself, and perhaps with the animal he kept stabled behind the house and which, whatever the weather, he rode each afternoon. Not, as you might imagine, a wild, black stallion but a handsome bay gelding, it carried him each day around the perimeter of his property as on Rogation Days the minister would lead his flock around the parish boundaries carrying Bible and cross. Except that he carried nothing but a brown leather whip with which from time to time he would tap the withers of a horse which needed no such reminders from a master whose path never varied.

A mile to the north, down the track which led to Norwich, was another building, set in open parkland. Here, a young woman was to interest herself in the fetid squalor of Victorian prisons. We know the past shapes all our presents but could it be

7

that the future casts a shadow back in time, bending our lives to fit its patterns? Certainly you could say that there was something of Elizabeth Fry in the woman whose home had once also been a hall, albeit a building whose music was in a minor key and whose chief characteristic was decay. She now lived in a farm marked on three sides by the river, the church and the minister's house. She was no country yokel. She might rise with the sun and perform the duties of a farmer's daughter but her mind was her own. Beside her bed were books of devotion. In the front parlour was an embroidery frame. Her parents were of the nobility but time and fortune and a kind of inherited lethargy had fretted away the symmetry of rank and wealth until faded clothes folded in a rusting trunk were the only remains of former days. Nobleman's hall had been exchanged for yeoman's farm and subtle daughter become milkmaid. It was she whom the man from Colney Hall met one winter's afternoon on the lane which passes the low flint wall beside the church. And his name? Let us call him what he later chose to call himself: Roger Chillingworth.

November had brought a first dusting of snow but now had come a sudden ice shower which angled down towards the earth. Hawthorn and may were rimed with a crystal sheath, branches of ash and elder dragged down by the weight of frozen rain. The wind which had blown from the south the previous night now swung round to the north-east. Above the church a metal cockerel turned its metal tail. It was no day to go riding but the ice without found its match within as Chillingworth dug his heels into the flanks of a horse which turned its head from the driving sleet only to have it pulled violently back by its rider. He rode through the woods which fringed his property and then looped round where the river's double bend seemed to spell out a letter in the marsh. Still he rode on, though he could no longer see more than a few paces ahead; but horse and rider knew this land as well as anyone so that they reached the ford without difficulty. Here, though, the water boiled over rocks now hidden beneath a twisting current. Slate black, it surged past bearing the tangled limbs of trees which danced around one another like so many broken-legged drunkards at a village fair. The horse resisted, pulling back from the tumbling blackness, and for a second or so it seemed that its will would prevail; but two heels in his ribs and the pistol crack of a hand on his flank drove him on. A crust of ice had formed on the bank and it was down this that the animal tried to step, a ballerina pointing a graceful toe towards the stage. Still it pulled back, its nostrils wide with terror. But the man forced him on, kicking his sides and slashing at him with a whip. As he did so a hoof slipped along and through the compacted snow onto a glazed rock. In fighting to regain its footing it turned sideways in the river and staggered forward. For a second Chillingworth clung desperately to its neck, smelling the dank odour of sweat and leather, before tumbling in a graceless tangle into the rushing water. For a moment longer he held on to the reins then let go as a pain shot clean and sharp through his shoulder.

In summer a sluggish stream no more than a few feet deep, by winter the Yare had deepened and widened until it moved with a slow force which was deceptive in its power. Hence its ancient name: Garw, the rough water. So Chillingworth was tumbled around as he reached for a footing and swept into the centre of the river. At first the sudden cold brought a clarity of mind so that everything seemed to stand out in surprising detail, despite the driving snow. For a second he felt calm, detached, almost confident. Even now it was barely thirty feet to the opposite bank. Then, amidst the rushing spray, he was slowed, sucked downwards as his riding-boots began to fill. He tried to reach a hand to them, his face staring blindly through the dark, cold water. Then, as he kicked out, hoping to force one off with the other, a branch, spinning round in its own vortex, struck him in the throat, stifling a scream he neither heard nor knew he uttered.

There is little doubt he would have drowned, absurdly, pointlessly, had it not been for a willow branch, weighed down with ice, which interrupted his passage and swung him gracefully to shore under the pressure of his weight, the current and its own tensile suppleness. Nobody came to his aid because nobody knew of this drama performed on an empty stage. Neither could he call out, his voice refusing to sound after the blow to his throat. He snatched desperately at the ice-encrusted reeds and struggled to pull himself on to the bank. When at last he succeeded he turned on his back and stared up into the driving snow which formed and dissolved strange shapes in the angled wind. The hand which held the willow branch was like a claw, frozen in position and streaked with blood. The white of an exposed tendon showed where the wood had cut into his fingers. Slowly the world came back to him and he began to shake. He pulled first one boot and then the other from his feet and emptied them of water before forcing them on again.

He looked behind him at the old farmhouse. A light shone dully within but it never occurred to him to seek help, though he could no longer stop his teeth from chattering. Instead, he climbed slowly to his feet and looked vainly round for his horse. It was gone, though he remembered its dark shape rising above him in the water, its eyes white and wild. To his surprise he found that he had been swept some hundred feet downstream from the ford to a point below the church and rather than fight his way along the bank, grey-white with ice, black-gapped with tree stumps and bushes, chose to walk towards the church whose shape he could just make out against the yellowing sky. As he walked he spoke aloud to see if his voice had returned; and the word that he spoke was 'No!' though why he could not have said. Pressing through the churchyard, where a yew tree had fallen, forming a less than triumphal arch, he emerged on the road where a young woman stood calming his horse which nervously shifted its feet in a cloud of steam, its rear leg lifted delicately and uselessly in the air. When he stumbled on to the road, wet and wild, the woman stepped back in alarm. By way of response he attempted an ironic bow but as he did so passed out in a dead faint. And the woman who watched him collapse, as a conjuror will disappear leaving only his suddenly evacuated clothing falling vacantly behind him? Her name was Hester.

I have, perhaps, presented this man as a combination of Mr Rochester and Heathcliff, as a product of the mind of Mrs

Radcliffe or Mr Poe. He was none of these. His science was the amateur dabbling of a man who viewed the world with ironic detachment. He had no secret in an upstairs room and had never been troubled by passion. Yet there was melodrama in his life, as there is in the lives of all of us, for what is melodrama but a disproportion between cause and effect, word and action, intent and response. He took a certain pride in his isolation, never yearning for the company of those he was convinced had nothing to offer him but contempt, this being the same emotion in which he indulged himself. Though the world we are visiting here – time-travellers careful not to disturb a single blade of grass lest by doing so we destroy the very history we express – knew nothing of later theories of science and the mind, its inhabitants were not innocent of the power of environment and heredity, though they might more readily have spoken of fate and curse and tainted blood. And had the villagers of Colney known of his past they would have nodded their heads in unsurprised acknowledgement of laws which needed no legislators to enact nor magistrates to enforce. For here is where melodrama touched his life. Roger Chillingworth was born not on land but at sea and not in quiet seclusion but a longboat off the Azores, just hours before his distracted mother slipped first into unconsciousness and thence into death. Discovered later by a passing schooner, in that same longboat, held in a dying man's grasp, he was delivered as in a second birth aboard a ship sailing far to the south, a ship on which no woman had set foot and the only gentleness was the roll of the sea and the mournful cry of distant gulls. Melodrama enough?

Returned to land he was delivered into the hands of a family of merchants who reproached him for survival and saw in his eyes those of the woman who had taken from them the son whom the sea had claimed a second time, a woman whose own background they feared and despised, though concealed from this alien child. His schooling was at the hands of clerics who themselves abjured the touch of women and taught an unforgiving creed. The one gift his family offered was a modest fortune when they died, left to him not out of love but because there was no other who could sustain their name. It was with that money, made, like that of so many others in Norwich, great and small, from the cloth trade, that he bought Colney Hall, severing immediately all connection with the company which, unusually, bore the family name and that of another, the latter thereby rendered bankrupt with removal of the capital on which success depended. As with so much else that he did there was no vindictiveness here; it was simply that such trade offered no interest to a man wedded to nothing but his own company. It was not that there was no humanity in him but that he had locked it away so securely in a forgotten room that he no longer noticed its absence. Somewhere there was a key, placed carelessly on a dust-laden shelf, but he no longer remembered where.

He returned to his senses in a makeshift bed by a fire which crackled and spit. He was naked under the rough blanket which held him fast like a lunatic, his arms tight to his sides. His clothes steamed by the hearth, a faint smell of scorching in the air. The lowering sky allowed nothing but a thin gruel of yellow light to penetrate the narrow windows. The fire alone, save for a single unguarded candle, set the shadows dancing.

Nobody sat by his bedside awaiting his recovery. That would occur or not and, besides, a winter ducking was not so unusual that it left anyone alarmed at a simple loss of consciousness. At a time of doubtful diet, when clothing could constrict and ice encrusted the inner windows of all rooms which lacked a fire, fainting was anyway something more than a literary conceit, though as yet the novel, which proposed it as a natural accompaniment to love lost and found, had not been born, narrative still requiring rhyme and meter when it was not a simple agent of divine instruction.

His inclination was to leap out of what passed for a bed and leave the house immediately before he should be discovered but strength had left his body. A door opened behind him as a burning ember spat out of the fire with the crack of a breaking twig. A heavy boot stamped on it.

'Thou art back with us, then.'

It was less a question than an answer and the man who spoke awaited no reply, kicking the cinder back into the hearth and leaving the room immediately, quite as though he had entered with the sole intent of extinguishing the spark. In a second, though, the door reopened and this time there was a gentler step.

'Thou art better, I trust, sir. Thou didst hit thy head as thou fell.'

Only then was he aware of a pain at the back of his head and, as he raised himself on one elbow, the room seemed to turn about its axis. He slumped down with a groan.

'Rest a while, sir. My brother will hitch the wagon when thou be ready but thou art welcome to stay this night should thou wish. It would be better to avoid the ford.'

'I shall leave immediately.' He corrected himself. 'I shall leave directly I can without losing my legs again.' Then, aware of his gruffness, 'I have thee to thank, I presume. My horse . . .' He stopped, too weary to offer explanation.

'He told his own story. A bruised leg, his withers dark with river water. And thou, sir, half man, half otter.'

Chillingworth blushed and hoped that the firelight would cover his embarrassment. 'And didst thou carry me?'

'Not I, sir. My charge was thy horse. And, since thou enquire, he is in the stable and I would guess will mend. My brother brought thee home, rather like a sack of corn, if truth were told.'

He relaxed, loosening the blanket round his chest.

'And would thy brother be so kind as to pass me my breeches and shirt.'

'Thou would do well to leave them awhile. There is still a deal of river to be steamed out of them.'

He looked at the woman who now sat across from him, the beginning of a smile, he fancied, shadowing her lips. And since he is looking at her let us do likewise.

Neither plain nor pretty, but with a kind of beauty nonetheless, Hester had, beyond everything, a sense of composure and grace. It is a minor miracle, perhaps, and a sufficient answer to those who believe that we are shaped by the nature of our past or the force of our present, that the smallest village can give birth to someone whose strengths and weaknesses owe so little to their setting or their time. Nor did her ancestry explain her character, for that had proved feeble indeed. It is true that Colney was no Galápagos but neither was her home a Puritan Dove Cottage. The Lord's name was respected here. A Bible stood in the corner of the room, like the foundation stone of the building, and was consulted for help to survive the day. But in this house the will was left intact and though Hester had no sister yet her sex was respected without condescension. Her once great family had adjusted to their new condition, which required that they live like farmers and survive as best they might by their own efforts. Though at times her father, white-bearded and bent by rheumatism, would put on the clothes of his youth, the white ruffles of Elizabethan England, a velvet cloak now worn smooth and dull with age, he and they acknowledged with a will the new necessities which drove them, though he less than they and they not without an occasional thought for the past.

Hester carried the bucket from the well, in cold weather as in hot, and cooked meal for the pigs, stirring with a stick of witch-hazel stripped from the tree. She laboured in the fields when the soil was heavy with water and swung the sickle at harvest when the husks rubbed skin raw around waist and neck. Yet if she was part of a family of men she also had her privacies and was respected for this, father and brother withdrawing each day as she wrote her most private thoughts, as many like her could not, in a diary whose lock she never turned. Her schooling had been in the hands of one who loved her but whose love she never recognized for what it was, such is the cruelty born out of ignorance. He was a cousin preparing for the Church and what a preparation it proved, forbidding himself to speak the only words that could set him free. Now we should label it suppression and file that fact away as adequate explanation. But, then, we think ourselves so much better versed in the ways of the heart and the mind's evasions than those who lacked the courage or the will to practise such a confident taxonomy.

Hester was just nineteen that winter, though her poise and quiet serenity made her seem older than her years, but there was an innocence to her which had never been tested since it was an innocence which seemed so natural in the quiet lanes down which her life had led her. At this moment her dark hair sparkled in the firelight but she was not so innocent as to be unaware of the fact; and as she stared into the heart of the flames her face seemed to glow from within in a manner which owed nothing to the fire where the grey ash bloomed into a deep red glow.

What Chillingworth saw of this I cannot say but something stirred in his icy heart as for the first time he found himself wondering about the secret life of another. He was no bigot. His contempt for others had nothing to do with their station or degree. He fancied himself a student of men and had a surgeon's coldness of manner, a detachment which he took for objectivity but which was closer to disdain. He sought to lay bare the simple mechanics of being. But, as the fire slowly restored his sluggish circulation, some inner part of him, long dead, came back to life as he looked at the soft curve of her cheek and the gentle flow of her body.

In the days which followed, Chillingworth kept to his house, the day's adventure leaving him with a cold which led within a week to pneumonia. Taking to his bed he sweated in the tangled sheets while, outside, the snow fell in slow, heavy flakes. From time to time his housekeeper pushed open the bedroom door, preceded by a bowl of steaming soup, but he either waved it away or was unaware of her presence. It was a further week before the fever left him and when he finally woke with a nagging hunger he fancied himself a changed man. For in that sleep of death what dreams had come.

He re-enacted his accident, this time dramatized on an operatic scale. In his fevered mind he was battered against brooding rocks and pulled towards a sea which, mysteriously, had moved twenty miles inland and now broke around the flinted base of a Colney church become Norman castle. Though his bed was soaked with perspiration he was colder than the ice which floated past his struggling body. Then came a woman who, stretching out her hand, caused the waters to calm and recede. She spoke no words but smiled as perhaps his mother had once smiled at him as the sea surged all about. Hour after hour he replayed this vision until its very rhythm became the essence of the nightmare. But each time her face came into view he calmed and lay still, staring unseeing at his bedroom ceiling, white, but filled the while with strangely moving shapes.

When, finally, he was master of his mind and the lurid fantasies of dream had shrunk to a nullity, one image still remained, that of a nineteen-year-old girl dressed in simple homespun staring deep into the centre of a fire. Anyone else, perhaps, would have recognized this for what it was but so thoroughly had he excluded from his life such possibility that he could acknowledge nothing but his need to meet again a woman some twenty years and more his junior.

If he was recovered, though, his horse was not and the snow now lay deep in the field. For week after week day differed from night only in the yellow-grey glow which seemed to suffuse the sky without ever focusing into anything as definite as a sun. A silence had settled on the world that seemed to carry one back beyond creation's dawn. The very whiteness of the snow, tinged yellow as it was by reflected light, seemed to offer the chance of new beginnings, a sheet of clean paper on which to write oneself anew. Indeed the language of rebirth and renewal, of purification and innocence, was familiar enough in a place whence many had departed for a New World whose name alone was token of the desire to be born again. There was a time when Chillingworth would have welcomed such enforced solitude, retreating to the herbs and chemicals whose secret codes he fancied to decipher, but now he longed to be in the cold air, with a horse between his legs and a mystery more profound to penetrate.

As ill-luck would have it that winter was the worst for thirty years. The first suggestion of a thaw brought fresh blizzards from the north until the river itself froze solid, save that a lantern held close to its surface could detect the slow movement of tench and roach and dace trapped far below. So it is, perhaps, with us.

We, too, need a lantern to light the depths beneath a frosted surface. Whatever the truth of that, life was suspended everywhere. Cattle and sheep were gathered within stable and barn but, even so, many were the farmers who found their animals stiff-frozen to the ground while in the church on Sundays there were those whose piety did battle with the cold as the lengthening sermon froze fingers and toes even as it was designed to bring rigour to the soul by threatening the fires of hell. Indeed, rigor mortis seemed more of a possibility to many who blew on their hands and stamped frozen feet on the hard stone floor.

It was the third week of March before he could re-saddle his horse, itself now fully restored and stamping its hooves like pistol shots on the frost-free cobbles. The thaw, though, was sudden and by the time he had reached the river it was in full flood so that all he could do was to look across at the house from which a twist of smoke rose into a pale blue sky. There were geese and chickens in the yard but no proud young woman to calm the troubled waters which separated him from his new obsession.

There was a bridge downstream at Earlham but the river was already overflowing its banks where it traced its vermicular path across the flat valley to the north. Indeed, even as he pressed his heels into the warm sides of his horse, nervously tensed for its first outing in six weeks, he could see where the water had spilled out like molten glass, reflecting back the blue of the sky and a flight of wild duck slanting in across a sunken sun to meet their reflections rising towards them from a silver-edged mirror. He swung around and urged the sweating gelding to a gallop. Water sprayed around him in an arc through which the full spectrum of colours shone, a travelling rainbow promising the fire next time. And the fire did indeed await both this man on horseback and the woman whose absence had become a central presence in his life.

As for Hester, she was no longer where he sought her. Just as we see the brightness of a star which may long since have died, exploding silently in the cold distance of space, so we fix our minds on a face which may have changed with time and a heart perhaps less constant than our own. The childhood sweetheart

17

remains ever fresh-faced, eyes bright, limbs supple. We spend a lifetime half expecting her return, searching each face, revisiting remembered lanes. But should those memories of youth collide one day with flesh and blood what disillusion would lie there; and if six weeks were hardly likely to have wrought much change he still subsisted on the only image he possessed, a woman seen but once and frozen thus, a daguerrotype in the mind, pensively moving but inert.

By the same token he located her where last he had seen her, as though she waited on this chance acquaintance for re-animation. The truth was more mundane since she had left the very day which followed his brief occupation of her kitchen, walking the five miles to Caistor St Edmund where her cousin Margaret lived among the relics of an earlier age, Caistor being scattered with reminders of the Roman occupation, an ironic commentary on the decline of empire lost on those concerned to forge their own. Margaret lived alone despite her married state, her husband being bosun on a ship which sailed out of Yarmouth, round the tip of England and out into the broad Atlantic.

By luck Hester arrived just before the storm which would have inhibited even such a country girl as she from venturing out. As it was she struggled the last half-mile blinded by the swirling snow and chilled by the sudden wind.

While Chillingworth battled with his fever and desperately sought her redemptive face, she, herself, the corporeal woman, gossiped far into the night with the cousin who had shared so much of her early life.

There is a communication between women which is quite unlike that between men. Beneath the banter and the gossip a relationship is laid down layer by layer, compacting into a rock as solid as granite yet as malleable as clay. In this rock everything is preserved, perhaps to surface later. It is not the content of such conversations which matters but the rhythm and the tone, the contrapuntal melody, and finally that phatic communion that has no need of speech. Yet, no matter how deep or secure it seems and is, there is a force which can undo such bonds, which had, indeed, when Margaret first followed a man who himself heard another voice, that of the sea. And though she matched Hester with her stories of Norwich and the local minister, the small change, in other words, of rural life, I fancy her heart was somewhere far away on the deck of a ship on a far ocean.

As you will have guessed, however, whatever difficulties fate or authors may choose to interpose, two separate characters, once brought together, will surely meet again and this is no less true of Hester and Roger Chillingworth, though I wish that I could say it were otherwise, for just as parents watch in dismay as sons and daughters reach out towards those who would do them harm, and must speak no words, so, too, does he who tells a story whose logic is implacable. Nor can men and women so introduced be permitted to remain indifferent to each other. Sparks will fly even from the dullest flint and flint is a stone in which Norfolk abounds.

I have told you of the birth of what you or I would no doubt call love in the soul of the one, if soul, indeed, he possessed, for certainly there were some who doubted it. Nothing strange, I suspect, in that. The driest scholar can be set aflame by a pale face seen in the firelight, by a smile which seems to come from deep within. More difficult far, however, to explain the birth of love in that other, so full of life, so anxious to discover all there is to know and feel in a world where everything seems new. Perhaps that was partly what drew her to him for he seemed the repository of all knowledge. He spoke languages as though he were in touch with mysteries which eluded her. She heard a music in the words though they meant nothing to her. For one who had scarcely travelled more than ten miles from her door, and in that resembled some nine in ten of her countrymen, he represented a world beyond the rising sun. And can we so misunderstand the human heart as to imagine that his deformity would do anything to one such as Hester other than inspire a gentle but intense protectiveness, a feeling that nature had required of him a price for the secrets it would divulge? Unlike many of her fellow villagers she, who read herself and had taken delight in letters and words since her earliest years, tracing them in the dust of the farmyard, running her fingers over the flowing print of Bible and prayer-book, had never thought to wed knowledge to the black arts. Perhaps she came to love not because of him but because of what he represented to her, and who can say that this is anyway not the essence of love as we reshape the object of our affection into the very thing we imagine ourselves to desire. What we love is the projection which we ourselves cast on the flickering wall of the cave so that one day when the fire which threw the shadow is extinguished we are astonished to discover just how diminutive the reality we embrace.

Then again, there is a rhythm to the natural world which is hardly hidden from us though we may choose not to hear its distinctive throb. There comes a time when a young woman decides that the moment is ripe for change, that she must move on, metamorphose. There is, I fancy, a clock which ticks inside us and at a given moment an alarm begins to ring. We suddenly see our lives like well-water held in the hands. As it begins to slip through our fingers we rush to raise it to our lips before it shall spill into the dust. So there arrives a time when a young woman will decide, with absolute assurance, that her moment has come and happy the man who stands before her at such a moment. Or, on this occasion, happy the middle-aged misanthropist, if happy is the word to describe the raw, bleak world which was summoned into view as a young woman hastened to her fate with an eye that sparkled and a voice which seemed as beautiful as the sun come after rain.

Whatever the truth of that, Hester began to change. Unlike many of the villagers she had never felt suspicion or fear of a man who evidently preferred his own company, merely an ironic amusement at his discomfort as he had emerged from his winter baptism only to collapse ignominiously at her feet. His desperate wish to flee their house when his clothes lay steaming at the hearth had done nothing to change her mind. How she moved from this detachment, from seeing him, if at all, only out of the corner of the eye, to something wholly different is a mystery which language alone can never hope to encompass. Neither did

Puritan society offer circumstances for such transformations. This was not Jane Austen's world of country vicarages and grand houses, of picnics at Box Hill or ballrooms where sensibility swept sense quite away. It was a spare time. A certain winnowing of the spirit had occurred and the eye was always open for a sign of the devil's work. But no society was ever devised where private meaning could not be sought in the interstices of public form. Time and opportunity present themselves the more particularly when time obeys other laws than those measured by balance and wheel.

When his housekeeper herself took to her bed with a summer fever he sent word to the farm requesting help with ministering to her. Thus Hester first entered a house which was to be, by turns, a museum of wonders, a home, and, eventually, a prison, within the time it takes for a sparrow to move from egg to a fading stain on the woodland floor. For two full days she sat beside the woman in an airless room at the rear of the Hall before, on the morning of the third day, Chillingworth, his hair, she fancied, carefully brushed, his manner as gentle as might be, invited her to see his study and its clutter of books and equipment. Childishly intent to interest her in every experiment, every theory, every fancy, he showed her books in languages she knew nothing of from countries of which she had never heard. He poured yellow, green and blue liquids on to powder, plant and fluid until the room quite filled with smells and smoke and sounds like a nest of adders disturbed by a scythe. Holding a kerchief to her nose she eventually fled the room even as he hurried after with a beaker foaming deep vermilion. At her behest the next day they dispensed with chemicals and looked instead through his books, some filled with strange ciphers, others in languages long dead. It was there that they came together, he offering to teach her words, a grammar and a syntax from another time; she, for her part, agreeing to submit to his tutelage.

Hester was a ready pupil. Her heart reached out for knowledge. For so long content that the parish boundaries be her own, she now longed for worlds unseen. He held her with his stories, seduced her with his experiences. So, by degrees, she moved from respect, to reliance, to, what she shocked herself by calling one day in her journal, love. But when you have never known such emotion before you lack the means to make comparison with true rigour. Pain cannot be mistaken. Scald your hand on the kettle and you have no further need of explanation. With love we move into another sphere. To be sure Hester had no novels, nor yet magazines to teach her the conventions of romance. You would imagine, though, that love would be unmistakable as the day. We all learn otherwise in time, though usually without much pain or cost. Love follows love, dismissing each in turn as falling short of its successor. Hester was not so lucky, for in truth she was in part the inventor of her own despair when later she gave other names to the tumult in her breast. For the moment, though, suffice it to say that her world had suddenly transformed and there was none other than this who had brought about the transformation.

It was as though Hester had been waiting, as though within her was a sleeper who had to be aroused. There had been moments in church when something seemed to seize her, when the blood throbbed in her ears and tears came to her eyes. She had such a capacity to love that she lacked only an object worthy of her commitment. For a while, as she approached sixteen, she had thought she was drawn to Christ. A whole month saw her fasting and praying long at night until her family feared for her health. But it was not a path she could take who loved the touch, the sounds, the smells of daily life. The cloister was no place for her. For a time she poured out love to the animals she kept and tended. She would brush and groom the ploughing horse, feeling the gentle shivering of its flanks, pressing her face to its tautly curving neck. There had been boys at harvest, glistening in the sun, but she made no response to their urgent stares. She scarcely seemed to notice the men she encountered, though they had noticed her these many years. Now had come this man, born out of a snow storm, baptized in a winter river.

'Art thou happy to live all alone?'

22

'Happy?' queried Chillingworth blankly. 'I am content, I think, nor am I alone.'

She looked away.

'And yet,' he hastened to correct himself, 'it has seemed that way these last weeks.'

'Even so? My company then makes thee feel alone.'

'No, that is not my meaning.' He shook his head, urgently, hearing no irony. 'Until thou came I had not felt the want of company. Now there are times . . .' He was not sure that he had made himself any clearer.

'I understand, though for one who can speak so many languages thou art a little uncertain of thine own. Thou dost not come to church,' she said accusingly, changing tack in a way he found confusing.

'I am not of that company.'

'All are of that company.'

'It may be that there are some who are not of that opinion. I would make a poor church-goer who am faithful to other demands.'

'I am glad at least that thou art faithful. It is a rare quality in men, I am told.'

Hester felt suddenly like a light-footed dancer who ducks and weaves about a maypole whose duty is to stand but still as others weave their patterns. She fancied she could play this man, so proud of his solemn knowledge, until he should bend to her will. She was not the first to make such a mistake and allow youthful vigour to feel superior to wisdom and power, nor the first to fancy her ease with herself, her sudden blossoming spirit, a product of love. For if he should prove such an excellent audience could it be for any other reason than a kind of enchantment and enchantment may spin a mutual magic. I am loved may require I love to complete its spell.

'Nor do we see thee at harvest feast. Dost thou not grow hungry of a summer's end?'

'I have been solitary, I grant, and now I see that in thy eyes it is a fault I shall try to find remedy.'

'And if thou shalt I shall be thy guide as thou art mine.'

23

'Even so,' he replied, as though some compact had been signed. 'We shall together, thou and I.'

Their eyes met and for a second neither spoke. For more than a second. And silence can be dangerous. Meaning may seep into it from another world. Such a meaning began to crystallize. A transaction began which would prove a bad bargain for both of them. How can we be so deceived in our own judgement? Is there no truth in feelings? Can we never tell the counterfeit from the true until the time has come to spend?

'Come,' he said, holding out his hand.

For a second she hesitated.

'Come, let me show thee more of my life.'

Still she hesitated and had she continued to do so much pain would have been spared and this story become another. But instead she offered up her hand and with it perhaps her soul.

It is not long since there were those who feared clocks, believing them to make time rather than mark it, as though the twitch of the hands stirred the very stars into being. Chillingworth kept clocks. There was no room in the hall without their fidgeting itch, so many abacus beads clicking off the tally of eternity. No two agreed and yet each beat out the same rhythm. Hester questioned him about such a collection when there was but a single time, but he did no more than smile and admit his fondness for mechanical things. Yet he never turned the clocks on the shelf to bring the hands of one to match another. It was as though they recorded each separately a separate world. Indeed, as time is the greatest enigma, perhaps they did, and since he was inclined to mystery perhaps the clocks were a clue to more besides.

One day, as she and Chillingworth stood in the sun and looked out over the valley, Hester heard two of them chime, one in the kitchen, one in the parlour, like animals calling to one another in the night but, an hour apart, they spoke in different languages, one on Amsterdam time, he explained, another on their own. How there could be more than one time, though, she was unsure for she imagined time as being like a thread of wool on a loom, held taut between sun-up and sun-down. And why should he live in two times at once, supposing he did not jest, as in part she believed he did?

Hester, who was now used to other clocks – the dandelion and the moving shadows of a summer day – remembered another, above the mantel in the place which had been her home until her move from hall to farm. It stood throughout her youth, its hands slightly parted about the noon and midnight hour, silent in a house of noise. It stood, she half suspected, as an image of her family's failure, halted at a zenith which was also a nadir. They had lost their way. Chillingworth seemed certain of his. They represented the past, he the future. And yet it was not that which stirred her. She was like a colt looking for the open field. She trembled on the brink of a life she wished to summon into being.

'And hast thou seen much of the world?'

'I have seen but little of it, if thou mean other places and people. Amsterdam. The cities of France and Germany.'

'That is not little to someone whose boundary is marked by Caistor and Yarmouth, and these be adventures in themselves.'

'Maybe so. But there are other journeys which wear out no shoe leather. I have no need of horse or ship to travel where I would go.'

'And couldst thou take me on such journeys?'

'If thou but have the spirit for it. Or thou couldst stay below on the farm and watch the world go by.'

'And I could do far worse. I have those that love me and whom I love, nor is my home to be despised.'

'Ah, Hester.' He spoke her name. She turned away. 'I had not thought to anger thee. I have no skills for pretty talk. I meant only that there is that in thee which reaches out beyond this place. Nor art thou without . . .' he paused, 'affection here.'

'Affection?'

'Thou seest, Hester . . .' He spoke her name again. 'I have but rough manners and an uncertain tongue. I am in need of tutoring. Dost thou know someone who might gentle my roughness?'

Hester knew. The pupil is to become the teacher and what flattery there is in that. And who so blind as those required to lead another through a darkness of his own invention. Chillingworth's clocks ticked on and, whether on Amsterdam or Colney time, the hands approached the hour.

Thus, one day, as July turned into August and they walked together through the woods which fringed the riverbank, there came a moment when logic seemed to hold them in its grasp, albeit a logic which had never had the sanction of the mind. The times might permit no declaration but not all communication has the need of words. Nonetheless there were proprieties to be obeyed. The fact that they could walk together at all was no doubt because they seemed rather more like father and daughter than lovers. Indeed, to be precise, the word love had never been spoken between them or even, in his case, entered his mind. They had never been alone together in his house, the brooding presence of his housekeeper the guarantee of their propriety. Besides, who would have suspected anything between a girl whose sensible beauty was in such stark contrast to the contorted physique of a man whom others shunned as assiduously as he did them.

There was a company he kept. In one of Norwich's twisted streets, which spell out a message inscribed by the line of ancient settlements, was an upstairs room beyond the narrow arch of Tombland. Here, along the cathedral wall, where horse sales filled the air with flies and noise, was a small meeting house, though not, of course, in any Quaker sense since they should risk hanging should they threaten Church and state with their rantings. Here would gather, twice a month or more, those who gathered for no other reason. Though this was a time when dissent from a fast-changing orthodoxy could bring swift punishment, the divine right of Parliament swiftly threatening that of King, there were those who fancied themselves obedient to other laws. Members of an ancient guild (not those dissolved by royal decree some hundred years before), they had their secret ceremonies and practices and recognized each other with such signs and gestures as were invisible to those who saw them without knowing such. A thread in their clothing might betoken rank or degree while each wore a ring whose labyrinthine designs were references to such arts as now we might perceive as sciences. If they sometimes reeked of magic (at a moment when witches were moved with dispatch to hell), which science does not which posits the invisible and asks its followers to believe? We live in a time of wonders no less than these. We know, as we do the time of sunrise, that the solid ground beneath our feet has no solidity at all and that we link hands back through time to creatures who would strike a terror into our hearts should we but meet them; and meet them we do since they are part of us and we are nothing but their children long removed. Yet this lineage is invisible. So was it then. It was simply that the invisible took different form. We know that disease and illness are the products of invisible powers, of tainted water and contaminated food. They knew the same except that the powers they suspected carried different names and moved among them in another guise. Which profession today does not surround itself with flummery, invest itself with power, hint at a secret knowledge and seem to conspire against those not privy to their craft? They were no necromancers, yet they summoned into existence that which did not exist before. Neither were they astrologers, though they did indeed stare into a future which could amaze. They were no doctors in a common sense. They had no faith in leeches or the normal remedies. Yet they had their skills with plants, could cure what faith alone could not and were interested in the frailties of the spirit. Though some, like Chillingworth himself, had travelled and indeed had formed their communion first across the sea in the gabled city of Amsterdam, eternally cold and eternally damp, the journeys on which they chose to go were not in space and time. They chose the inward track. They were fascinated by the internal landscape of the soul as the Dutch artists were concerned with capturing the landscape of the face and body. I do not mean to imply that they practised their skills or lack of them always on others, still less on themselves. Their concern was not only with the mind but in the mind.

It goes without saying that this company was male. Witches might be women, tipped over the edge of the rational by denial and constraint, breaking through the silence of their role into a babble, a flow, a torrent of language, vomited up from a stifled soul, or more likely offered up as a sacrifice by those who suspected their intuitive power, their capacity to read the world with their emotions. More likely still they were simply victims of malice, self-righteousness and cant, the tempters of men returned to the work of the devil which had brought death to the world and separated man from his God. But men had no such vulnerability. They could pull around themselves the assumed protection of their gender: a gnomic wisdom, a catechist's enquiry into faith, an intellectual abstraction which nullifies the risk of free thought.

Yet there were those in this city who watched this group of men, who noted the signs with which they greeted one another and, if they lacked the skill to read the meanings they contained, saw other coherences in this sinister cabal. For one, at least, of their number was a Jew who assayed silver, fashioned cups and plate and buckles for shoes which even in this plain time were to be seen adorning the feet of those whose faith and therefore grace was great. And Norwich had a memory for Jews.

Here was committed a crime which would resonate for centuries. Not the crime which started the story on its way but the crime which was the story, for story-telling can be the source of deepest evil as well as the grace with which we staunch the flow of fear.

In 1144, at Thorpe, beyond Mousehold, in a clump of willows where the road meets the river, was found the body of a young boy. He was tied with strong twine in a series of intricate knots, his legs doubled up to his chest. His body had been pierced like that of Christ and was in a state of some decay. Today we would suspect the unsubtle refinements of perverted lust. Then such things were practised but seldom named and there was, as chance would have it, a more visible and more useful candidate to hand. As in many other cities of the realm Norwich was the heart of a Jewish community, permitted, as Christians were not, to engage in usury, which is to say in lending money to finance their own eventual destruction. Even today there are streets and sudden passages whose names recall the wealthy ghetto which fuelled the city's growth. But the Jews, the Christ-killers and deniers of Christ's divinity, sat increasingly in the shadow of a great cathedral, an aching tooth in the mouth of a just and bold people. The Norwich miracle plays, performed beyond the cathedral walls at Tombland and St Peter Mancroft, recalled in motley the assassination of God by those whose money-changing tables had been overturned by the gentle hand of Christ. And just as a boil must be tolerated as the pus gathers within so the purging needle may lance its heart and void the corruption, so someone seems to have decided that a time for purging had arrived for those whose loyalties lay elsewhere and whose mystic symbols hinted at a secret plot against powers visible and invisible. The word began to spread that a Christian child had been the victim of a rite of sacrifice required by a faith so tainted as to need fresh Christian blood to live.

So the story began. An embryo compacted in the shell, black stubs of wings pressed close against a body where a heart had begun its ominous beat. For the most terrible of narratives was invented not in the heart of savage Russia, bent on pogrom, not in the Eastern empires, whose barbarian ways shocked no one, but in this quiet corner of a crooked wood on the edge of a city itself on the westward edge of an ancient empire. Here the dark-furled creature began to tap against the shell. Having sucked dry the yoke it thrust itself through its flaking prison to go in search of carrion.

So there were those who watched as Chillingworth entered through a heavy, studded door, to be followed by his fellows in a quiet confederacy. At a time when others fixed their eyes on God there were those who focused theirs on the product of his works, on the poppies of the field and belladonna, on mineral and distillation, on creatures turned inside out with sharpened steel, on rocks which carried at their heart a past encysted in a whorl of flint. And those who watched sent their reports and those who read them filed them away should ever private meeting become public conspiracy.

Perhaps they might have shown more immediate interest had they known, what none knew and none suspected, that there was in that chamber not one Jew but two. For that was the cause of the special hatred felt by Chillingworth's adopted parents. Their son had been wooed from their side and taken to his watery grave by one who denied Christ's divinity and took his life. Behind the name of Chillingworth, and that of the family which made him their own, was that of another. The loss of his father meant little to him. He was but part of a family whose charity he accepted with ill grace. That other was unknown, her name forbidden. One more secret for a twice-born son to explore.

For a time at least he was truant from his lodge, distracted by thoughts other than those of a man of the mind. In one afternoon with her father he had secured consent to a marriage which none but they could understand and even they found as unreal as the shapes sometimes formed by the river mist at dawn. Who can hope to understand love or what, for a while, we choose to characterize as such. It is true that discrepancy of age mattered less to those more attuned to the necessities of nature but the man to whom Hester contented to join herself was almost as mysterious as the day he had risen from the water only to fall at her feet. She had, though, never met his like before and he offered to open a door for her which otherwise would have remained closed tight. What she thought she might be to him it is impossible to say. She was of an age when certainties are announced only to be exchanged for others within the month. Perhaps, for all the happiness of her early years, she recognized the unyielding and unalterable nature of a life which offered little beyond eternal repetition, and though before she had never felt that an imposition, he had held out to her such visions as to breed discontent in the most constant soul. She lacked ambition in the modern sense, would never trade contentment for new ways; but contentment could never quite sum up a spirit that leaned, as hers did, into the future, that felt a wind coming towards her from another time and place. So she chose to call love what might rather have been characterized as a need for change, a desire to break away, to search out something new. Besides, love was not so beribboned with fancy in the country, in a world gone severely practical.

And what of him? Not so hard to fathom, you presume. A distorted body and slipping into middle years, bereft of company except that of an embittered crone. Who would not wish the warm body of a young girl, a light in the kitchen and one more besides in the bedroom? Yet it is doubtful that he saw it thus at all. Perhaps they were mutual victims of their mutual self-deceit; and yet he told her once that what he felt was never love. A curious honesty, perhaps, made him speak so, but, since we seldom hear what we have no wish to hear, Hester thought it no more than play.

Whatever the truth, as harvest was gathered Hester and Chillingworth were married. Their names were joined in the register and in the minds of men as that of God, though it seems that God did that day look away and when his glance returned the deed was done. The church was bedecked with flowers but perhaps among the petalled colour was a black and violet berry which leaked its poison in the air. Smell the nosegay and feel the vapours spread, and how could Hester know that such knowledge was concealed in the scent of columbine and rose?

No relative or friend of his was present, so that one side of the church was in a kind of shadow, the empty pews offering neither colour nor yet the fitful movement of those who turned about to greet their kin. But, on the other, family, friend and childhood playmate laughed away regret with smiles and tears, as raindrops will sometimes fall from out of a cloudless sky. The groom was as gracious as could be, for a man who had so little intercourse with others, and raised several glasses on the lawn of the Hall where they later sat in the summer sun. When the guests at length departed and the last jiggling lamp had crossed beyond the ford then husband and wife looked at each other as husbands and wives have always done, with a mixture of shock, and fear and, on her part, a sudden joy.

There are country ways with wedding nights but by some unexpressed agreement this couple were left to themselves alone and it seemed would have been content to sit outside the whole night through had not rain begun to fall, heavy drops of water splashing on the tables set amidst the brittle grass. Together they entered the house, though not hand in hand, and together mounted the stairs, but the fate towards which she moved was not that about which she had dreamed. So the night which was to have begun their marriage ended it. No word was spoken the whole night through. They lay together staring at the ceiling, the very one at which he had stared in his winter fever, until he fell into a fitful sleep and she looked across the room to the window where the cold, disdainful light of a million stars shone down until they slowly blurred and dissolved into a tear.

How could this have been? Had he so mistaken his feelings and hers to believe they had made no more than a simple contract to dwell side by side? He, who was so versed in knowledge of all kinds. Had those early years, perhaps, disqualified him from understanding women's lives and his books reduced all passion to the mind? Or had, perhaps, the potions, pills and roots so drained his being that he lacked both will and means to make this girl his wife? Or could it be that his affection had been shaped by those hands he had grasped in societies which shunned a woman's touch? Whatever cause or reason, this night's epiphany was void.

★

The world is to end tomorrow. For days men and women have moved through the countryside towards the sea to be present at an end which requires of them no movement. They carry red ribbons which stream in the wind, tongues of colour which anticipate the flames to come. No one knows where or when the prophecy was made, or by whom, but time is assumed to be slowing, to flow like honey. Some dance a kind of parodistic jig; others put one foot slowly in front of the other as though measuring out their remaining lives.

Hester had watched them from the hillside where she had not been pierced by nail or spear, not pierced at all. But time had already begun its surcease for her. The end they sought and feared was already in sight for one, like she, who had suffered but bore no wound, who had longed for a wound, believing it to be the doorway to life.

They moved by the river, shouting out a joyous name in a saddened tone. The name of God echoed through the valley. At moments they would fall to their knees in nettle and marsh, dark clumps of humanity amidst the green grass. Each second stretched until it sang with tension.

In her heart she, too, longed for the end. And were the signs of last times not there aplenty? It was a surprise to feel the ground still beneath one's feet and what more unnatural than her own wedded and unwedded state? A cloud had passed over the sun nor did she expect it to fly on its way. Time had stopped its journey, as it seemed, and this rag-taggle band of prophets treasured a secret which would soon be secret no more.

The day dawned. The day progressed. Sunset came with a flame of red. But as the darkness gathered, a single star, pin bright, shone down, and then a thousand more, ploughing their regular furrow, rising as bears, embracing as sisters, populating the universe. A new day came and those who had skipped and run and walked their way to the edge of existence turned slowly about and stepped once again in the footprints made in meadow and lane, burdened with the knowledge that history was not done nor they released from the terrible beauty of life.

Hester watched them return. For two days they passed, some weighed down by sins committed in the shadow of expected death, others by a poverty new-born of efforts to win their way through heaven's door. A clock had begun to tick again and the hands had recommenced that relentless circling which measures out despair and hope alike. She heard the striking of the hour from behind her in the Hall and then the striking of another, keeping a different count. She existed, it seemed to her, within the space between the two, somehow within time and yet beyond it, too, both performer and audience in her private drama.

As a child Hester had sat among the spinach and the kale and sprinkled salt upon the glistening slugs which smeared a silver path across the green. She had watched them wince, shrink

33

within themselves and die. Chillingworth had sprinkled salt on Hester's soul.

There are summers which have barely slipped into autumn before the shadow of winter advances its chill. The smell of camomile on the stove becomes the sharper as morning mists begin to sparkle with a sudden ice and frost to wither bean on vine and break the brittle velvet of blue pansy. It may be thus, too, with you and I, as with a young girl who goes to bed one night with bright eyes and eager spirit only but to wake into a world gone strange and cold to her fingers' touch. It was so for Hester. The world had changed and she drew a cloak about her for the chill.

In the days that followed she watched for a sign of true gentleness but it was as though her marriage day had completed some experiment and that now there were other investigations to pursue. He still took some pleasure in her company but, as with a Christmas puppy which quickly outgrows its novelty, she commanded ever less of his attention with each day that passed. By degrees, she came to realize the extent of her error as one who dives on a hot day into the cold depths of a spring-fed lake. The sudden chill can paralyse the heart so that such a one may never take warm breath again. Hester had discovered the danger in such depths and fought to reach the surface lest she drown.

It was not cruelty at first but a baffled incomprehension which characterized his attitude to Hester. Seen from afar, even as regular visitor to his house, she had been to him an object of mystery and desire but that desire was of the mind, though he had failed to recognize as much as they simulated the processes of love. But, then, what greater mystery is there than love itself which slowly smoulders, bursts to flames, and then extinguishes itself as men are said spontaneously to combust from some superfluity within and leave only a stain behind? While offering the appearance of mutuality it stems from the deepest self-regard as each seeks completion by colonizing another. Such, at any rate, were the convictions which Chillingworth began to commit to a diary in his study, a heavy volume, secured with a clasp, which he first opened the day after his wedding night, even

34

as the magpies pecked and scraped at the pewter dishes on the tables beyond his window. In a single night she had moved from being the subject of his love to being the object of his study, a further cipher of nature to be broken, another aspect of being to be dissected for its elusive meaning. If no change in the human heart is quite so sudden – for surely he understood little, at first, of the transformation of his feelings – yet change there was, as a caterpillar becomes a death's-head moth.

What of Hester herself, proud, independent Hester? She was a maid, as innocent in the ways of love as any woman may be raised with the Bible on the table and a fear of sin fixed in her heart. Yet she was a farmer's daughter, or at least was such since nobility had bowed its knee to necessity's rule. She was a witness to nature's urgencies. Just as the shadow of the church fell across the barn so she believed in the sacredness of natural things. She had seen the horse in the field and the fowl in the barn pursue their natural needs, and there were feelings in her that a whole society had persuaded itself never to name but that were real enough, so that the barren nights pressed upon her spirit. But she was not born to be so readily broken, neither did she want for those gestures of concern and affection towards her husband as would have stirred even a St Paul. Nor was he wanting at first in his simple courtesies to her, in a clumsy fashion seeking to recompense her for what both came quickly to recognize as the error of their union.

It is our nature, though, to blame others than ourselves and, as summer turned into autumn, with fruit dropping to the tufted grass in a maze of wasps and with a soft miasma rising each dawn and dusk from a sluggish river thick with green and yellow weed, so a coldness began to enter the house on the hill which had begun to resemble a prison to those who lived within. Chillingworth retired more often to his books and the acrid smell of vapour seeped along the darkening corridors. Indeed, from time to time, there was a strangeness to his gait, an uncertainty to his gaze, when he emerged, which made her wonder if he might not have taken into himself some of the poisons he distilled from the berries which he gathered at the water's edge and the still stranger plants he cultivated under cover of glass at the southern extremity of the house. He resumed his meetings in Norwich, saddling his horse in the late afternoons and not returning until early the following morning: and there were those who watched.

Even now, before the match was lit, riders splashed by night through September fields dark streaked with dew. The earth flew. Conspiracy spread like bindweed. There were names on lists and lists on plain oak tables where men met in a candle's wayward light. The taste of coins was in the mouth and within a year or two they would summon for the reckoning. 'Sing,' they would say, to the boy who stood before them. 'Sing?' he would reply. And so they would kill him, the children of traitors being traitors themselves in the womb. 'Sing,' they would say, and he would see the glint of moonlight on steel.

And still the riders, with doors closed fast against them which would open soon. Milestones would be broken. Kingship is a greased axle. The wheel turns and we turn with it. Soon, in a thousand ditches, broken spokes.

In every city there were those who watched each face for loyalties which might prove disloyal. They watched here, and one they watched rode out each day and climbed the stairs to a room where the sounds of horse sales mingled with words which had no meaning to the man who bent at the door and listened.

There would be those who stood, in fair weather and foul, on hillside tree-stumps and spoke their minds, surprised they had the minds to speak. All save women, who must keep their peace or feel the shadow of witchcraft pass across their brows. There would be those who spoke and those who listened until listening became a crime, the names all in a book and the book to be thrown down one day and opened. And on that day a blood-caked fingernail would move downwards and press its edge, a half-moon sign, in the paper's weave. That mark might signify interest only or perhaps suspicion or even death. These will be precise times, exact. Walk carefully if you must walk at all and speak only in plain language for that which is not plain may be the cause of your demise. 'Sing,' they would say and God protect he who did not know the song.

I danced for the scribe
And the pharisee,
But they would not dance
And they wouldn't follow me,
I danced for the fishermen,
For James and John
They came with me,
And the dance went on.

Dance, then, wherever you may be,
I am the Lord of the dance, said he,
And I'll lead you all, wherever you may be,
And I'll lead you all in the dance, said he.

Nor were the changes in Hester unremarked by her family for
though, like all of us, she was unwilling to confess to others the
very errors of which we accuse ourselves, so guileless was she, so
unpractised at the arts of deception, that they should have been
insensible indeed if they should have failed to see the unhappiness
written on her face. But those were times when a married woman
was a kind of chattel, invisible to law and powerless to intervene on
her own behalf. Her voice was not heard nor her feelings
considered. Family love was real enough, nor did the heart grieve
less sharply for the girl-child laid to rest in an early grave than for
her brother who might lie by her side, but there were governances,
laws and customs which interpenetrated one another as birch twigs
laced together form a basket impervious to water. Such governances sealed off half the populationn from its rights. Heads might
shake in sorrow and regret but there were few who thought to
challenge a fiat sanctioned alike by God and man. So Hester grew

more desperate and with the approach of her twentieth birthday a determination began to grow in her that she must leave this place, abandon a man into whose hands she had so foolishly entrusted her life. She felt with a sudden passion that a life of possibility and light had been blighted as a rose is cankered by a worm: but where was she to go? Her family was only four furlongs distant while even her cousin was no more than five miles away, and yet she had no more right to freedom than had the people of Israel in the hands of the rulers of Egypt.

It was then that she thought of another place, remote and distant and born of imagination's need: a promised land across the waters, where the past might be forgotten and sins forgiven, and a line be drawn across a life. Suddenly a light seemed to glow ahead of her, a door had swung open through which she might pass if she could only find a way. Yet what convinces as idea may not prove practical as deed, the idea itself being content to be its own fulfilment. Knowing that escape is possible, escape itself no longer seems required and, indeed, once Hester had arrived at this solution to her problems she immediately became happier with her plight.

What is cruelty? The wanton, unnecessary inflicting of pain? Perhaps. But there is a cruelty, too, in indifference, in the withdrawal of love, in the stifling of the human spirit, in a cold and clinical gaze which carries no commitment, no offer to treat, no hint of remorse, no suggestion of life. What is a prison? A constraining encirclement with impenetrable walls? Perhaps. But there is a prison, too, in companionship denied, in enforced solitude, in youth yoked to age without solace of love.

As winter began to drain the world of colour, and grey clouds to press ever closer to the earth, Hester felt cruelly entombed. To be sure her husband in name offered her no violence and barred no door against her excursions but she felt herself marooned in a sea of isolation. And he had changed. It was not simply that the clumsy and endearing suitor had withdrawn into privacy but that privacy had become so intense as to border on insanity. At times she would hear his laughter through the door of his study yet when he emerged there was never a trace of a smile on his face. She saw letters on his desk in a strange language, letters half concealed and yet insufficiently so, as though his distracted mind was not even equal to concealment. Once a man came to the door late at night and she heard voices raised. At breakfast she asked after the visitor, for they still exchanged words, albeit none that bore on the pain she felt, only to have him deny his existence. She even longed for the presence of the housekeeper, long since dismissed: but even this consolation was denied. And so she laid her plans.

In the spring, when a soft heat seemed to breathe from the fields and the hedgerows were yellow-green with new shoots, she begged leave to visit her cousin in Caistor and set out on a journey which itself lifted her heart. Everywhere was new life. In winter, in the fastness of the Hall, she would have seen in this an irony, but now she was a country girl again taking pleasure in a country world whose seasonal rhythms carried their own compulsions. If winter encloses, driving the cows from the meadow and man to his hearth, then spring liberates. The air is no longer heavy with threat or brittle with cold. Winter has no smell but that of the kitchen and the fire and the dank sweat of washing darkly hanging by the flames. Spring is a nosegay; not the sickly sweet perfume of summer, with poppy and wild rose and evening honeysuckle, but the subtle freshness of green things newly unfurled, of a world swept clean by storm and flood to emerge as for the first time. Within a mile of leaving what she forbore to call her home she walked with a new confidence to her step. At Cringleford she stopped to watch two turquoise and azure dragonflies, their wings ablur, weave coloured arabesques above the surface of a stream once more transparent and coolly green, and heard the song of thrush and blackbird echo in the valley. She saw, too, cattle sway heavy down a narrow lane, released at last into the open fields.

But for all the pleasure that she took her mind was firm. She took it as reminder of that which she had lost and carried her conspiracy within her as though pregnant with the spring child she might once have expected to bear. When she arrived at the cottage the rare presence of her cousin's husband seemed a confirmation of the rightness of her plans. Thus it was that, after supper, as they sat in the shade of an apple tree, its blossom pink with life, she asked about his voyages and about one destination beyond others.

'America,' he said, 'nor that's a voyage I like, Hester. Three times I've made it and each time some calamity. Once to Virginia with those who've ruffles on their sleeves and money in their souls, and twice with a party so pious as to drive me to drink and more; and both ruffles and homespun vomiting in the ocean as though to leave themselves a trail to lead them back to home. And each time a man lost. It's not a voyage I like.'

'And what if I should wish to take that trail,' enquired Hester. 'Would thou take me by the hand and guide me there?'

It will be imagined what followed. Incredulity. Reminders of family, of duty, of danger. Only in retrospect do we see those who left for the New World as heroes and heroines, pioneers, the vanguard of the future. Then they seemed to many as extreme in their views as in their actions, malcontents and adventurers or pure in their faith but simple in their minds. Stories of death by pestilence and disease, by bitter winter storms and snakes, had long since reassured those who never themselves have ventured a journey above a dozen miles. Even so her cousin had to admit to a community of souls fast growing on the eastern shore while refusing to carry Hester thither on his ship. Yet they recognized her desperation and the transformation effected in a bare eight months. They offered what we offer to such people in despair: patience, hope, the need for reconciliation, resignation. She told them nothing, of course, of the fact that they were husband and wife still only in name. Nor was this simple modesty or the fact that such things were then cloaked deep in darkness, a secret unacknowledged almost even in its execution. The fact was that she knew so little herself and having no comparison was unsure whether this should be strange or no. Nor did she mention love since this was not a word that could be spoken without pain and self-accusation for her own former self, the one which had walked by the river's edge with a stranger and imagined him a friend and lover yet. This self was now as much a stranger as he who refused to share her life or even the time of day while love was no longer a language which spoke her condition. Her natural language now was tears, and that night, through wattle and daub, a true husband and wife heard the quiet sobs of a woman who was a girl again, the girl with whom they had both once played on riverbank, in the stooped caves of corn and through the barn's dark shadows. Nor, by morning's light, were the tears hers alone.

The conviction grew in Hester's mind that hers had been no marriage, and search as she might she could find no fault in herself except to have entered into a pact against her soul. There are many who would have settled for the consequences of such a mistake and this not simply because of the fiat of Church or the intangible power of convention. There is a lethargy of spirit born out of despair, a consolation to be sought in habit and in rectitude itself. Pass a glass over the soul of rich and poor alike and you will find few where true contentment leaves them blemish-free. Yet, determined though she was to break through the bars she had conspired in forging, she stayed her hand, in part believing in the power of her own gentleness, in part trusting to the change she sought in him, though by now doubting that she wished for such a transformation. And some consolation was to be found in the diary which she wrote and into which she spilled her thoughts as Catholics do to priests. The very action of the pen seemed to calm her. Each careful letter forced a concentration which led her close to trance. Her troubled mind relaxed as wrist and fingers shaped to form a truth which pained her so long as it was locked within. She found release in the process of expression, spoke in silence what she could not speak aloud.

Unbeknown to her here was a connection with the husband with whom she believed she shared nothing more than a growing desolation. For he, too, would retire to write in a book, though he retreated to a locked room when he took up pen and ink. But where he wrote with a cold and careful mind, in characters so small and cramped that none but he could decipher them, she wrote with flowing hand and spilled the lifeblood of her heart so that she might see what she knew but could not utter in the light.

Hester found in writing and in words a means to unlock a world of feeling and thought she had not thought she could express, yet she never fell into the error of believing that those who lacked these skills lacked also the feelings they express. For in the churchyard lay two sisters and a brother, who now kept company with their mother. She knew the pain that death brought to those who stand around each fresh-dug grave. She knew, too, that at such a moment words crawl back into some cave of the mind aware of their insufficiency. Indeed she suspected that words may stand between the self and its expression as she reached for a phrase which could precisely render her conflicting feelings.

Whether the same conviction was embraced by he whose pen scratched his report by candlelight I doubt. As he wrote of the doings of the Cabal on Tombland Alley, as he called it, I suspect he had no thoughts of the magical power of words nor still less of their insufficiency. His prose weighed heavy on the page, listing times and names, as writers of almanacs might identify the phases of the moon and the state of the tide. Yet, like all functionaries, he knew there was a power in what he wrote if others chose to read there a meaning which touched the affairs of state. In a city in which, until recent times, a third of the population had been 'strangers', refugees speaking French or Flemish, cloth-workers who preserved the secrets of their trade, suspicion of conspiracy was general, and conspiracy was not without commercial logic. They lived apart, operated their own cloth halls, worshipped in churches of their own: the Dutch in Blackfriars Hall, the French in St Mary the Less. Each deployed their own defensive force, with pikes to pin a truth too subtle for the general, too crude for those of other faiths. So that the presence, in an upper room, above the gateway at Tombland's entrance, of three secretive men and a Jew meant money in the hand for him who chronicled their passing. The forces then preparing civil war were breeding here. Still to come were Edgehill and Marston Moor and Naseby. A king defeated and Parliament triumphant would soon leave nothing safe. The ground was trembling and there were those who would not meet

42

the eye of passing friends for in such times friends will pass apace to settle business best not known or deny the very bone and sinew of that friendship forged and sealed in other times. Heresies and treacheries were hatching like flies on a dung heap. Bureaucracies have longer memories than those who compose them. They find comfort in thick parchment and rough vellum brought by courier to their collective door, for all lines cross at the point they inhabit and thus testify to their own significance.

As it happened Chillingworth plotted no revolt, no more, he assumed, than did his companions. They were adherents neither of the King nor of such other parties as might choose to call a king to book. They were more revolutionary than revolutionaries can ever be who debate only who might possess the power rather than what the nature of that power might be. They shared the clerics' belief that the material world is void but not because they looked to heaven's light. They took the world as sign, as but the outward vesture of a system which denied its meaning to the eye. There was a politics to that, of course, since neither rank nor appearance left them overawed but to Chillingworth, and his fellows, as he assumed, their politics wore no sword and buckle nor preached sedition in the streets. It was likewise why their very heterodoxy was a boon for he who would unlock the riddle of the universe has need of as large a bunch of keys as can possibly be possessed. It was also why they could not rest content with any single craft or skill. Every experience, every object, every material thing existed to be dismantled, disassembled, in a search for meaning which itself might prove mere illusion. Thus Chillingworth distrusted even his own responses. It was not only the blunt, corroding effects of the noxious fumes he so often inhaled which made him increasingly oblivious to his cruel indifference to his wife. As time progressed and the shock of a passion he had not known himself capable of feeling wore off, so she became another part of that deceptive state of being which others chose to see as reality but which he had come to regard as fantasy. To embrace her was to allow deception to have sway. What signifies this beauty, he would ask himself, what signifies this woman in my house?

These were times when scolds had their tongues depressed with metal spokes and liars theirs branded with a letter 'L' so that they should speak their crimes. Each word would thus contain its denial. Who can declare her innocence whose very tongue proclaims her guilt? And most such were women whose power resided alone in words, as it assuredly resided in little else. But there were others who doubted the wisdom of speech, shunned words which might render them into the hands of those who would inscribe their names on documents which might deprive them of access to speech at all. Some, though, saw in words a power which could topple kings and disassemble a nation, saw in the flow of ink on paper, in the echo of words in private and public places, a force which nothing but the blunt fact of sharp swords could neutralize.

Chillingworth was a pupil and a master of words. In his diary he wrote in a code partly transliterative, partly transpositional. He relied on his knowledge to move from one language to another, while regulating the shifts according to mathematical formulae. A member of a kind of conspiracy, he had to believe that conspiracies informed the universe. He once spent a month endeavouring to find the principle which determines the fissures which appear on a page of writing and which run down the text like a crack in a great building. Could it be, he wondered, that such white scars might themselves be a form of language, speaking from the other side of some lexical divide? Might the necessary crudity of words be shadowed by a subtler grammar which slid directly into the sensibility and there affected transformations in being itself?

He believed in the alchemy of language. He thought it possible that as gas may become liquid and then solid in turn, if only the correct reagent be found, the correct combination of elements and circumstances, so words might become things. It was a matter of identifying not merely the words but the cadences, the sonorities, the volumes, the concatenation of languages, the rhythms which might suddenly unlock the mystery. The gap between word and thing was an irony he sought to neutralize. He searched for the word which would make the thing.

As a consequence he would make such noises in his study as might lead you to imagine he communed with the devil. At one moment he would sound like an animal in pain, at the next recite a line from Virgil or enumerate simple numbers in German, French and Dutch, and at such a speed as to create a kind of fractured song. He would speak in tongues or vibrate his own. He knew and could prove that sound alone could smash a glass, that some invisible force locked up in his voice could fly through the air as fast as a musket-ball and yet in such a way that none could see. He had merely to make visible what was closed to the eye. Alchemy had occurred; it was simply that it could not be seen for what it was.

There were those then and there have been those since who believed that there are secret texts which may take the sensibility through doors of passion which are closed in the realm of fact. He was, perhaps, one of those for whom words have the power to arouse where images do not, where, indeed, insistent flesh does not. Certainly there were texts on his shelves, in Latin and Greek, which ventured such privacies, books which none but a few could venture to read without threat to their souls. But for him such volumes were not the stimulus to passion; they were the source and substance of passion.

He believed there to be a language in which lies could not be told, whose words could not be articulated if they were placed in the service of deception. Could but such a language be located and a people bound to fluency in its ways, the whole nature of social intercourse must change. But was it, he wondered, a mere matter of discovery or would this state of total clarity, in which a bright light would be made to shine into the darkest corners of experience, be achieved by slow degree? Words, perhaps, might be purified, language clarified until all imperfections should be expelled. He pursued purity, therefore, but saw no limits to the mechanisms which might be deployed to enforce such a purity, for purity may require the fire.

He saw Hester as a pure being contaminated but little with coarser elements. By instruction, though, such elements might be eradicated, such adulterations expelled, purged. She was a spiritual being contained by a physical vitality which blurred her finer self. To release gas from liquid, he had learned, might require either heat or vacuum or some combination thereof and what might apply to fluid in a flask might apply, too, to a woman whose evident desire for physical contact restrained her from spiritual release and threatened the ethereal state to which he himself aspired. He dealt with the elements only that he might find a means of liberating himself from them; she, because she took pleasure in them. He showed her a violet flower, which in combination with certain fluids, could be made to render a surface free of insect life. She would turn it in her hands and insist on the beauty of its enfolding petals, the thick, sweet smell as it was bruised in the crucible. He thought her fanciful in caring for surfaces. What lay beyond was his domain. Each object was a hieroglyph to be decoded, a mystery to be explored, a paradox to be resolved, an instrument whose mechanism must be exposed.

He believed, too, that language might be a path down which it would be possible to walk to the future. Those who study the past sooner or later grow weary of its inflexible substance and hope to catch a glimpse in the mirror of what yet might be. The future tense, he felt, already gave substance to tomorrow, set out the scenery for a play whose possibilities were thereby in part defined. Words were a means of making the world what it was not. Yet here was a dilemma for a seeker after truth for just as he knew that substances may masquerade as their opposite, beauty contain poison, sweet blossom bring forth bitter fruit, so, too, with words.

And as he travelled further into this territory of the mind, where mere speculation became the apparent bedrock for further conjecture, so he began to walk ever closer to the edge of a precipice whose danger was its own attraction. He believed that there might be a word which, if pronounced, could precipitate chaos and destruction, plunge the world into a kind of cleansing conflagration. The search for that word was a flirtation with the deepest inferno, a holocaust which beckoned him on for how else to discover that word unless by speaking it, no matter in the faintest whisper. So the world would end with a word, as it had sprung into being with another. Nor did he fail to contemplate what that word might have been if only because its reverse might prove the key to unmaking.

Such was the state of mind of the man to whom Hester had wedded her destiny and from whom she now felt the need to part, even as he had closed a door in his heart which fate and a beauty of the spirit had momentarily opened.

But still Hester waited. Once again the fields beneath the Hall clouded with butterflies, a shifting palette of red and blue and yellow shimmering in tall grass and round the heavy-headed poppies. Striped caterpillars, which had looped and stretched along bindweed, hardened into stickybuds, inert, impervious to light and rain. So, too, with Hester, who spun about her a protective shield and lived her life within. Her resolve, once so implacable and firm, began to falter once again.

Summer passed to autumn. Geese and swans gathered their kind, ran splashing over crystal water and launched into a softening sky, their wings sighing as, in perfect Vs, they cut a graceful vector to the sun. Fieldmice gnawed their way into shed and pantry and the fields themselves, now shorn of wheat, lay baldly under gathering clouds until flint set them aflame so that they glowed throughout the night. It was a time of ripening and completion; and though civil strife seemed gathering its tinder for the sport, here resolution seemed in the air, along with the smell of smoke and the rich stench of fecundity as the first autumn mists seemed drawn from the very earth itself.

I doubt, though, if Hester would have been moved to resolution herself had she not entered her chamber one dank November night, when her husband had ridden into town, there to discover her diary on the bed, its pages strewn around. Her inmost secrets lay thus exposed and violated. Not a word had he spoken as he passed her on the stairs but stared at her with what seemed like hatred. They had grown used to silence but there was such a ferocity in that stare that she had stood trembling long after the thud of hooves had faded far away.

There is a quiet place in the lives of us all to which we retreat. It has a door with a lock to which we alone possess the key. What if that key should fall into the hands of another? Love, after all, may open a door long barred against the light. And what if he who enters offers no love in return? Hester had handed a silver key to the one who stirred her heart and had watched as he turned it in the lock. He flashed such a look at her as would chill the soul and stepped into a privacy which was the essence of her life. The horror was that he now looked through her eyes and felt each first stirring of feeling and remorse. He knew her through and through. He had penetrated her mystery until there was no corner into which he had not pried, no subtle sensation over which he had not passed a coarse and calloused hand.

She sat now on the bed, like a bride amidst the scraps of paper thrown by village folk. Her deepest fears, her longings, her desires were written here and now he had knowledge of her far deeper than had he been her true husband. She realized, too, that thoughts of flight were written here, thoughts she must abandon or execute at once. Yet how? For all that she had thought so much on this and spoken to her cousin she lacked the detail to effect plans which had more of fantasy than reality about them. For a full hour she sat immobile, her mind bewildered, her soul in despair, but at last a terrible clarity swept through her and, slipping on a cloak and heavy shoes, she set out through a clearing night towards Caistor.

'But what shall become of thee there, Hester?'

'What shall become of me here?'

'Has he struck thee, then?'

'No. The blows he delivers are not with the hand. I cannot stay and where should I go but to a new country.'

'To thy family. Thou shalt return home to them or come here to me. There is no need to leave. This is madness, girl. And thou shalt wake up tomorrow and know as much. There are plenty worse off than thee.'

'I cannot face it here, Maggie. There I shall be born again. No one shall know me. I can be myself.'

'But we shall miss thee so, Hester, and thy father . . .' She broke off, knowing as well as her cousin that that father's mind was more fixed on the past than on the present.

'Maggie, I have looked at the river and I see me there sometimes. This is the other freedom that beckons.'

'That be a sin, Hester.'

'It is a sin to live a lie. It is a sin to greet each day with despair. He is not the man I took him for. There are times I doubt he is a man at all. There is in him something I may not understand. But until tonight I had no fear. Now I cannot stay a night more. Is John at Yarmouth?'

'Oh, Hester.'

'Is he, Maggie, is he?'

'That he is, but not for long. I know thou spoke of this before but John and I thought it were but fancy.'

'And will he take me, dost thou think?'

'It be fancy still, Hester. Thou may not leave us who do love thee. They are severe there, John says, and they will surely find thy secret out.'

'And should they do so, what of that? I am resolved, Margaret. I will go and if John will not take me then I pray that there be others that will. Shall thou help me or no?'

The answer was not in words but tears as the two young women clung to each other, each filled with her own thoughts, each remembering a past they had shared and aghast at a separation that would pain them both.

For ten long days and nights Hester waited. The ship outfitting at Yarmouth would not sail before the start of the third week of November and she must needs maintain pretence until the moment came to flee. Neither spoke of the diary nor of much else besides. He seemed more inward than ever and withdrew each day into his study. But he had read her plans and whether or not he took them for mere fancy no longer rode to town, sitting by the fire each evening and staring at her as though she were Mary Queen of Scots waiting for the moment of rebellion in her Norfolk prison. Each day her fear grew greater lest opportunity of escape should be denied. What he might do she had no means to tell but that he would wave her on her way was beyond belief.

At last the day arrived when she would have to leave. The ship was to sail on the morning tide and it would be spring before it returned and she had chance again; but he seemed no less restless than herself, pacing his room all afternoon. Then, when she despaired and had almost resolved to confront him with her plans, he strode past her in his cloak and, minutes later, rode off in the gathering dusk.

The next hour was a frenzy of activity as she rushed from one end of the house to the other, picking up and discarding a shawl, a dress, a flower pressed flat which brought back memories of another time. Margaret had already sent a small ship's box with clothes and a handful of coins to await her at Yarmouth but she had been unable to remove anything of her own for fear of discovery. It was those few things which she quickly gathered together and placed in an ample bag, those and a plain dress of Norwich cloth which one day and in another land would be emblazoned with scarlet stitched with a fine gold thread.

The night was clear and crisp with a frost fast-forming on the ground as she set out to cross the town to reach the Yarmouth road. Family goodbyes had long since been made, and family tears shed on many a day. She had resisted all arguments and restrained her brother, for whom a simple confrontation seemed adequate solution to her plight. Difference in rank alone would have been enough to carry him to prison. She had twenty and more miles to go and little more than nine or ten hours to complete her journey. Her father's horse was lame and she had no desire to implicate him in her escape. But she was strong. A farm child is used to walking and her resolution drove her on, that and a fear of pursuit. Nor was her fear without grounds for her husband had made provision for her flight, stationing a man among the lichen-covered graves at Colney church.

As luck would have it, though the winter rains had yet to fall, and the river was consequently low, she chose not to cross the ford which would take her past a home where a dear father and brother went about their business. She set out instead to follow the river's western bank towards Earlham, and though the man who watched saw what he thought to be her in the field, her black cloak made her indistinct and he hesitated to raise hue and cry before he had himself crossed the river and confirmed his suspicion. By the time he had returned to his horse, tethered between forge and church, Hester was already approaching the deserted streets of a city which seemed to glow with pale silver light.

Even so when a man in a broad hat tethered his horse at Tombland and summoned Chillingworth from his upstairs room Hester was not yet two miles along the road to what she could still think of as freedom. Barely a quarter of an hour would have sufficed to bring husband and wife face to face and who knows what would have followed from such confrontation. Indeed, in something rather less than that he reached the milestone by which she had momentarily rested and which indicated to those with the skill to read that they were now only eighteen miles from Yarmouth. But there he was halted. For as he had set a man to watch over Hester so that man whom others had set to watch over him had assembled those who, seeing him leave that mysterious and secret band in their Tombland conspiracy and take the Yarmouth road, had set off in pursuit. With his mind on the one ahead of him, who planned her treacherous abandonment, he heard nothing of those behind until, riding on either side of him, they forced him to a halt. Drawing their own conclusions from what they had seen, projecting their own meanings, they were no more and no less absurd than those who have defended the state throughout the centuries by reading the text of life awry.

Either way they halted Roger Chillingworth on the Yarmouth road and led him back to town, looking the while over his shoulder at the riverlike path which shone wetly in the moonlight.

The ship lay low in the water, a lantern swaying slowly on each mast. On the jetty, figures moved in the semi-darkness. From a distance the vessel looked absurdly small and frail but to Hester, cut through with cold and numb with fatigue, it represented hope and freedom and safety. The grass was slippery under her feet and she could no longer distinguish the path worn down by cattle and traveller alike. This was no feeble victim, though. There was iron in the woman who made her way towards the harbour, clutching in her hand a carpetbag which contained all she possessed in the world besides those few belongings waiting in a sea-chest far below. If she stumbled from tiredness, those three faint lights, yellow stars in an inverted universe, drew her down towards her destiny.

Those who stepped on board the ships that sailed the high seas at that time knew that there was no certainty about voyage or destination. It took more than religious faith to set out on vessels that would sit with ease within the stomach of Leviathan. Stout timber may float and seem at one with the surging sea but all who sailed knew that the sea could claim its own. Even those who lived with it, who acknowledged, too, its moods and its secrets, knew that their lives were not their own. The country is fringed with granite stones which list whole families lost in the deep waters of the northern sea and the blue-grey swell of the western ocean.

Hester thought nothing of this. Her mind was on her possible pursuers riding along a Yarmouth road where she herself had walked these ten long hours. The air was cold and a mist was gathering off the shore, even as the sky lightened from the east. A sudden weariness gripped her. So near to safety she felt the pressure of a night in which her life seemed almost to have run its course. As she came into the town, so the harbour disappeared from sight, the three false stars eclipsed. The houses were tight closed and silent, though ahead she fancied she heard the dull shout of a command and, as she turned a last corner, her shoulders aching from her burden and her feet torn by the uneven road, there before her lay the low shape of her salvation.

She saw her cousin as soon as she was close enough to distinguish the figures on the deck. Tall and broad-shouldered, he was carrying a sea-chest towards the prow as if it were nothing more than a lady's reticule. Resting it on thigh and ship's side he raised a hand to greet her but she lacked the energy to respond. A young boy pulled at a rope which lowered the lantern on the mizen-mast. The pale light of dawn was spreading from the east and he had been ordered to snuff out the candles which had illuminated the deck in yellow puddles of light throughout a long night. Upending the chest, her cousin strode the length of the deck to greet Hester, who stood now on the grey stone quay like a diver poised before a plunge.

*

As Hester walked unsteadily along the rough double plank she had the sense of crossing more than a few feet of silken sea. The woman who set foot upon the *Hope* could not be the same as she who stepped uncertainly from Norfolk soil. Behind and ahead was a vacancy and even the wood beneath her shoes offered no solidity, grating softly as the ship eased at her mooring. Some changes in our lives pass unobserved but here the symbolism was clear and as she stepped down upon the deck, her cousin's warm arm around her waist, she knew that Hester – child, daughter, bride – was dead, while another Hester was struggling to be born.

He wished to hurry her below but she was too fearful of Chillingworth's arrival to turn her eyes from the distant road. So, as a last heavy bale of Norfolk worsted was carried from the quay, she looked back to where she herself had stood a bare hour before. Knowing nothing of his fate she feared he must arrive and claim her for his own, and yet there was a quietness about her as though, after much struggle and peril, she was resigned to her fate. Holding hard to a thin rope which disappeared above her, she looked at the lightening sky. The last stars shone sharply still, swaying gently in an arc as the tide pulled at the ship. Their very remoteness gave her a kind of reassurance. Nor did she forbear to rest her mind on God, despite the fact that she might be thought to be challenging his law. But, then, doubtless, had she been of a mind to quibble, she would have reflected that she was no wife nor ever had been such and that a ceremony is without meaning which is entered into in bad faith. What, anyway, should she presume he had in his mind who had offered her no hint of married love? As the planks were withdrawn and shadowy figures on the shore bent to the ropes, the last links with her former life were cut and who can believe that she was anything but relieved and terrified in the same instant.

Ahead she heard a scrape and thump as oars were slid into rowlocks and then the first regular plash as a longboat took up the strain and slowly urged the *Hope* away from shore. A lantern in the prow cast its flat light on a circle of dark sea but as they cleared the quay and edged towards the harbour entrance so to the east the first light of dawn revealed a faint line where sea and sky a moment before had been sealed together by darkness. With a cry and a further splash the line was released and, to the sound of a dull thud from above, the sails took up a sudden off-shore breeze. The ship itself shuddered for a second, as though resisting the open sea and the wind that would commit her to it, then seemed to dip its prow into a phosphorescent mist which clung to the surface of the water. Behind her the land receded and seemed to sink to meet the ocean as she felt the wind fresh upon her face. With a swelling heart and hot tears in her eyes she turned her face to the future.

Her cabin, when at last she descended to it, was small but would have been smaller still had she shared it with the mother and daughter prevented by illness from joining the voyage. As it was, though she was far from tall, she had to remember to avoid the heavy beam which divided the space in two, a huge squared piece of oak which she found oddly reassuring in its solidity. Beside her bed was her sea-chest and, beside that, table, chair, bowl and jug. This was a ship on which cloth took precedence over everything and no concession was made to women. Indeed, women had no existence. Everywhere was roughness, severe right angle, tortured wood, hard-edged reality. But reality was what she fled. Reality or its shadow. Now she opened her arms to a promise. But there had been another promise. She closed her eyes, shutting out the parchment-yellow light, then opened them again. Still the bed, still the table, still the bowl and jug. So, she thought, I am here and not there. I am alive, after all.

She sank onto the bed, exhausted, tears starting to her eyes.

Alone, and embarked on a voyage into the unknown, she felt a sudden sense of total abandonment. A woman's vulnerabilities double and treble the anguish of a man's, and though Hester had an inner strength which few men, I think, could equal she saw nothing ahead but danger and despair, nothing but the possibility of a life become its own destiny. Something in her wished to smile. How else account for her desire to fly, to rise up on wings into her own imagining? Something in her wished to weep. How else account for the rain which seemed to fall on her soul, cold, unforgiving but curiously refreshing? So, she thought, it ends. So it begins. If only beginnings did not imply endings.

She would have slept immediately had the ship not suddenly lost way, waves slapping hard against the sides as, above, the sails snapped in the wind like a carpet beaten out of doors. Why had they stopped? Was she to be caught, after all? And if she were what could she do? Did his word carry weight a mile at sea? She drew the wooden bolt on the cabin door. It struck the metal hasp with a sound of finality. Then she pressed her hand against the rough-grained planks of the door and slowly, purposefully, pushed it open and stepped into a narrow space lit neither by candle nor the light of dawn. Ahead she could only just make out the steps which led back to the deck and, holding the flat of her hand against the wall, edged forward until her shin struck the bottom of a staircase which rose steeply above her.

Even in the few minutes she had been below deck the sky had lightened more and was a pale pink to the east, the white horses on a distant sankbank tipped with flame. Towards the shore, however, and it was thither that she directed her gaze, it was still dark and it was a moment before she could pick out the boat which moved steadily towards them. Where the oars touched the surface luminous green and white circles formed and dissolved in silence. So, he had found her after all, pursued a woman he disdained to notice in her own home. She felt that it was she who moved towards him and not he towards her. Destiny was a point midway between them while the stars turned away, fading into their own indifference.

At the prow of the skiff was a muffled figure, while behind him two men pulled at oars which now began to catch the light from the eastern sky.

'We'll just now miss the tide,' said a voice behind her in the shadows.

'Art thou in such a hurry, then,' replied another.

'Yes, yes,' she whispered to herself. Then she felt her cousin's arm around her again.

'Don't worry, my dear. 'Tis nothing but a passenger come late. With eight weeks or more ahead 'twould be churlish to leave him to wave us on our way.'

Wave, wave, she thought. There is no waving only a pushing away, a thrusting out. Then, as the boat neared them and the two men shipped their oars, Hester could see from the way their passenger held himself that this was not the twisted form of her husband, though his face was lost to her in the shadow cast by the ship. Involuntarily she raised her eyes to the distant land, now lower in the sea but just catching the full rays of the rising sun so that it seemed ablaze with fire. She could see neither horse nor rider, nor would she at such distance. No hint of pursuit. Those who watched for the beacon warnings of Armada's approach did not look as keenly as she but there was nothing except the English coast shining like gold in the morning light. Brightly vacant. Brilliantly without. When she looked down again their belated passenger had already clambered up the side and plunged into the dark interior; but it was as though his shadow remained, the reflected light of the sun leaving a translucent scar on her eye which faded before she could recognize its existence. That absence was a reproach and an invitation except that neither could be recognized as such. A moment, an instant that can be extended by words, has no more duration than a snowflake drifting down onto a kitchen fire.

The young man who leant on his oar to push his skiff away from the sloping side of the *Hope* looked up at her, caught her eye and smiled, then walked with perfect balance to his place and settled himself and his oar for the pull back to shore. The sea now seemed to boil up against the side as though heated by some invisible furnace, so powerful was the counter pull of tide and current. It seemed to her as though the sea were braided like a rope holding them in place, an anchor preventing her escape, and as skiff and ship parted she could not be sure for a second which one was moving or whether each was breaking free at once. There are such moments of disorientation which reach out to us all and for a second send us spinning around the edge of a vortex of time. But, then, somewhere at the heart of the mechanism, a stopped clock began to tick, the braided rope snapped in two and history recalled its destiny. With a dull crack from overhead the sails took the wind and the ship leaned over and turned about its length. Behind, the flaming land flew away like a festival firework; ahead, once more, the sea, and a new day.

As the *Hope* swung round towards the south, sailing first parallel to the Norfolk and then the Suffolk coast, past Lowestoft and Southwold, Aldeburgh and Orford Ness, with its swirling banks of seabirds, its powdering of gulls and terns and geese and ducks and solitary hovering hawks, and on towards Ipswich and beyond, Hester knelt at her prayers. She knelt on the hard wooden floor of her new and temporary home and tried to centre her thoughts, her guilt, her confused feelings, on God, who made both the world she left and that towards which she travelled, who had given life even to this soul who searched in vain for communion with her maker. In her confusion and remorse she hunted her memory for evidence of her own dereliction. Did she but know it she cried and laughed and turned a strand of her hair around her finger. But she was inward, a deep-sea fish, blind, afraid that to surface was to die, searching out redemption by simple instinct and need transformed to hope.

Outside, the wind was freshening and the sky blue-white. But in the cabin there was no light save that of a lantern which swung with the slow roll of a vessel which leaned into the wind, shadows lengthening and shortening, ebbing and flowing. There was no light, either, in that searching soul. Yet, though tears cool-scalded her cheeks, she could find no other path than that which she had taken, no sin but foolishness and youth, and when she finally stumbled to her bed some two hours later she felt both

57

purged and clean. Invisible in the gloom two dark stains marked the oak floor where her knees had bled into the wood, but she was unaware of pain, unaware of anything, indeed. For, after a night of fear and flight and physical exhaustion, she fell into a sudden and deep sleep still fully clothed from her journey.

You may imagine the dreams which now sailed full-masted through her mind, the images which floated through her consciousness, like the gulls of Orford Ness, riding the wind. Whatever function dreams may have, this day turned into night took Hester on a wild journey through her life. Fragments of her childhood blended with a future made not of memory but imagination. She saw for the first time the light of love in the eyes of the one who had tutored her, and cried for the knowledge, stood again beside a church as a demon from the deep stumbled on to the road. Harvest and seed-time met in her brain as never in the world of nature, and behind it all a subtle cadence as, unbeknown to her, water slapped gently by her head and the ship swayed slowly in the strengthening current. Bubbles of air, stirred by the prow, swept along the side creating a gentle tumbling sound which entered her mind as a music which seemed so natural she never questioned why it was heard in field and by stream.

She slept through that day and the night which followed, oblivious to the dull thud of canvas shoe and bare feet above her head, as to the words of command which from time to time became part of the dreams which surged and retreated like the tide. Then, at dawn on the day that followed, as the *Hope* left the Thames estuary on its starboard beam, she awoke. For a second she lay in bewilderment. Her lantern had long since extinguished and she lay in the purest darkness with only sound to offer a clue to her situation. She was like a child in the womb with nothing but a distant heartbeat for comfort. Then, she knew. For a second she opened and closed her eyes to distinguish the darkness without from the darkness within before swinging her feet carefully to the deck, surprised to realize as she did so that she still wore the clothes in which she had entered the cabin. Though when that might have been she could not know. What she did know was that she felt reborn. She, who had knelt as a guilty woman, had risen from her bed with sore knees and aching body but a pure heart and revived spirit.

By touch alone she made her way across the cabin, remembering to guard her head against the beam. Drawing back the latch she opened the door. Even the thin, grey light which reached her from the open hatch further down the corridor made her narrow her eyes, but after a second she walked uncertainly forward, as yet unused to the motion of the ship, and climbed the stairs to the deck.

It was to be the last fine day she would see for a week but it shook her in its beauty and she, who was used to a landscape of field and fen, saw for the first time a scene so epic in its grandeur that it caused her heart to race. For all around her was the sea. Wherever she looked was the curving edge of the world, and space. There was no middle ground. She, whose eyes had been drawn to tree and church, whose natural setting was hamlet or city square, the bustle of market or the quiet gentleness of willow and stream, now looked out on a vast emptiness. She knew, of course, that she could not be far from land but she knew, too, that ahead lay the true ocean whose dangers were real enough. Today, though, the sea rose and fell gently and far away was the thin purple line of the horizon's curve. Above her head gulls circled and dipped, swooping down by the stern where the waters tumbled. Again the ship was aflame, offering a harbinger of what was to come: red sky in the morning, shepherd's warning. Hester loosened her hair and shook it free, so that the wind caught it and blew it across her face. The deck seemed to hum beneath her feet, a vibration which made it feel alive and she a part of something more than herself.

Another day, and Land's End appeared briefly in the distance, a smudge of grey to the north as the clouds began to gather. Then it was gone and with it a final link to a distant home. Hester, on deck again, and joined by her cousin in the stern, felt a shiver pass through her. One commitment was left behind, another was forming invisibly in the western sky.

'Thou must be used to waving goodbye to thy home, John,'

said Hester, holding her hair away from her face with the back of a pale hand.

'Before I married it were all an adventure. New lands and all. But now it be different. I've a home.' He faltered, looking quickly across at her. 'But I have no other trade. I could work across to Amsterdam and there's fishing, too, but there are those made for home waters and others for the oceans. I'm for the oceans.'

'I, too, perhaps.'

'Thou? This is no woman's world, Hester. Thou shouldst stay close to the hearth.'

'Is that to be my fate, then?'

'It's the way of things. Can thou hoist wet canvas, hold the wheel when wind and current are contrary, climb to the mizen?'

'And can thou bear a child, John? Bear the pain of it? We are stronger than thou think nor more foolish. No, nor less. We are not so different after all. And I have a liking for wildness.'

'Well, there's wildness enough where thou art going. Dost thou know what lies ahead, Hester? The people are honest enough, I wouldn't deny, but they are made severe by the place. The seasons are hard and so too is the ground. There's forest to be cleared . . .' He broke off, not because of any alarm on Hester's face, for there was none, but because he recalled that this was to be her home. 'Ay, but there are good people, too. And no armies, nor yet no beggars come to the door.'

The shadow of a bird fell across them for a second as they stared down into the water, a sudden coolness like a grace bestowed and then withdrawn.

'John,' asked Hester, looking across to the dark opening of the hatch, 'who was he who joined us as we left? Why did we stop?'

'A passenger like thyself. The Captain had a message he were to come but we were else to miss the tide and wind. He were lucky in the end but gold is a great encouragement to courtesy so we had the courtesy to hove to.'

'Yes, but who is he?'

'Ah, that I don't know. Another pilgrim, no doubt. Besides I needn't tell thee these are times it's best not to enquire too far.

The world is not what it was and there are those who find it better to be elsewhere. Like thee, lass. But he will doubtless be companion for thee. There's none but thou and he aboard and there are long days ahead. Not that this be a time for voyaging. I fear the weather is not set fair, Hester. I hope there be something of the sailor in thee, after all.'

'But the sky is blue.'

'So are some men's eyes, but don't put thy trust in them for all that. Besides, there are clouds behind us. Thou hast been looking in the wrong quarter.'

'I've never been on any water deeper than the Broads and that only for a childhood treat.'

'Well, this will be no treat, my lass, and I should tell thee now. There's sickness ahead and times thou will be afraid, because there's times everyone's afraid and times everyone is sick. I should fill thy lungs with good English air for I doubt that thou wilt stir from thy bed for a good few days to come. The wind is freshening from the north and I can feel we're in for something strong. Thou wilt have thy taste of wildness soon enough so that even the world to which thou goest will seem tame.'

If forecasting weather is the sign of a natural seaman then cousin John was the best of the breed, for that night a wind blew which caused every plank to creak. The rigging sang and screamed as though a soul were in torment. Waves were no longer white-capped rills through which they would move like a sledge through snow. Suddenly they became hills and valleys and then, by degrees, so it seemed, mountains and crevasses which rose above them and sank far beneath. The ship itself appeared to have taken a mind to smash itself to pieces, hurling itself from the top of each crest, each peak, to the void below. Nor did they take a direct course, cutting through this fearful terrain, but moved crabwise forwards so that Hester was flung from one side to the other of the bed to which she had swiftly taken. Had she not followed instruction and lifted the wooden sides of her bunk she would have spent her time falling to the floor and climbing back again. The bowl and jug slid back and forth and she lacked the will to secure them until, following a brutal collision of wood and water, the ship seemed to halt in a kind of violent tremor and jug and bowl each smashed to the floor.

For the first hour she had thought that a firm mind would defeat a rebellious stomach but that was a conviction which quickly proved false and this girl, who had spent her life on as even a piece of land as the Lord and England has to offer, outside of Lincolnshire, found herself falling and climbing without ever leaving her bunk until, finally, she was indeed sick and went on being sick, as it seemed to her, for the best part of a night and day.

To say that she was sick is like saying that those who suffer from the plague are unwell. So they are, but unto death and there were times when death itself seemed to have its attractions. She had been sick enough as a child. Sullied food and wild fruit had had their effect; but nothing was to compare with this. For the world itself was in perpetual movement. Those who are sick on land know that however they feel the ground remains stable, though it seems to fly about them. Here, nothing was stationary. There was no normality from which to diverge. Again the candle flickered and died and though her cousin came to re-light it several times and enquired after her health, she could offer him no reply beyond a groan. From time to time she fancied she heard a cry from the next cabin but there was little comfort to be found in another's suffering which did nothing to alleviate her own.

The storm continued for eight full days and it was only on the last two that she was able to take a little gruel and sit in a chair. When she looked in a small pocket mirror which she found in her sea-chest, the face which looked back was so pale and hollow-eyed that it seemed like that of a corpse. The pressure of so much vomiting had raised a dark swelling under her eyes so that she looked twice her age; and Hester, who was as vain as anyone, wept to see herself thus, though ironically this was proof of her recovery since but a few hours since she would have cared nothing for her looks.

The storm had done real damage. A tangle of rope and shredded canvas lay limply on the deck, a jagged spar beside them. Just as the *Speedwell*, setting off for the New World from

Plymouth, had been forced back to land by a damaged hull, so the *Hope* began to take water, and when Hester finally put her head above deck few had any time for her as they went about the business of repair. It was with a certain pride that she noticed that she alone of the two passengers was on deck, though her own legs seemed likely to betray her even as she braced herself against the ship's side.

The storm was followed by a sudden calm. The sea rose and fell like a cow's belly after milking but the wind dropped quite away and within twelve hours was still as a midsummer Broad. Where a few hours before wind and wave had crashed about her, like canon on a battlefield, now the hull acted as one huge sounding board, magnifying each creak and crack and rasping rumble. But little else was still as the crew began to saw and hammer, to plug the leaks and strengthen the planking. It was then that Hester was introduced to the Captain.

He was tall at a time when this was scarcely an advantage on a ship designed for smaller men. The *Hope* was barely three hundred tons and built, it seemed, on a Lilliputian scale. He wore a dark jacket cut away behind so that two tails seemed to flap in the wind. His face was weathered and creased like an old map folded and refolded and she seldom, thereafter, saw him without a clay pipe in his hand, though she never saw it lit. His eyes were narrowed as though staring at the sun had half blinded him. Each night during the five they were becalmed she heard him pace the deck above her head, like a metronome ticking its regular beat.

John brought him across to the taffrail where she leaned looking at a man working in a cat's-cradle of ropes strung over the side, all his tools in a heavy belt about his waist.

'Mistress,' he croaked, in a voice rough from shouting in the wind. He nodded towards her awkwardly, looking, indeed, quite past her as he did so. 'Thou art welcome aboard. I hope the storm did not affright thee.'

His embarrassment was infectious. She inclined her head in answer to what she took to be his courtesy.

63

'Why, sir, I must have known occasions of greater terror but none such come to mind.'

He nodded again, as though the answer had proved apt. ''Tis not a season to choose for such a journey.'

'Indeed, sir. But we do not always choose our moment nor yet our destinies.'

Again the nod, as though he were a schoolmaster intent on testing some homework set the night before.

'Is this calmness after a storm the manner of such things?' she asked.

He plunged his hand into a coat dark blue and streaked with salt. The hand re-emerged, clutching the long-stemmed white pipe which he moved towards his mouth. The gesture was not completed. Instead he stabbed the air vaguely with it, as though writing on the wind.

'There is all manner of things at sea, mistress. Surprise is all. She is sly and has her tricks. Thou hast seen her wild but not yet as wild as she can be. Then again, thou doubtless think this still but she has a stillness which is like a kind of death and thou wouldst swear that all the life there is had vanished from the world. Not a fish breaks surface and all the air is sucked into the sun. Thou hast seen but the part of it.' He broke off, embarrassed, so it seemed, by his sudden fluency.

'No, go on, I pray thee, Captain. John has told us tales but few, I fear, because his wife might worry so. But I am here and would wish to know about a world so new to me.'

He nodded, though more to himself than to her. 'The land and the sea are night and day, thou might say. On shore the seasons come and go by the calendar. There is a seed-time, a time for growing and for harvesting, and though the wind may blow and rains come, they break upon stone. Thou may look at nature's power from a cottage window with nothing to fear but a lightning flash. Here there are no seasons. Winter, spring, summer are all one. In a single hour I have seen sun which draws the moisture from the deck like the spirit of the dead, then rain and wind and snow then sun again. And the sea like a living wall, higher than the mast above you. Here is no stone. Here is no window, and should the wind flatten our mast, as perhaps it does the wheat in thy field or the oaks in thy wood, there will be no replanting with the next spring and no hand to throw the seed.'

He broke off again, no doubt aware that he might terrify the young woman who had, indeed, had he but known it, been rendering up prayers for her survival these many days. He waved his pipe towards himself. 'But, as thou seest, this old oak has yet to fall and I would exchange no moment on this ocean for a lifetime of safety on the shore, for safety is a kind of death as it seems to me. Here there's a deal of respect between the sea and those who sail it.'

'Thou speak of it, sir, as though it were alive.'

He had begun to turn from her as though the interview were at an end but at this he turned back, a curious light in eyes which wandered for a second as he seemed to stare through her.

'Alive? Can thou have slept through these days? We are but mites on the wild cat's back. We are the wheat; she is the soil. Stand on the deck, watch each wave that comes, hear the music, aye, the music in the staysail, see the mast bend before her and thou wilt not doubt she is alive. But not as thou or I for she will be there when we have gone. She was and will be. There was a time, it is said, when she was worshipped as a god. We live in wiser times but what is our God and he does not contain the living heart of creation itself. Thou seest there is a pagan in me.' He smiled, if smile it could be called, which was halfway between a scowl and a laugh, gave one of his peremptory nods, and turned away, his hands clasped tight behind his back, the white pipe between them like a sheep's stubbed tail.

Though still enamoured by the novelty of the scene before her, Hester was unused to being idle. Part of the misery of her past year was that she had missed the daily routine of the farm, even the physical labour of the field and barn. Now the sailors around her had suddenly turned carpenters and smiths and the air was full of the rasp and thump of plane and hammer while she had little to do but wander in her new environment and watch the sea, black-green and still.

65

One man, who worked with a plane on a piece of oak planking set across two trestles, had thrown his shirt amongst the shavings, curled like petals on the deck. Despite the pale sunshine, which barely took the chill off the November day, he laboured in nothing but breeches and canvas shoes. But the most remarkable aspect of the man, to Hester, who had seen men aplenty so attired at harvest-time, was the pictures and strange designs picked out on his skin. For there was hardly an inch of his flesh not covered by tattoos. His body was like a lexicon, a volume of heraldry, an artist's sketch-pad, a cipher book. The pictures and words, or so they seemed, flexed and moved as he worked the wood and Hester found herself staring with total fascination.

On his back was a series of reptilian creatures which twisted in such serpentine ways as to seem to spell out words, though what they might be was beyond the comprehension of one used to reading simpler texts. Along each shoulder, and disappearing under each arm, were what appeared to be astral signs or even such foreign tongues as were spoken by those who had never known Christ's salvation. After a minute or two he became aware of Hester's gaze and with a smile put down the plane. It was the first real smile to have greeted her since she stepped aboard and in a second she was the self she had once been, laughing as he turned about with such evident pleasure, holding his arms above his head. He flexed his muscles so she might the better see the gallery he contained.

Every part of his body seemed picked out in red and blue, each design running into its companion as though part of one comprehensive narrative. And as he turned so they seemed to animate. Mythic beasts appeared to leap over hillsides, rivers to flow and words to articulate. So comprehensive was this body turned art that his own outline, the clear division between self and the world, began to blur. A ship, for such there seemed to be, rounding the narrows of his waist, appeared to wish to sail across the ocean which stretched out behind him, while at the top of his head, which was shaven almost to the top of his skull, was a single eye which stared back at her with a fierce unblinking intensity.

'Thou art a picture, indeed,' she said, seeing that even his bare feet carried their own insignia.

He grinned broadly and turned around once more before returning to his work.

'He do not speak, mistress,' said a fellow-carpenter, pointing to his companion with a sharp-edged chisel.

'Is he from Amsterdam, then?' asked Hester, for whom all strangers met in the streets of Norwich were Dutch.

'He is not from England, right enough, and would speak nothing of our language did he speak any language at all, but since he was born without a tongue to speak he is twice dumb.'

Hester's smile vanished at the thought of one so cut off from intercourse with his fellow-man.

'Oh, don't worry, mistress. He can understand as well as thou or I. Can thou not?'

The man grinned back and nodded vigorously.

'He even uses them pictures to make his meaning clear. There's a rising sun and elsewhere a moon and what I takes to be love and hunger and such like, though others take different meanings from those same marks. Those pictures be his tongue. Thou wilt see him point to them, though by now there is no need.'

'And he is quite happy,' observed Hester, falling easily into the habit of speaking in the third person of one you imagine impaired or from another land.

'Thou mean his smile? That betokens nothing. It be there fair weather or foul. The same affliction that made him born without a tongue fixed his face so. The day that he will die he will greet death with a laugh and doubtless fool him as he fools all those he meets. There be others who smile and are false, who mean thee harm. There is no harm in him, no matter the fierceness of the marks he bears. Thou hast seen him in the day. By candlelight there's pictures cannot be seen in the light of the sun. Some trick by the heathen who marked him so makes creatures stare out at thee in a candle's moving light would send a shiver through thy soul. But shouldst thou but look at him the terrors shrink away. On every ship there's one who becomes a kind of charm. He be that man on the *Hope*. That eye of his never sleeps. It watches over us all, even in the dark; and there are those on board who think it searches secrets out. Such will tell him things they would never tell another, knowing he has no voice to speak and so no power to betray. Nor can he lie, neither, for he can never say that which is not nor can his face pretend to feelings and so deceive. The smile is constant and true. I never sailed with better man nor never with one I would trust as much as he.'

'And what is he called? What art thou called?' asked Hester, correcting herself.

The smile beamed back at her. He pointed with a stubby finger, itself seemingly alive with swirling figures picked out in pinpricks of colour. The design at which he pointed seemed to signify a heart, though one pierced through with arrows, or perhaps it was some animal and those its horns, or maybe a sea creature and the lines attached its fins or waterspouts. Or perhaps . . . Hester realized that the image seemed to metamorphose with the changing light or the angle at which he stood.

'That is thy name?'

He smiled back at her.

'We call him John, though on the *Charity* he were Peter and before that Matthew. It be all one to him. He will answer to anything.'

'Well, John, I must not keep thee from thy work but I thank thee for showing me such strange wonders. There are none of these where I come from.'

In a curious way she felt the safer herself for this man's presence. Like the crew she felt some strange significance in one who spoke not with his tongue but his very being.

As the men continued to work in a pale November sunshine filtered by a thin, white haze, she saw on the far horizon a point where the line between sea and sky seemed to kink into irregularity, a smudged comma. At first she took it for the tail of the storm as it pressed on to serve other vessels as poorly as it had served them. But, as her eye returned to it, as a tongue to an ulcer in the mouth, so she fancied it to have grown until she thought it might be land. Then it would disappear again until she had convinced herself that it was nothing but a departing cloud.

She looked to see if her fellow-passenger would emerge but there was no sign of the hooded figure she had seen huddled in the prow of the skiff off Yarmouth harbour, a place which itself now seemed part of another world. Other things had changed, too. A ship which had seemed to tower above her when she had walked aboard along that narrow plank now seemed to have shrunk to a small island in a vast and empty space and, quite suddenly, she felt a rush of loneliness and despair. Home and friends had disappeared so completely that it was as though they had never been. The fixed points of her life had been removed and her navigation was now to be on oceans in which no markers indicated safe passage. She sailed on seas more threatening than those which had caused her such distress this past week. What rocks might lie ahead she could not know.

There was a cry from the stern. A young sailor stood with one foot on the rigging and the other in mere air and pointed to the very sign she had taken for land. The others on the deck lay down their tools and looked astern, shading their eyes. The captain, pipe still in hand, clumped slowly past her to stand beside the sailor whose hand was still extended. Pipe was exchanged for telescope as he steadied himself like some figurehead. A second later he collapsed the telescope with a snap which echoed round the suddenly silent deck.

'Ship the longboat, mister,' he ordered, 'there's work to be done.'

No one questioned the order or sought explanation, moving instead to a low flat boat which rested on the deck. Hester watched in some bewilderment as it was swung out over the water, and then lowered on squeaking pulleys until it smacked into the sea, dropping the last few feet. Men tumbled over the side in silence, suddenly intense, focused. To Hester it was like some ritual played out in mime. A rope was thrown up from the boat and the young sailor, blond hair swept back into a bunch secured by a ribbon, walked it forward to the prow as the men below pushed away from the side and began to lean back against the oars. The rope tightened as they moved ahead and swung in front of the ship, becoming taut and sending a line of silver droplets sparkling into the sea. For a second nothing happened, as the blades dug down into the grey water, but by degree the ship began to move, though without the sounds to which she had become accustomed. The rope chafed against the wood but with neither wind nor waves and such slow passage there was an uncanny silence as though theirs were a ghost ship drawn on by the living dead.

With her cousin in the longboat there was no one to explain the mystery to Hester. It was clear that the distant object, which now stood out more clearly, less a comma than an exclamation mark written on the line of the horizon, was the cause of all the action. Not knowing the nature of her role or the propriety of asking questions she stood and watched in some bewilderment, feeling apprehension but unsure as to its source. At last she could stand it no more and approached the Captain who looked first to those who strained at their oars and then to the eastern sky.

'Captain, forgive me if I should not speak but what is amiss?'

He straightened up for a moment and without turning spat out a single word: 'Privateers.'

'Privateers? And what might they be? Pirates?'

'Ay, pirates.'

'But how do they hope to catch us with no wind?'

He turned to her at last and as to a child explained. 'First, my lass, there may be wind there and none here. I have seen two ships no more than a chain's length apart, one with full sails, the other flat becalmed. There is no single wind. There are currents in the wind as there are in the sea and they move where they will.'

'Perhaps they are rowing as we do.'

'I think not. Their sails are full.'

'But the wind must fail them soon.'

'Perchance, and I pray it will, but we are taking water still.'

'We are sinking?' she asked in alarm.

The Captain shook his head, as much in exasperation at the question, it seemed to her, as in denial. 'No, but I must finish repairs and, as thou see, my carpenters have turned seamen again; but I must recall them soon or the water may begin to damage what we carry. And were that to be we might as well hand it to those who anyway are closing on us apace.'

She glanced over her shoulder and recognized the truth of what he said. For the first time she fancied she could distinguish a ship. Certainly, what had once seemed a line of grey now had a touch of white to it. 'And hast thou encountered privateers before, Captain?'

'That I have,' he replied, lifting his hand to a weathered cheek. 'Mr Jones,' he shouted to the young sailor who leaned forward in the prow, pouring water from a canvas bucket on the rope which rasped along the wood, 'convey my compliments to our other passenger and suggest to him that we may be in need of his assistance. Then break out the arms. And thou, mistress, I must ask to go below if they approach. They will not treat thee with kindness.' Then, to himself, in a low murmur, 'I had not thought to find them so far west.'

'I believe I can serve my part.'

'That thou can and thy part is to remain below deck and leave us to do what we may.'

The distant ship was clearer now and she could make out masts and sails. Their own progress through the water was distressingly slow. She watched a patch of weed glide slowly the length of the ship.

'She's losing way, Captain,' shouted the young sailor, who suddenly seemed like some Adonis to Hester now that he stood between her and danger.

'That she is.'

Hester herself could see that the rime of white at the base of the bow, which indicated its progress towards her, had disappeared.

'They're getting out the boats. Two of them.'

'Then they must catch us,' said Hester, half to herself.

'By no means,' replied the Captain, who had walked a few paces off but heard her nonetheless. 'By no means. There's but two hours to sunset and providence may take a hand.'

And providence did. Above their heads canvas stirred like a creature newly born. All three looked up and as they did so a figure emerged from the cabin below. It was Hester's fellow-passenger. He stood, his white shirt unbuttoned, hair ruffled in the strengthening breeze. He was pale enough but when Hester looked at him in the flat light of that November day she felt a physical shock. Perhaps it was the moment of threatening danger and possible escape, but never before had the simple sight of another set her heart to race.

'Call in the men, mister,' shouted the Captain, and then, to the man who stood by the hatch, looking, as it seemed to Hester, as sick as she had a few hours since, 'We'll outrun them, yet, Mr Dimmesdale. I had thought to put a sword in thy hand but there may yet be no need. For all that, thou wilt turn to and aid us, if thee please. The wind may yet find their sails again and we must ship the boat and set our own sails.'

Ahead of them the men had ceased their rowing and with what little sail was set the *Hope* was already drawing abreast of them. Her fellow passenger, as pale as the canvas which now began to fill, set about aiding in the recovery of the longboat and, as the men clambered back on board, hauled beside them on the ropes until, dropping grey droplets on to the still greyer sea, it swung upwards and inboard. By the time they had begun to set the sails, however, those who pursued had halved the distance between themselves and their prize. Hester could now make out the faces of individual oarsmen, though not the ropes which connected them to the ship whose sails lay slackly from their heads, so that it seemed as if the larger vessel followed the smaller as a cuckoo pursues a foster mother a fraction of its size.

Though at home she had wondered at rain which fell on one side of their home but left the other dry, she was still amazed that their own sails should now be filling and their ship croaking and moaning with life while hardly half a mile astern another had to be pulled forward by muscle and sinew. And though they began to pull away she noticed that several sails were still not set. It was as though they were accepting some deliberate handicap. Was this, then, some game that they played to rules she could know nothing of?

'Are we safe, then, cousin?' she asked, as he passed her by, his face beaded with sweat.

'Until the wind should reach his sails. We dare not set all ours, Hester, until the leaks be plugged. Our greatest friend is darkness. Our greatest enemy is the water in the hold. Say a prayer and then another. We have need of them.'

With the sails now set and the wind pulling them onwards the best part of the crew disappeared below to complete repairs, leaving on the deck the Captain, two seamen in the rigging, Hester and that other whose appearance had so disturbed her.

At this point, with the privateers' ship only waiting for the wind to find her sails, with the *Hope* letting water in her hold and the mysterious passenger at last on deck, it must seem like a story ready made. No wonder, though, for there is something about a voyage which draws the story-teller. The sea is more than physical space, and lines of latitude more than marks drawn on a map. No one steps off a ship the same person who stepped on. You go towards the future slowly. On shore the days soon pass. Here they stretch towards the horizon. There is something about the sea that those who have never ventured on it may never know. Time requires a shoreline, a departure and an arrival. The horizon is a proposition, merely, a receding edge of perception. We are drawn to the ship's rail and who has not played, at least in fancy, with the notion of a downwards plunge into a cold enclosing spray. The sea is a beginning and an end. No gravestone there for the sailor who slides down a board and plunges, weighted, into the blackness of ocean deep: one who was and is not, whose resting place never rests.

On board ship all time, all morality, all customs and conventions are in suspension. Here we meet with no past, no burden of knowledge or ignorance, no ties, no prohibitions, no fears, save those engendered by the sea itself. Here, hands may touch which on shore may never intertwine. Here, words may be spoken which if spoken on land would terrify the soul. Here, truths may sound clear even if they be truths but for the moment.

There are stranger things at sea, Hester's father had said when a two-headed lamb was born or the sky gleamed with flowing waves of colour. And now she had the proof of it. The *Hope* began to catch the wind full astern, driving before it, while the sails of the pursuer still hung limp and useless. Even as she watched, however, so the two boats which towed the black bulk of the privateers' vessel, as children will lead their blind father, began to turn away. She caught the glint of light on oars which were quickly shipped and watched as the men climbed spiderlike up the ship's side. A sharp order from the Captain and their own men tumbled onto deck, uncoiling rope and pulling together until the remaining canvas was hauled into position and unfurled. And what of the leaks? Not a word was spoken but the ship responded like a deer with dogs at its heels.

'They have the wind, sir,' shouted a voice from high above. And so they did. Half a dozen white flowers blossomed amongst her masts and once again a collar of ruffled white was visible along her prow.

Even with the thrill of the chase Hester still found time to look at her mysterious companion, though now there seemed little mystery about him. He worked readily alongside the seamen and if his hesitations showed that he was far from practised at his profession yet he took instruction readily, one moment pulling at a rope, the next emptying canvas buckets of dark water. His hair was long but not that of a royalist; it was rather that it wanted cutting. His face seemed pallid beside the leather tan of the sailors, like the underside of a flat fish. His shoes were hardly suited for the deck and after a little he kicked them off. His black breeches were gathered at the knees and soon were soiled, as was his shirt, by the spray which began to swirl in the wind like grapeshot. Indeed the sea, a moment since flat and entirely tractable, was now flecked with white, while the sway of the ship about its central axis indicated the beginnings of a deep swell.

Yet, keenly as the *Hope* cut through the waves, she could not shake her pursuer who had begun to close again, though it was difficult to pick out details in the deepening gloom. The storm, it seemed, had swung in some great arc only to return from a different quarter.

'Don't worry, Hester,' said her cousin, briefly at her side. 'If we can continue a little, the night may save us. There'll be no moon tonight.'

And it was true, for though the distance continued to shorten it was as if a well of darkness had begun to rise up from the east, a darkness which soon engulfed the following ship, itself already but a grey outline on a grey ocean, and then themselves. There were indeed to be no stars in this night nor silver moon. Everywhere was darkness and Hester nearly lost her balance as the wheel was spun and they shifted course, the sails above her throbbing like a hive of bees. The wind had slackened but still drove them in the darkness. She felt a hand on her arm.

'Thou must go below, Hester. By morning we shall have the whole ocean to ourselves.'

'But what of the water in the hold? Are we not still in danger?'

'We shall finish repairs in the morning. Now, below, and keep silent, for even in the wind the sound of a voice may carry where that of ship and sail do not.'

The same firm hand led her in the darkness to the hatch and aided her as she reached for the stairs which led below. She turned about and climbed carefully to the lower deck. But as she reached the door of her cabin and lifted her hand to the latch she was conscious of another presence.

'Is there someone there?' she gasped, afraid to speak but afraid equally to stay silent.

'There is, indeed. But none save thy companion. They have sent me below as useless to them and I must confess I am grateful for it.' A hand brushed gently against her back and was gone.

There was something in the voice, so quiet and assured, that calmed Hester's fears at once.

'Tomorrow we shall meet. But for now, I fancy, we both have our orders to obey. May God watch over us.'

She heard the click and rasp of the latch and she was alone again, though not as alone as she had felt but a moment before.

Some time in the night she woke, a dream of familiar faces in unfamiliar places fading instantly. She listened in the darkness. The ship had lost way, rocking gently. Above her she heard the dull thud of bare feet and a slithering sound that meant nothing to her but amorphous threat. Then, the squeak of pulleys. So, the boat was being swung out once again. A few moments later it struck the water, as before with a sharp slap, almost directly in line with where she lay. A curse, quickly muffled, sounded clearly, quite as though the ship's side were made of parchment rather than oak. Then the soft splash and swirl of oars, a regular pulse so close that it seemed a part of her. She waited as the sound faded ahead but was too exhausted to capture the excitement of the evening before and as the *Hope* responded sluggishly to the invisible rowers and arpeggios of bubbles chased along the keel, so she slipped back into sleep.

She woke suddenly. Her cover had slipped invisibly to the floor and she was bone cold, but what made her suddenly alert was a noise which had somehow commenced in her dream but echoed in reality as she was shaken into consciousness. Then another seemed to explode inside her skull. Her brain, still fuddled from sleep, struggled to make sense of cold and sound and fear. Plainly they had been caught and those were musket-shots, but why now this silence, complete and utter as it seemed. There was a sound, however; it was simply that her ear was tuned now to the percussive power of gunpowder. For again, distant and indistinct, came that familiar plish-plosh and she felt the ship begin to swing about. She lay, uncertain what to do, whether to rise and join those on deck or stay in her bed and invent a story to account for what she heard. An hour passed.

There was a gentle tap at the door. 'Hester,' whispered a soft voice. She lay for a second, her mind full of confused images. 'Hester.'

She swung her feet to the cold deck. By now she was so familiar with her cabin that she moved with the assurance of a blind woman, reaching for the cloak folded neatly over the chair beside her bunk and feeling with her feet for the cloth slippers beneath the table. She edged towards the door with her hands outstretched, though she knew no obstruction endangered her. Her hand found the latch immediately and she eased it from its clasp, for what privateer would choose to knock and speak with such softness: and then she stopped, shocked by a thought which had never entered her mind until that second. The Captain had said that it was unusual for privateers to be found in these waters. Yet someone pursued them and there was one who might have cause to do so. Could it be that the husband she had banished from her mind and heart could be reaching out to bring her back?

There are thoughts that come in the night which in the light of day we would laugh away in a second, perhaps because there was once a time, before light and fire, when the night held terrors real enough. But the thought of Chillingworth stayed her hand for only a second. She unlocked the door.

'Hester, thou art to have no fear.'

Her cousin's voice alone would have stilled whatever fears she might have had. It was gentle and low and calming and seemed to reach inside her.

'We are in a thick fog and thought ourselves well free. We had been rowing some four hours and changing course like a rat in a barn but whoever guides their ship seems to think much as we.'

His whispered voice was so low that Hester had to lean close to him in the darkness. She detected the sharp smell of a man who had laboured while she slept.

'It was while we rested that we heard their voices. They seemed to come from everywhere. Then we passed through a stretch where the fog had quite disappeared. The men took to the oars again to pull to the other side but one of my fellows in his haste missed his stroke and fell back. Unfortunately he cried out. It was enough for someone among our pursuers to discharge his gun, and, whether in fear or eagerness, one of our number fired his.'

So, she had indeed heard not the first but the second shot.

'Then the fog closed in again. They never saw us, I think, and there is no means to tell in what direction we might lie. It were chance they came upon us, I am sure. Anyway, I am ordered below to tell thee that no sound must betray our position and no light appear, not even in this dungeon, for some glimmer of it may escape. Even the sails are furled lest they betray us.'

She listened less to the sense than the sound, the tone, the quiet assurance.

'I must leave thee now. Have no fear.'

A moment later he was gone, leaving her nothing to do but lie in the dark like a blind woman living by sound alone. For an hour she lay, her heart beating wildly, but even fear and excitement give way to tiredness and, by degrees, she slipped into a restless sleep. In that sleep came a dream that seemed so close to truth that though the memory of it faded with her waking yet while she slept it had a reality which would not be denied. It was a dream in which her mysterious companion came close to her, an angel and a devil at the same moment; but, as she struggled with her contrary feelings, she was awake again, aware of another knocking at her door. She quickly swung her feet to the floor and opened it, expecting her cousin to be returned, but the voice which came from the darkness was not his.

'Mistress Hester. I have been asked to sit with thee. The others are required on deck. There is little I can do either there or here but if I may but stay with thee we shall doubtless both feel the better for it.'

She seemed still in her dream, for why else should she stand aside so that he might enter in? But stand aside she did and felt him brush against her in the dark.

'And it please thee,' she whispered, 'there is a table and two chairs.'

So, here she was, still night-attired and inviting into her room a man of whom she knew not name nor status, nor nothing else at all. Such, though, may be the pressure of the moment, the power of circumstance and danger undefined. She reached out in a darkness near to total, but for the slightest suggestion of a grey uncertain shadow. Her intent was but to guide but when their fingers touched Hester gasped at the coldness of the hand which grasped hers in the dark.

'We may not talk, save in a whisper, I'm afraid.'

'There will be time aplenty for talk, sir. Now we must wait. But who is it I shall be waiting with?'

'Ah, yes. We have never yet been introduced. My name is Dimmesdale. Arthur Dimmesdale.'

'And I Hester . . .' She hesitated a second, who would not speak the name of the man she had left behind. 'Hester Prynne.'

'Mistress Prynne.'

For some minutes they sat in the darkness, listening to the breathing of the ship, like a Leviathan turning slowly in its sleep. Forbidden to speak in anything but whispers, they listened to the voice of the *Hope*. In the distance the regular kiss of wood on water, followed by a carillon of bubbles strangely magnified by the hull. From time to time the sound of the Captain's boots on the deck added a heartbeat to the illusion of a living creature.

They sat, thus, staring sightlessly at one another until at a distant sound or a sudden movement of the vessel, he reached out a hand and grasped her gently round the wrist. The effect was as immediate as it was unexpected. The accumulated anxieties and tensions of a year seemed to pour into her heart as though the winter rains had burst an earthen dam. From somewhere deep inside there came into her throat a choking sob and in a second her whole body was shaken with disturbing tremors. Her breath came in sudden gasps and she clung to the anonymous hand as a drowning person will seize upon her rescuer, and, indeed, since they were sworn to silence, with much the same potential effect.

'Mistress Prynne, Mistress Prynne. What is it that so distresses thee? The danger will soon pass. We are in safe hands, as I believe, for we are never without God to guide our thoughts and keep us safe.'

But she was past hearing, past responding, and certainly beyond a simple platitude. She was on a dark and threatening ocean of her own, discovering emotions she could never name. Pain, grief, guilt, none of these could begin to describe a feeling which the mind alone could neither contain nor yet explain but which had awaited only the touch of a human hand to release.

Perhaps it was the darkness, perhaps the danger within whose circle they were held, perhaps the very anonymity and invisibility of the cabin, but he ventured what elsewhere he would not and she responded as elsewhere she could not. He rose from his chair and in a second was beside her. She fell forward, half in a faint, her head pressed into his shoulder, her arms reaching round to draw this comfort to her. There was no sexual charge to the embrace. He felt the fluttering life of a wounded animal in his arms; she the simple refuge of another's care. He held her as you would a child who had woken from nightmare.

Then, still more strange, as the sobs began to subside, she began to speak in a broken voice, scarce above a whisper. The words seemed to come from somewhere outside herself, though the thoughts were from deep within. She required no prompting nor needed any response. In this gently moving darkness she conversed with none but herself. It was one long narrative, a confessional, in which she spilled into the night the events and feelings of a year that had turned her from an eager girl to a woman forced to take her own life in her hands. For the man who listened, and whose presence she seemed quite to have forgotten, it was a tortured story told in a broken cadence as each thought tumbled and crashed into another. She gasped for breath as though she had been granted only these few moments to tell all there was to tell. No sentence was complete before she abandoned it for another, rushing onwards to some conclusion which never arrived. She spoke with total familiarity of places and people with no meaning to him precisely because she spoke not to him but herself. The absolution which she sought was not from another; it lay in speaking aloud what had been locked away in a place so secret she had thought that neither she nor others would ever visit it.

She spoke of Chillingworth, but not with any bitterness. It was herself she blamed for falling under his sway, for thinking she had the power to change his will, for assenting to the eclipse of her own freedom. Nor did she fail to mention the nature of her wedding night, for she was in some trance quite as though a conjuror had instructed her to display her inmost self as simple necessity, laying aside inhibition and doubt.

At last she began to slow. The energy which had driven her on with such a powerful and random force seemed to exhaust itself. And at last a kind of sleep came over her and, as it did so, her grip relaxed, for until then her fingers had clung to his arm until he winced and once cried out in pain.

It can only be imagined what this silent and invisible companion thought as for half a night he listened to such a melancholy and scarcely audible cry of anguish. Perhaps it held a dark mirror up to his own soul. Certainly he grasped her now sleeping form to himself with a gentle passion which suggested understanding. And as the movement of the ship told him that wind had once again sought them out on a flat and murky ocean, he lifted her, as one would lift an exhausted child at day's end, and, moving carefully in the unfamiliar room, laid her on the bunk, separated from his own only by stout oak planks. As he did so, and despite the prohibitions of his faith, he made a kind of sign above her forehead, a sign invisible in the dark which betokened the forgiveness which she did not know she sought.

As he opened the cabin door a chill, grey light seemed to seep into the room like mist. He looked across the room towards the figure who lay on the bed, hair tumbled about, dress hanging down to the floor like a curtain. Her face was turned away but in that moment he felt a tenderness which had never invaded him before, he who had listened to many another private sin before this night.

Dimmesdale left the cabin no less changed than Hester. For several hours, as the *Hope* tracked backwards and forwards to escape an invisible pursuer, he had listened to an invisible woman, her words pouring from her mouth into his mind. For all the pain it betokened and for all the desperate energy of its delivery, it was a story told with such simplicity, devoid of craft, that it moved him greatly as he sat in the dark and the desperate music of her voice washed over him. There was no self-pity in what she said nor yet an effort at self-justification, but when, from time to time, tears briefly interrupted her song, for that, in retrospect, was almost how he felt of it, his own eyes filled with tears. He had thought himself, until then, a strict moralist. He had been taught to guide his feet down narrow paths, to pity the sinner and hate the sin. Yet, when she denied the truth of a sacrament, he never doubted her right to make such denial. He felt, as she, that the marriage she described was no true marriage nor this flight from obedience other than a journey fully justified. Nor was there trace of pity in his heart. Was he not in flight from obedience himself, and did he not feel justified in his journey to another land?

The morning light was insubstantial and flat as he stepped on deck. At first the whole ship seemed deserted, sailing onwards without a human hand to guide her passage. But then ahead, towards the bow, he saw the dark figure of the Captain, arms folded behind his back like some huge bird of prey watching for a beating heart on the forest floor to carry to the treetops. The fog had gone, blown away by a fitful wind which played a game with the canvas, at one moment ballooning it to pregnant life, the next leaving it flaccid, detumescent. Of their pursuer there was no sign, though the visibility was poor. A yellowing sky, tinged grey-green, seemed to plunge into a sea the colour of black ink barely a mile or so away, though, a landsman, he could no more read the signs of the ocean than a mariner can tell elderflower from may.

The ship sailed on, heading towards a still dark western sky, as though there were some invisible rope which stretched ahead on which a phantom crew continued to row. Though he should perhaps have been desperate to know of their situation, the efforts of the previous night and his own deep exhaustion from the inward journey on which he had sailed in the darkness of the cabin beneath his feet, had left him drained.

He was started from his reveries by a hand which took his own. So abstracted was he in staring at the sea that he neither saw nor heard the Captain's approach.

'They have left us, sir. If ever they were there.'

'Captain?'

'The sea has many memories. Sometimes those memories are displayed before us.'

'But the shot?'

'Perhaps our own, echoed back to us. I once spent half a day shouting to myself. Fog is like a varying liquid: here like water, there like molasses. Sounds will sometimes echo round amidst it and then come back from another quarter, doubled, trebled, and in a different voice. Then there's creatures that call out like a woman in pain or sing like a young boy at church.'

'But it was real. I saw. I heard.'

'We sometimes hear and see what we will. But, yes, it was there indeed. It is no more, though. The thing itself was real; it is the meaning of it which I mistrust. A privateer so far west seems strange to me. Whatever it was, though, 'tis gone. And partly thanks to thee, though thy hands, I judge, will have suffered for it.'

Dimmesdale looked down at his hands and in the strengthening light could see that they were indeed torn and stained with blood, though these stigmata gave him no pain.

'Thou hast a landsman's hands and more besides. They be gentleman's hands, I think.'

'Not gentleman's but scholar's, perhaps.'

'Well, scholar, thou didst well, but look to those. Keep them in use and, when the flesh has healed, knead in some beeswax or within a day or two thou will not be able to hold thy pisser. Good morning to thee, sir, and I were thee I would take to mine own cabin and then to my bed. Thy shipmates have gone that way this hour since, though they will be back at work while thou wilt be dreaming of this night's adventure.'

Hester slept deeply as though enchanted. Night and day had been reversed but what more appropriate for one whose life has been turned so completely inside out? She slept a dreamless sleep, quite empty now of secret pain. The ship rolled slowly in the swell but she barely moved, lying deep in a silent void. She had crossed some meridian invisible to the eye but real enough for all that. When at last she rose and climbed the now familiar stairs to the sloping deck she felt reborn. Nor did she feel embarrassment when she saw her companion of the night before, his hands with rough bandages, walking unsteadily on the after deck, for though she remembered little of what she had said in the darkness of her cabin she thought of him as a source of comfort.

'It seems my hands do not take to honest toil, Mistress Prynne. Too much labouring in the galleys.'

'Do they pain thee?'

'No, they have been treated by an expert physician.'

She raised an eyebrow, knowing none such in five hundred miles.

'The very man who makes our meals apparently attends to all

the body's needs hereabouts. He cooked up some yellow paste which smells as vile as rotting meat then spread it with a stick as though it were pork dripping on bread and wrapped them as thou seest. Three days, he says, and they are mended. Meanwhile I walk around with a bear's paws, unable to tie a lace or lift a spoon. And my companions at the oars show not a sign of distress. This voyage, it seems, will acquaint me with my failings more than a thousand sabbaths in pulpit or pew.'

What could Hester do but agree?

'Thou art wearing thy dress of yesternight?'

'I have but two dresses in my wardrobe. Thou shall see this one for weeks to come, washed through until it be the colour of yonder grey clouds. It were white once and would be now but for the small matter of some privateers.'

'It is a perfect dress and I can see that it has aspirations to whiteness, as do we all, but I fear it bears my mark.'

'Sir?'

He turned her gently round with his bandaged hand to reveal a stain. 'It was only this morning that I realized the condition of my hands. I fear there is blood here.'

Hester endeavoured to look behind her, as a dog will try to bite the flea from its back, but could see nothing. There was, however, such a mark, a splash of red which caught a sudden morning sun and seemed to shine out from a whiteness which had indeed survived the honest dirt of shipboard life. The shape, though, was not quite that of a bloodied hand, though there was something of that about it.

'Oh, it will wash away. Salt water is the cure for that, if little else.' She smiled her absolution and for a second was picked out by the sun, appearing from behind the very grey clouds to which she had pointed but a moment before, and for a second she seemed suffused by a soft red light, though the low sun which barely rose above the eastern horizon cast a long shadow besides. 'Now I must eat, for I feel I have starved myself this month. Does thy cook have a solution to this problem, too?'

But he heard nothing of this remark for he still looked at this glowing figure before him and he, too, had felt that electric shock which had passed through Hester when he touched her, as it seemed, but a moment since.

It is often so that a problem which seems beyond solution when we retire to bed no longer seems such with the morning's light. So was it with the privateer. All eyes had stared into the darkness awaiting the first sign of God's daily grace. When it came, a soft silver touched with palest pink slowly lightening the eastern sky as a watercolour swept across a damp parchment will spill its transparent sheen down the page, they were alone on the ocean swell. Still they looked, until tears started to their unblinking eyes. It was only some six hours since the night had been punctuated by the pistol shots and two since the fog had slunk back into its watery cave, but for all that could be seen they had the world quite to themselves. No word was spoken, quite as though they were still under the interdict to quiet their tongues, nor did any venture to the galley. They seemed instead still to await the echo from a cannon shot. High above, in the topmast shrouds, two sailors, back to back like twins whose flesh was fused, looked steadfastly, one into the night, the other into the new-born day. From the deck below it seemed that neither moved. They appeared like some creature guiding them to their destiny. Yet move they did, turning their heads slowly and looking for some sign of menace, a mark where a second before there was none, as we may feel the smallest swelling in our body which may one day take our life. Nor did they think to find what they sought by a direct gaze. For they knew that the sight is keenest at the periphery, that there are things which we may see out of the corner of our eye which will forever remain invisible should we stare at them straight: we discover truth at the margins of our lives and most clearly speak that truth when we tell it slant.

But no cry came from high above nor yet from below, until it seemed almost as if the privateer had never been. An hour passed and then two, until the whole sky turned the jaundice yellow which had greeted Dimmesdale's appearance. The two sailors at the topmast separated and resumed their separate beings but to be replaced by two others who fused themselves anew and continued their vigilance. Down below the smell of gruel drew others to the galley, and Hester, too, took a small pewter bowl and fetched herself breakfast from a cook scarcely taller than herself who had to stand on a stool to ladle the thick, discoloured porridge. Returning to her cabin she sat alone and ate with an enthusiasm which could have little to do with victuals which tasted of nothing except burnt oats.

By noon priorities had changed. Leaving the lookout to watch for renewed danger, the Captain set his men to complete repairs, a task which continued through that day and into another. Hester watched in fascination before, at the end of the second night, retiring to her cabin. There, seated beneath a swaying lantern, she reached into the bag which she had borne some twenty miles and placed her diary on the table's top. It carried but a single entry, for sickness and adventure had kept her from her desk. Now, though, she set about a kind of ritual which required its niceties. She placed both pen and ink before her, setting them out with care, and before committing the night's events to paper read through what she had written before the storm had discouraged her from further writing:

I am on board the Hope *and the very name doth lift my spirit to the stars. We are at sea but a few hours and already what came before is but a shadow. A fear has dropped from me like a cloak. I am myself again or if never quite that self then another, bright and clean. I may smile in a mirror once more or might had vanity such a thing to hand. I travel from that I know to that I know not of but have quite lost my fear, though fear of another sort has been my companion here as sky and water are wont to change places so often that my stomach is quite undecided.*

I am the only woman on board and which fact surprises me since I believed there would be others, but none is there who offers ought but courtesy. I am all of a spin and that not for the changing wind and erring current. So much that was me has been lost or traded these last few months that I am not sure there is residue sufficient. But stars and sea make no judgement, no, no more should I who am rescued from perdition. I doubt that had I remained but one more day I should have lacked the will or courage for this venture; but there is a time when the fruit is ripe and must fall no matter the convenience of the farmer. And so

I live in this narrow cabin and must watch the horizon each day for a hint of what I will soon inhabit. I am the daughter of tomorrow and must abide my inheritance. There is another . . .

There the text ceased. She stopped and stared ahead at the lantern, her lips pursed, a dark curl fallen damply across her forehead. In the distance she heard the liquid sound of a song as, closer to hand, she was aware of the regular slap of water on wood. She dipped her pen into a glass bottle of black ink and continued.

There is another on board who near did miss the ship. He joined us as we drew away from Yarmouth. I thought him sinister at first. But he is sinister no more. Merely a mystery. And mysteries have their fascination.

I, who have such a father and such a brother cannot rail against men. Yet I have learned that there are those to whom we are but jewels to be kept in the shadows and looked at behind closed shutters or not looked at all, daisies to be picked and left till our petals shall drop one by one. We are songbirds in a cage. We are . . .

And here she paused again, pen poised, the black iridescent ink bleeding at its tip.

We are what they would make us and not what we would be.

Where the full stop was placed a blot of ink spilled and she watched as the swaying ship teased tendrils out on either side, so many spider's legs.

Such was he who spoke of love but built a prison with his smiles until he might have no more need of smiles, nor of me. He tossed me in the fire like the peel of an Indies' orange and I perished there with the briefest flare of flame, a blue heat that died so soon to cinder.

She then wrote of the privateer, of the fear and the thrill and the final salvation. Then, as sleep began to press upon her, she turned to the day's events.

I had thought that fire and water were enemies. I had thought that a vessel made of wood, with woollen cloth stored in its hold and canvas blossoming from its masts, would have shunned the flame. But not so. Today I waked to the bitter smell of tar and a new song from those on deck. When I ventured forth it was to see a great iron cauldron raised on yellow bricks with flames beneath it in a kind of metal tray. Above, like some native cook rendering human flesh into soup, was the silent man whose tattoos spoke for him. The flames reflected in his eyes. And

87

always the smile saying that he knew more than his fellows, as certainly he knew more than he could tell.

Around his waist was a leather apron, scorched black in places as though he sought to extend his hieroglyphs on to his very clothes. Nor was he alone. Others stood beside him, similarly attired, like members of a secret society discovered at their terrible oaths. Each carried a kind of leather mop with tasselled end, like so many staffs of office, and stared into the oily liquid.

They were about the business of repair so that in a way fire did remain an enemy of water, as they caulked the longboat and disappeared below deck, carrying leather-bestreamed poles of steaming pitch. Every now and then a shout of pain would echo round the ship as a splash of tar burned the skin and, indeed, I now remembered the odd marks carried by some members of the crew, strange blotches which were perhaps mementoes of earlier such accidents.

The work continued all day and into the night, presided over throughout by the smiling man who stirred the bubbling black sulphur with a wooden paddle, as I have stirred a Christmas pudding in another life. As the night came – suddenly, here, not with the grace of even – so the ship seemed lit by a dull red light as the flames shrunk back into glowing cinders which by turns burned white in the scurrying breeze or winked a dark eye in the stillness. Still the men laboured, their shadows cast upwards on the billowing canvas or stretched before them on the deck so that they seemed to step on their very lives. It was as though the Hope were crewed by phantoms who haunted a world which prefigured hell. They no longer sang the songs of morning. A day's toil had rendered them as mute as he who presided over this affecting ritual. I alone was not a participant, or rather I and my fellow passenger. For with nightfall he emerged, a cloak drawn tight against the evening chill, quite as though he felt no heat from off the furnace. And, indeed, there was a sudden chill, though I had not noticed it till then, for though my face burned as from the summer sun yet was my back as cold as marble.

The fumes, which I had breathed all day, may, I think, have worked in some mysterious and subtle way upon my mind for as the sky darkened and the stars began to prickle the heavens so the scene in front of me wavered and flowed as though I watched it through a thick glass window whose whorls and bubbled imperfections shaped the world beyond. It appeared a kind of dance in which the figures moved with such a slowness and deliberateness that it quite disturbed and dismayed me there. They seemed to move like flies trapped in honey, swimming in their own sweet death; and I would reach out a hand but could do nothing for those so enmired who would as well perish in the sustaining clarity of their prison as be smeared, wing-bedraggled, on some flaking sill.

I stared as from a great height and felt a giddiness in my belly which was part terror and part unexplained ecstasy. And, as I watched, so my mute friend seemed to come alive as, in the shimmering heat, the pictures on his body began to animate, to beckon and to dance. They looked back at me, or so I thought, over shoulders themselves like mountain peaks. Springs started from smooth rocks. Hands, separated by the forgotten illustrator, touched. As he reached for more fuel and placed a black wafer in the crucible so the word LOVE emblazoned on one muscle of his chest was brought together with the word HATE on another so that the simple admonition LATE was spelled out in the red glow, before separating again. In the dullness of my thought I felt some private message was thereby offered me, though whether it might be a comment on my long-delayed decision or some warning as to something still ahead I could not say.

Thus had a day of breathing brimstone clouded my mind until I could scarcely trust anything I might think or see, while a terrible opiate lethargy had fallen on me. Certainly those who had laboured throughout the day seemed a somnambulant crew. They bore no relation to those who had run up the rigging in a sharp-edged wind or pulled at the ropes, pipes in mouths. These men marched to a different tune, indeed marched not at all, but were as those woken from a deep sleep who move their limbs to avoid the door lintel but have never quite relinquished their grasp on a favoured dream.

Eventually I came below, as the fire began to glow less brightly and the wind to stiffen from the north. Even so my unknown companion stayed on deck staring, as it appeared, into the dying embers there to seek out the answer to some riddle in his mind.

It is some hours later and sleep remains a stranger. I had thought that the sounds of the ship and the slow rocking of my wooden cradle had become a part of me but I have lain these several hours and listened as one at a deathbed harkens to each hard-drawn breath. There is at my heart a *terrible emptiness as though I had lost the very axle of my being, and it is true that all that was dear to me has gone along with the bad. I am a blankness on which the world must write; and yet there is a shadow of writing here, is there not, as though an oversheet of paper had been removed and left its ghost behind. I am capable of love, I know, and if that love has been misplaced what am I to make of that? Does love not carry its own legitimacy?*

But why should such thoughts assail me here who am removed from affairs of the heart as from the company of all I have known and cared for? I am betwixt and between, a summer flower pressed in the leaves of a forgotten Bible left beneath the stairs. One day perchance a hand will retrieve it and open it for a text, so letting in the light. But shall I recover the shape I have lost or the form and colour that once was mine? Or shall I remain the remnant of a discarded past, as thin as the page which presses me, to blow in the wind, a butterfly's wing in the dust of a lane, quite filmed over, no longer to bear the weight of its need for flight.

Such are the thoughts of a nether hour. The candle is quite out and I must to my bed again so as to bear the brightness of another day and learn to shed no tears for what has been and can never be again. There is a strange consolation, though, in the words I write, as though at last to see before me my inmost thoughts or even to record no more than the day's events were to render life into my hands rather than to see it wash away like a wave on the deck, thinning into a wash of cuckoo spit only to slide back to an anonymous sea. So I bid thee goodnight, my diary, who art my oldest friend.

Who may enter another's heart? We live side by side for a lifetime and remain strangers. At some level we commune only with ourselves and, deeper still, may keep secrets even from this self. What did Hester think of that stranger who plays so little part in her narrative? Was there no hint of a sympathetic chord, no suggestion of a stirring hope? So, lovers delight to explore the moment of their meeting, playfully seeking the second of their first enchantment. Such games, though, are a summer's pleasure, a gentle torture as they imagine the time of love's inwash. Mere chance becomes a destiny.

There must have been a moment, though: the inclination of a head, a smile, a glance held longer than it should until the world begins to narrow to a still, bright point. She wrote a diary for her eyes alone and yet could not trust the intimacy of her own utterance, the privacy of a word written in a dark place at a dark time of night where no owls shriek and the day's eye has closed to all. Tell me, Hester, could it be that love is already implanted, that mystery alone has proved sufficient to turn your face to the wind where the sea spray tastes of tears and a name may be spoken aloud without fear of over-hearing? Or is it too soon and must we watch a little longer for you and he to begin the small matter of your exaltation and your slow but still certain dismay? Very well. I see from your demeanour, as you sleep, that you and we alike must abide another day, talk somewhat more of sea and sky. But the time is close. We are at the very moment before the flower opens and the bee drops downwards through a heavy sky towards its destiny.

There is a rhythm to shipboard life quite unlike that on shore. Bells ring, men pull together on tensioned ropes, sing songs with a thumping beat and wistful air, sway with wind and wave. To be sure there is ritual, too, and the sombre repetition of habit on land; cows to be milked at dawn, the hard-baked soil to be weeded till sundown, and there, too, bells may toll the Sabbath and the passing of life. But at sea rhythm is a part of muscle and sinew; it shapes the very thoughts of a man who stands on watch and sees creation rock gently around the centre of his being.

There is no solitude, such as comes a thousand miles from land; no companionship, such as that forged by danger or the thought of depthless ocean and topless heaven. Thus we were lulled once on an inward sea, soothed by the gentle hiss of blood and the reassurance of echoing heartbeat. Did we believe, then, in a world beyond, in meaning to be born with birthing, and, if not, did we think darkness our fate and a watery bed our only resting place? Perhaps the echo of all that sings in our ears, as current and tide carry us beyond the imagined.

The sea drives you within. There are many whose lips move as they stare over the side, speaking to themselves or the drifting spray. The sea is an ear that listens, a confessional for those in need of grace. It was so with Hester who felt such lightness of the soul that she would scarcely have been surprised to drift away on the wind. Guilt and recrimination had thinned to transparency, tumbled in the infilling curve of the ship's wake. The water was purification and anointment, and when, one night, it, and the ship's spars, seemed to flicker with a blue flame in the cold, clear air, she felt as though the Holy Spirit itself offered absolution. For Hester, the sea became a church, not stark and stripped of joy like a Puritan sepulchre, not dark flint and gloom like her Colney chapel, but bright with the inexpressible, pulsing and swelling with meaning which had no need to move through language to understanding.

And why was Hester, raised on the self's denial, one day to make love to one not her husband, as I am compelled to tell you she assuredly will, and why did he, a man of faith, so forget his vows? You might as well ask why we are as we are. That we are so is beyond doubt. The acceptance of that has a certain consecration. Denial is a denial. Nothing comes of nothing. Is the coming together of a man and a woman not a route to the spirit? It, too, has a rhythm, the rhythm of the universe. The waves of the sea breed life and the passing of the moon through its cycle provides the metronome beat to creation's necessities.

We live by commandments we inherit, as we speak words shaped by other mouths. These are not our imperatives but the catechism of the past. What is ours alone is our inmost passion, the slow erupting truth of all our senses orchestrated in a single moment's pure reflex. It carries our signature. Yet where our own truth conflicts with custom's lore we bow the knee and strike our breasts and wish away our own true selves for the sake of nothing more than habit crowned as king.

It is useless to try to explain why we do what we do. We live by rules or do not. We punish and reward ourselves in roughly equal measure. What is vital for one is without meaning for another. For one person, guilt is the lash to strip the skin; for another, transgression liberates the soul. We live in the interstices of time. Love knows only the moment, as does death. Who has not inhabited those spaces and watched amazed as others come and go and live inconsequence as though life could be anything but the pressure of a hand or an eye softening with love. The sun shines, teacups rattle down the days, rebellion, riot or the sad gavotte of repetition are chronicled with care. But for those entwined, who seek no more than one another's breath or the touch of skin on skin, there is no time and the arrow will not strike its target, always halving the distance, never to arrive.

The *Hope* sailed in the interstices of time. For all the rhythm of the passing days, those on board inhabited their own country beneath a sky where the very idea of minute and hour were no more than a gentle irony.

'Stand by to come about,' shouts a single, clear voice, and, with no more than a tightening rope and the cannon-shot of canvas, time is reversed and space itself revisited. As the plough on land so the ship at sea bends back on itself in rictus.

At sea you hear the sounds of the world's blood easing its way through the body of the earth, the sounds of breathing and stretching. At sea there is terror, as nowhere on land. At sea there is peace, as nowhere on lake or mountain or plain. Below you is a depth of sea, above the cold sky beaded with the frost of stars, the unimaginable past summoned by an unheeding present. The mariner's timepiece can have no meaning as a silver light from yesterday's yesterday throws a shadow on a deck bleached white by salt. And though the compass needle trembles around magnetic north every sailor knows that if you travel far enough to north or east they both become no more than their opposites. As do we all, returning whence we came.

There are other seas than those which break upon deserted beaches or fill the sculpted coves of ancient Devon. Certainly Hester was adrift on more than a literal ocean, reborn to more than an Atlantic surge. As the *Hope* made her crabwise advance against an angled wind or drove before a gale, so she felt ever less resistance, ever less pull from the past, ever less need to reproach herself with images which now swept away in the flowering wake of a solitary vessel.

After the incident with the privateer, whether phantom or real, the voyage fell into a pattern. The west seemed to draw

93

them on like a lodestone. For two weeks the wind, so fitful and dangerous before, blew steadily from the northeast. The pale breasts of the sails filled; the prow dipped deep into a blue-black sea. Birds, which had once circled and dipped around tensioned masts, had long since departed, save for a single tern which seemed to hang on the air for one bright timeless afternoon, finally disappearing with the failing sun so that there was no movement in the sky as a first distant star shone down.

Hester now divided her day with the scrupulous care of a legal clerk. Each morning she would rise with the dawn and walk about the deck. Now her eyes sought out not the eastern but the western horizon. Then she paced about her temporary world, as she had once walked each day to the gates of Earlham and back for the sheer pleasure of being abroad. She took her breakfast alone. That done, she would brush the floor of her sea-borne room quite as though she were still in her Colney home, before returning to the deck, there to meet, as though by arrangement, her fellow-passenger. For though her first real encounter seemed to have been but in dream, there had followed another, in a world more tangible and real.

Had she chosen to read the entries in her diary, as she did not, seeing each day as a story complete in itself, she would have encountered a narrative there which might have surprised her still. For along with descriptions of porpoises, which tumbled and turned beneath their bow, of the curious shining which seemed to set the sea alight at night, of the strangely shaped fish which flew through the air and sought to swim across their deck, of the graceful mending of sails by hardened seamen, sat in rows like grandmothers around a fire, was the slow unfolding of another tale having to do with a meeting of strangers which became an encounter of friends and then something more. Page after page was filled with descriptions of his looks, his remarks and his actions, written with a sloping hand in a sloping cabin in the middle of a sloping ocean. But in between were other observations, born of the world she saw.

One sailor flew a kite from the afterdeck this noon. It had the appearance of a dragon with a tail which twitched most convincingly in the wind. With every agitation of the air it plunged and soared until all on board watched it with deepest fascination. Even the Captain stood awhile, pipe as ever in his hand, and enjoyed its twisting turns. It did, indeed, seem quite alive, a child of the wind, born when it blew and fated to die when it should cease. And methought that there was something of ourselves in this, freely moving with a lively spirit and yet pulled along by the ship below, firm anchored by a length of twine. Such is our freedom, too. Our destination is laid down by our Lord, announced before we board. We do but exercise our permitted flight and wait the moment of the sudden calm which ends our dancing and will mark our fall. Though to disprove the allegory I wrought a sudden gust put such a pressure on the line that it parted quite in two and the dragon had the freedom of the skies, rising ever higher until it dwindled to our eyes. There were many who looked for it long after it had disappeared from view and a curious sadness filled the ship as though we might have lost one of our own. Freedom, then, is possible, it seems, but it may have its dangers, too, as we rise alone but into an empty sky. Without that length of twine is no one witness to the daring of one's flight nor yet to feel the pulsing tug of life.

There is something about a voyage. Action and consequence seem separated. Proximity, occasion and time conspire to breed incaution and much more. Thus it was that one day, as they walked together round the deck, he turned to her and opened a door to a future they would both regret.

'Mistress Prynne, it seems to me that rather than I sit in my splendid privacy and thou in thine we might make better of our meals were we but to share them, though if privacy is what thee wish . . .'

'No. I had thought the same.'

At breakfast on the following day, he knocked on her door, entering her room in fact as once before, in Hester's mind at least, he had entered it in fancy, and for both of them the dismal room seemed to fill with light, but still she failed to ask herself why her heart beat so nor yet why he smiled quite as readily and as long as he did.

When the meal of biscuit and tea was done, and the cores of

two shrivelled apples stood in the centre of two empty plates, he took the lantern from its place, for morning and evening were all one below deck, and put it between them on the table.

'It seems to me, Mistress Prynne, that if we are to share this voyage together we had best share the story of our lives and to that end, with thy permission, I will recite me of the events which have brought me here.'

'Thou need tell me nothing, sir.'

'Ay, and if I should tell thee nothing how should I learn from thee what I would know? No, the truth is that I am a minister, summoned to Boston by a band of men and women of whom I know nothing and who doubtless expect a great deal more of me than they shall receive. A church awaits me and therefore I await a church.'

It would be difficult to explain the impact of those words on Hester who had imagined everything but never that. Something implacable seemed placed between them, nor could she say why this should matter so. He seemed to sense it for he reached out his hand to take hers, but she pulled back as from a fire. He let his hand rest there a second in a silence which threatened to fill the cabin. Then he got to his feet and began to pace the narrow cabin.

'In truth, Mistress Prynne, I am a narrow man who likes a plain and simple world, though I was born to more. My father was a king's man to his soul and we lived a life of neither want nor pain. Our land was bounded on the north and east only by the sea. Half a day's ride would not take me to the western edge. I was giddy with the thought that I must command so many lives as fell within those bounds, who felt so little right to do so. Do not mistake me. There was no cruelty, *is* no cruelty, in my father, nor yet a lack of generosity, but I yearned for stricter discipline, for a mind that held to sharper limits. Then I fell into a sickness and for two years they despaired for my life. A fever would come and go and bring me close to death; and in those moments I would see visions of the saints as clear as I see thee. These were but dreams, no doubt born of the fever, but when they left me I would cry to bring them back again. Yet they were not dreams of glory. No angelic hosts lifted me to the heavens.

Quite otherwise. These were simple men who came, who shook their heads at one who lived for nothing but another day to pass with riding out in a world I was told I owned. They were dreams of suffering, for I saw the arrows pierce their flesh. I thought I felt the pain of crucifixion, not in my own flesh but in the eyes that turned on me.

Why should I have longed for visions such as these? For others, I fancy, they would be nightmares to be driven out by the day, but for me they seemed a truth which filled me from within. These were men like myself, for all they streamed with light which sometimes seemed to blind me. They were men who knew the purpose of their being, for whom each rock, each ear of wheat, spoke its meaning, contributed to some whole I could approach only by becoming such as they. I know they were but summoned by my illness. I ate little at such times and my family feared for my sanity but that is when truth may enter in, when all else has been laid aside and the pleasures of this world abjured. I began to read, who anyway could not venture out. I took such a pleasure in my books that I did not doubt the rightness of what I did, but the very severity of words, so simple and contained, was what drew me to greater efforts. My father was a stranger to such habits, preferring to feed quite other appetites. My mother, I fancy, saw it as further evidence of the sickness which had, however, now begun to leave me.'

Hester leaned forward in the gloom, staring at a man who seemed scarcely to be aware of her presence.

'They celebrated my recovery, while in my heart I longed for the sickness to be reborn, for with the illness had gone, too, my visions. The books were my link to those images, vivid yet contained; and so, I suppose, a logic was born out of those years and I went as a scholar to Cambridge where they offered the severity I sought. Cold stone, cold water and at times cold hearts greeted me there; but this was what I yearned for, at least so I supposed. Why it should be so I now find a mystery. But I suspected every sign and symbol of excess. I ate a simple fare, refused to see the beauty of the world and suspected those in the church who thought to enter God's kingdom along a path strewn with idols and relics. I began to meet with others of like mind and to see around me a conspiracy to be redeemed only with a conspiracy of my own. We looked to strip this life of falsity, quite as though we knew what falsity to be. We wished to build a new Jerusalem in which souls reborn could walk along simple lanes closed in only by God's pure love.

'But we live at a time and in a place where such thoughts can seem dangerous, nor were we innocent of the fact that there were others who saw in our ways a threat to be met with necessity's cruelties. Hester, outside the honest world from which thou comest our England is alive with those who plot the downfall of their neighbours. I have come to feel, Hester . . .' He corrected himself. 'I came to feel then, and now feel stronger still, that there was lacking in our hearts one spark without which no true flame could burn. Love, Hester. We spoke of love of God but in our hearts was a coldness which could never have engendered life. By then I was committed and there were those who knew my plans and did not wish me well; and so I am come here pursuing certainties I may no longer be certain that I feel.'

The candle flickered inside its glass, bending their shadow selves in grotesque courtesies. She who had looked for strength in him now felt his need for the understanding she had sought, but when he looked into her eyes neither held the gaze, for there are prohibitions which become a part of us and may not, we think, ever be transgressed.

All on board, it seems, turn fishermen whenever they may. No sooner is duty done than they are with rod and line searching out the deeps for nature's plenty. Strange are the creatures that they hook. I have seen a fish that blows itself quite into a ball so that scarce any of its features can be distinguished. Yet another, brought up from a great depth, where several of them had combined their lines to fish, seemed to swell to bursting and then collapsed in a mess that stank within five minutes. And they have told me tales of stranger creatures still, some large enough to devour us all, if they are to be believed. But I have seen enough to know that God's creation is more multitudinous than ever I had suspected, while even the wisest man must remain a dunce who contemplates the varieties of life, known and unknown. Nor, I have learned, is human kind one thing and there are stranger creatures, too, among our number to trawl up from the depths. Yes, and I have netted one of these, I think, or else I should not be here to write such words as these as the Hope rocks me near to sleep beneath the moving stars.

The weather changed. The wind shifted to the north and all warmth was drained from the world. One day the sea was black as damson at full season, the next a pale white green, but, whatever its colour, it snatched all heat from body and from ship. The rigging began to rime with ice and the prow to grow a kind of white statuary which the crew beat with wooden clubs, quite as though they were attacking some citizen caught stealing a penny or eating from his master's river.

Then there came a day when they crossed a line invisible to the eye, between the land they left and that to which they sailed. A ceremony was required. Hester sought to demur but the Captain asked her to humour the men, for there are few as superstitious as sailors who, in their danger, had, he explained, retained certain propitiatory rites which would grant them better passage. He himself, he suggested, was of a more modern mind but it would be a foolish officer who did not indulge his men on such a trivial point. Hester doubted whether he was quite as free of superstition as he claimed and, as a country girl, was not herself immune from a necessary obeisance to the gods of nature, long since supposedly traded for the carpenter of Nazareth. There were trees in the meadow which were never to be cut and dark circles in the field within which magic could be practised and no scythe was to be used. In fact, if witches were to be hanged for indulging in their arts it was hardly possible to doubt that such art existed or that there were those who responded to their incantations. Rare was the cottage which did not hang above its door a horseshoe or bunch of herbs to ward off an evil as real as the sheep found with broken leg or the mildew which descended on a crop where no taint had been the night before. Since life itself depended on the season's regularity, what harm if that should be helped along by small gestures to powers not acknowledged by the Christian calendar.

Nor was the church so lacking in wisdom as to refuse such practices, where possible turning them to its own purpose. So, propitiation to the gods of the harvest was brought within doors and a pagan Christmas celebrated as the day of the Saviour's birth. It is the essence of such symbols that they retain their mystery and lose their origins so that we accept them without thought. It is bad luck, we know, to view a new moon through glass, to walk beneath a ladder or to break a mirror's silver face, and I suspect that there are few, today, for whom a faint shadow does not pass across the mind when they transgress such taboos, even as they deride those who live their lives by these injunctions quite as though they lived before wisdom had dispersed ignorance and faith replaced fear. How much more so then when defences against nature were few and when invisible forces did indeed seem to move through the land breathing pestilence and death?

So, Hester consented, as did her companion, now rarely from her side, but they were to be largely spectators, or so they were informed. The young sailor was their principal object, being dressed as some lord, with a wild array of clothing, including a shawl begged from Hester herself. He was seated on a chair in a shallow pool of water formed by a canvas sheet roped at each corner. Hester and Dimmesdale were required to preside, two mock magistrates in motley costumes, he holding a trident in one hand, she a cloth jerkin with fishes' tails sewn on by expert hands.

'Thou art the first,' explained the Captain to Hester, 'and thou, sir, art the last. He is the one who must be brought into thy kingdom. As to the rest of it, I don't understand a thing. It is some invention passed on from other ships and times. It will be over within this half hour. I shall be below. I do not favour such behaviour as slackens discipline, but without it they will be praying aloud with every shift of wind.'

Thus, Hester and Dimmesdale watched as a mock baptism was performed with freezing water coloured red with some dye made up by the men from berries evidently carried on board for this purpose. There was a roughness to the ceremony which seemed to border on cruelty. Although the water had been heated some, and steamed like a cauldron on the fire, it quickly lost its heat and the young sailor's teeth began to chatter, though whether from cold or fear was hard to say for one of his fellows now produced a prodigious razor with which he scraped a soapy lather from his face.

Nor were the two passengers exempt, for they, in turn, were required to take their place and though they were treated with more gentleness their clothes, too, bore the marks of the dye as a token sprinkle of blood-red water was dropped slowly on their heads.

The ceremony left all in a brighter mood, the more especially as some spirit was served hot from the galley to all participants. They were slapped on their backs by sailors they had only seen from afar before and felt that they had now become part of their true fraternity. Such is the power of signs. We may not understand them but we grant them their authority.

But if there was magic in this ceremony it was magic of a curious kind for two days later the young sailor, blond hair streaming like flames in the night, fell from the frost-encrusted rigging on to the dark deck below. Like a broken-winged bird he flew downwards, arms and legs outstretched, feeling the cold air liquid on his face, his voice snatched out of his mouth to whisper amongst the shrouds which now were shrouds indeed. No one saw him fall nor heard anything but the dull, disordered impact as he struck, already, by the sound, disassembled, carelessly disordered with limbs flailing the air.

When they found him the blood had blended with the red dye of but two days since. That blood sank deep into the grain of the deck, turned white by wind and rain as by the scouring brushes of men; and despite much further brushing it remained throughout the voyage, a dull bruise in the wood. He himself was sewn in stiff canvas by fingers creased and flaking. Two days before, the canvas had marked a mock birth; now it was a sign of last solemnities. Thus parcelled up, he was laid upon a plank which reached out over the side and the Captain and Dimmesdale both read verses over him. The canvas was weighted with an iron last, on which it was the sailor's habit to shape shoes, as did his father at Norwich market. Then, as a wave lifted them up towards the sky, two of his companions began to raise the deckward end of the plank so that when she eased down into the trough his body should slide into the waiting sea. And so it did, though, for a moment, it resisted the pull of gravity as though in death he would cling fast as in life he had failed to do. A moment later, and with a sudden convulsion which seemed to come from within the bag itself, it slid forwards with a sigh, never quite reaching the end but slipping to the side and striking the ship before plunging into the dark sea below.

For a moment or two it seemed to sail like a smaller version of the *Hope*, for in falling through the air, his second fall in as many hours, air had forced its way through the gaps left by rough needlework and the canvas filled with air. Indeed, a sudden wind swung it round in a circle and it began to make some way. But, by degrees, the canvas took the water into itself, darkening and letting out the air in sudden belches. It slowly settled lower before turning end on end and sliding like an expert diver into the depths, leaving no sign behind.

Though these were men used to death, men who recognized the power of the forces with which they lived, they were strangely moved by the young man's end. The Captain himself brushed away a tear with the back of a calloused hand while Hester realized that she had herself not known his name until she heard it spoken over the plain grey bundle on the deck. Jack. Yet she never after heard it pronounced other than as Young Jack and so he would continue for as long as his shipmates should live. Young Jack would be Young Jack in fifty years and it was his youth which made them so subdued; but it was evidently something more than this. It was that a certain innocence had gone out of their lives. They had taken pleasure in the knowledge which they had passed to him. For those with sons at home he was a substitute, an image of those others. For those with none he was the son they might have had. His ready smile and friendly disposition made him the one whose company they sought. For he had heard none of their tales, would believe any wonder they might claim to have witnessed and by his junior status thereby enhanced their own. He had flown at last with the angels and there were none who did not feel that he had joined them in their flight. But hope was gone from the *Hope* for many a night until routine, the rigours of their plight, and time's necessary oblivion, forced other matters from their minds. Hester, though, was not the only one who found herself glancing astern with a tear in her eye as she remembered one so bright and able launched now on such an inhospitable sea.

Nor was this the end of Young Jack, for three days after the burial, when all had ceased to look for him on deck or high above against the swelling sail, the ship suddenly lost way as she refused to answer the helm and but for some speedy work above the listing deck might well have snapped a mast. They lowered a man in a simple loop of rope to see what cause there might be; and as they waited his report there came a scream which cut through the hearts of all that heard. They quickly pulled him to the deck, imagining that some shark had reached up to take him to the depths. But when he came on board, eyes wide and mouth agape, a greater terror seemed to have seized upon him. For what he had seen and what, at last, he gasped out, was Young Jack himself, the canvas of his shroud wrapped round the rudder and he staring up at the ship as though he would climb on board to resume his life among the living. They took the sailor below where he remained a full week more. Nor did the Captain send for him nor order him to work; and when it came to clearing the fouled rudder he allowed that they should draw lots to look on him who now could look on nothing more himself.

The current, it seemed, had swung Jack and his shroud beneath the boat and such little air as remained had floated it up beneath the rudder where the cloth, but poorly sewn, had opened and been snatched up as the vessel got under way. When Hester and the others had looked far behind them for Young Jack he thus remained on board the *Hope*, no longer as a sailor but as a passenger at last. And did we but know it we, too, carry with us what we thought to have left to time and memory. It lives with us and will, whenever we imagine ourselves free, present itself anew.

Today, in my cabin, as I opened this book to record such thoughts and incidents as might seem worthy of recall, I was startled by a sudden movement. From out the corner of my eye I saw a flutter which left me afeared for no better reason than the movement itself. It took but a second to resolve this mystery and to still my heart for there settled on this page, even where I write these words, a butterfly, its velvet gentleness shimmering as it twitched its wings open and closed. A sudden colour enriched the white page and stirred my heart, though this time with wonder rather than fear. Such beauty and of such short life, for if a momentary warmth had given it life, the cold of a December night must end it. It stirred and, even with the sounds of shipboard, when I put my ear to the page on which it inscribed a wavering line, like a walker on a rope, I could hear the faintest scratching, a stirring of life where no flowers bloom and neither bee nor bird beat the air.

Its wings, which opened and closed as though at the behest of some invisible filament as it trembled its wayward path, were marked with a strange design, a cabalistic sign. At one moment it seemed an insignia, at another a kind of face. I have seen mechanical mannequins through the diamond windows of a Norwich shop and something of their jerky simulation of life was reflected here by this insect whose beauty was in vain and whose marking spelled out no message that others could read.

I thought to gather it in my hands and release it in the air above but the chill and the wind would surely destroy it before I should have returned below. Yet what was a longer life here on this white page surrounded by a sullen darkness? Was a brief life under the stars not better than a day spent where beauty has no shine and a mate is not to be found?

I suspect there is a moral here for me, though I lack the skill to seek it out. Certainly I feel some kinship for this creature whose high-hinged legs now tickle the palm of my hand and whose wings brush against my fingers. There is a dust which it leaves, like a daisy's blossom. Do I do damage, I wonder, by thus robbing it of this subtle patina? Is it shedding its life, mote by mote? Am I no more than a thief of another's life? Do I kill what I would protect?

Then, a sudden stillness comes. It has fallen on its side, its wings closed against the light. I breathe gently on it, hoping to suffuse it with the life it has so suddenly surrendered, but all that I effect is a slow opening of its wings as it settles in death. It seems to acquire a thin transparency quite as though another breath would send it on one last looping flight, as doubtless it would but with the cabin's floor for its destination. So we all live out our brief lives with no more idea of nearing our goal than this sad creature searching for its kind far from the place it took for a home. It leaves my blank page now as blank as it was before and with its secret messages still locked within its beauty so that none has nor never shall know why it had its being or that it died so far from the light for which it yearned and the company which had once seen it fly in a cloud of moving colour. As the last living evidence of my former life, I place it within a plain white kerchief against the day when I should close it between the pages of this diary so that it should mark not only a place but a day and a life.

Sailors may seem strangers to words. They are hoarders of language, frugal, storing it against a day that never arrives. Grammar and syntax are washed away with the cold sea spray. Theirs is a world of things, of ropes and iron and skin-smooth wood. With the wind in their ears they quickly learn the redundancy of speech. Their vocabulary is not that of others. Step ashore and they become as children, pointing, gesturing, bemused, as it seems, by the everyday, uneasy with the commerce of speech. On board all is control. Words are commands to shape their actions. On shore actions shape their words, as liquor and licence give voice to passions which stand in place of intercourse of a subtler kind. Their thoughts are their own. What they share is labour and a situation. Nor do they read anything save the sky and the sea, though there they discover a shaping narrative which may move them to tears as much as any poem may a lady in her parlour. Certain words they do speak, words to ward off evil. Other words may not be spoken since they may have the power to precipitate the evil they describe.

Their possessions are few yet none the less cherished for all that. No sailor will touch another's sea-chest, closed as it is against the world. Nor are these compacted with necessities. On the contrary, they are where secrets are stored, where memories are hidden that will stir a heart on the edge of despair. One man's chest contains a polished stone, another a spoon with an initial letter coiled about its handle; still another a piece of cloth worn smooth and transparent with handling. Each contains a story, enclosed within its form, and each thereby shapes the space which surrounds it, for stories may not be contained within themselves but press upon the world from which they are abstracted. See one of these men but hold the stone, feel the embossed curve of metal on thumb or pull the attenuated material across a weathered face, and you know that a story is being repeated within the mind in a voice silent to all but he who feels the sudden need of conversation with the past. There are times when what is not said echoes about the ship, for in truth do we not all exist through placing ourselves in a tale which we whisper to ourselves when our lives seem to fade to a thin transparency? Were we not loved, once? Did we not wake to a day whose memory is as fresh as the moment it was sealed within our being? Perhaps that stone once felt the impress of a lover's foot or stands in place of a country long since slipped below the horizon of a western sky. Perhaps the spoon was laid beside a sleeping child, the sole clue to a family which turned its back on an intrusive truth. Or if not so in fact how much more powerful when born out of necessity's invention. There is, perhaps, another country where untold tales are spoken aloud, a country which shadows our own and where what we but imagine becomes a truth. For we too easily believe that what is known is all that may be true and what is seen must stand superior to what is invisible but which is felt, nonetheless, like a wayward breeze on a cloudless day. Are there not moments when a muffled bell strikes a phantom hour and we set our course by stars invisible to the eye which sees but an outward sky?

Those who hoard their words may be taken for simpletons, and some may be such. But there are others who are none of this, whose heads are abuzz with chatter but who let none spill into a heedless world. They think their thoughts, they watch and wonder, knowing that to speak is but to borrow another's words and thereby deny the truth they would convey. We may dress in another's clothes and in a poor light look as they but we do not thereby become those we do but imitate. It is so with words. They seem familiar and will do to have the salt passed or order a shoe mended. But to speak of feelings, of despair, love, loneliness or hope they are but betrayers, deniers of the truth were truth itself to be netted like fish in the sea. There is a territory where no words suffice.

So, the Captain in his cabin unrolls his charts, placing a brass weight shaped like a whale at one end and another, shaped like a unicorn, at the other so that the corners curl inwards but the centre stays in place. Where the oceans front the land there are marks aplenty, shaded lines and codes, words and images betokening safety and danger alike, showing ports of call. But in the centre, where the ship must sail for weeks on end, are no marks at all save the name of the ocean written large and clear as though the word could render it anodyne and secure a passage from one realm unto another without remit. The word conceals what it may not tell for there are no words for this vast expanse. There is only the knowledge which unfolds with each passing day. Nor will today's safe passage under a blue and certain sky guarantee such to another who must make his way, as best he may, without benefit of advice or path marked out before. As each ship's master is on his own and must converse but with himself and his God so are we all, for what is true for us may not be so for another and advice may be but a lure to danger's door. We are translators all, intent on bridging the spaces which lie between us, but my heart is not thine, nor do my eyes see what others do. We both may call the sea and ocean blue but is thy blue mine or mine thine when already I know that the word alone is set to describe such a shifting spectrum, for never were sky and sea one blue and never yesterday's colour what today's appears nor what tomorrow may yet proclaim.

There is a truth, then, in silence, which is why the picture-man was felt so wise and why the sailor in his bunk may turn to the wall and there address another who is but a projection of his need for understanding rather than speak to those who sit with their long-stemmed pipes and remember a past they shared with none here, even should they then have stood beside them, or if they did never shared as their language might suppose.

Yet there was on board one who spoke, who at each day's end would sit with his comrades and, as the light faded and the air seemed as brittle as clear ice, would spill into the night a soft cascade of words. We say that such men spin a yarn, quite as though they teased out a single thread from a mess of wool, as though they conjured into being the filament which would one day form a cloak to keep us warm. And perhaps they do. For we speak, too, of a story's thread and may, I think, draw such fables and fancies around us to charm away the cold, though the chill be deep within.

Every ship has its story-teller. Nights are long and the spill of lanternlight invites forward a man who may stare into the flame and speak of other times and places. It is his profession quite as much as that which he performs in the rigging in a nor-easter and as necessary to his survival, and that of those who watch and listen. Story is our grasp upon the past. It tells us that we have lived before and so may live again. 'There was a man . . . In a village, long ago, as snow fell and the wolves howled . . .' So it has always been. A circle of men and women. A fire. One dressed in furs and carrying, perhaps, a stick or a kind of wand, sits before them and speaks into the night. 'There dwelt in these lands, in times past when there was darkness and no flame fluttered like a bird in a cave, a man. And the man's name was . . .' A child in a crib stares up at a face and listens to the rhythms, the tonalities, the music of a voice which tells lies which have the sound of truth but which is not truth since the truth alone cannot suffice. The *Hope* had such a story-teller and one evening Hester sat among the sailors, in a cabin full of the smoke from pipes which glowed in the dark like warning signals seen from a great distance off. She and her companion, for thus they were now taken to be, were invited there, or such she took to be the import of the gestures made by a smiling man whose body animated with a thousand stories itself. She sat beside Dimmesdale, so pressed against him, indeed, that she felt both unease and a disturbing quickening of her pulse. Propinquity weaves a spell less subtle but more powerful than any other.

'There was a time, it is said, when there was no sea, when men and, yes, women, too, would set out in the summer sun to walk where the salt waves break and out beyond and across until by winter's end they were come wither we now make our way. This be long ago, long before our Saviour died. Oh, there were seas enough, then, but in another place, far away where men had webs upon their feet like albatross and tern.'

'There never was such a time,' objected one of the youngest of the seamen who had yet to learn the limits of knowledge.

'And was there not? And wert thou there then? Thou seem a little too near to sprouting thy first beard to speak so sure on this or anything.'

Those around him nodded sagely and Hester felt something grave in their response to so modest an objection.

'It may be and it may be not. What we do not know and may not prove to those who believe nothing they have not seen may yet have been. There be only one who has seen the beginning and will see the end. Nor do I think the end can be far off when those so young seek to instruct their elders.' He paused, looked around steadily, then began once more. 'There was a time when there was no sea. And those who crossed be there still and thou wilt see them when we land for they have feathers in their hair and go without clothes and have arrows and spears. And I have seen arrows, or their like, before, my friends, back where we have left. I have seen them in the soil where they lay. How came such, my young master,' he asked of his questioner, 'to so distant a place when we know that none has sailed there until these last years? Nor is that land beneath us without its human inhabitants, if human they may be called. For there were those who still toiled across the mountains and the plains when the waters did return and they were left below. Many died and went to meet their maker but there were those who breathed the waters who once had breathed the air. And they will welcome all those who go to visit them, for if thou but fall into the sea whole, and not with a musket-ball in the breast or a cutlass slash about the heart, they will take thee to their cities.'

'What of Young Jack,' asked one of the men, hidden in the gloom of a cabin in which pipe smoke stung the eyes and lanternlight sent all swaying, 'will they have welcomed him?'

There was a silence, if ever there is silence on a ship which seems to groan and cry, as wood stretches and chafes.

'There is another who welcomes thy companion. He is at peace.' It was Dimmesdale who spoke, in a voice low but firm. 'Nor is this but a story.'

'He is at peace,' said the story-teller, 'for death hath that effect on all. But do not speak ill of story-tellers for I fancy thou art one of us, though the story thou tell we have heard before.'

'I speak but the truth.'

'No more than I for what we cannot see we must take for truth or believe that this be all there is and our fate but what we may hold in our hands or spy with our eyes, even though it be from the masthead. And hast thou not whispered in a maiden's ear of what may be but is not yet? There is none here who is not a teller of tales, for without such we are no more than sails which blow in the wind or hang loose like a dead man's shroud according to the moods of the weather. Thou hast whispered in a maiden's ear, hast thou not?'

There was a challenge in the voice which Dimmesdale could not but feel and had they been able to see, as in the uncertain light they could not, they must have detected the blush which suffused not only his face but equally that of his companion who felt that the accusation must be directed no less at her who they suspected, no doubt, to be a little more than friend if a little less than lover.

At the turn of the month they sighted the first ice, a mile distant on the port beam. Pale blue and green, it sailed past them on a voyage of its own. Its weight alone meant that while the ship rose and fell, pitched and yawed, in the broken sea, it sailed with the grace of a swan on an inland lake. It hardly matched the state of Hester's mind, which was neither cool nor placid.

Nor were her emotions, which, could she but have allowed them to be distilled into words, as she could not, would no doubt have shocked her out of mind. But what is not spoken, what never enters language, may perhaps be evaded or denied. Certainly Hester had yet to give a name to how she felt for to do so would be to confront a truth best left obscure. There is a pleasure in secrets kept, even from oneself. How else account for the smile which played around her lips as, unknowingly, she hugged a knowledge to herself she did not know that she possessed.

As for Dimmesdale, certainly he was a man transformed. He, who had led a contemplative life exerting himself, if at all, only on horseback or, more likely still, reaching for a book high on a library shelf, had discovered in a night's rowing a pleasure even in the pain and exhaustion of such labour. In exchanging the languid Cam for a threatening sea he found himself in awe not only of the natural world but also of his own capacity to respond to it. He stood on the deck, braced against the wind as Heathcliff might have stood on a Yorkshire moor to shout out Cathy's name into the void; but no name passed his lips. These were masters of repression, deniers on Olympian scale. They were informers on themselves, ready to bear witness at their own trials. They needed no accusers other than themselves nor any court in which to plead their guilt. So, Dimmesdale never shouted Hester's name save, perhaps, somewhere deep within, beyond the hearing of the subtlest listener. All he knew was that he greeted each day with delight and thought each moment lost not spent at her side. What was plain to all, certainly to those who travelled with them on the voyage, was not plain to these two who shared many a secret thought but not the one whose utterance would have driven them apart. And there, of course, is the truth of it for there was a danger here. Like the crystal ice which seemed to glide with such delicacy through the metalled sea but whose jagged underside could open up the ship like a surgeon's knife passing through slow discovered flesh, so the gentle smiles and new-found courtesies could send them plunging to an ocean floor no less deep than that which lay below them now. For if neither chose to name the source of the transformation in their lives, or even allow it to enter their consciousness, there might yet be safety, though can it be that they were really unaware of how close they came to that ice which burns?

Does temptation not always have a smiling face, else it would scarcely serve its purpose; and where should we be without temptation to test our steel? Lead us not into temptation: and yet was not Job tempted in the wilderness and Christ himself? We are plunged into the flames and thence the water-barrel to harden us and drive out our impurity. And is there not another thought that we must entertain? For where should we be without transgression, where without sin, at least as conceived by those who would instruct us in realities. For now they sailed under Galileo's heavens, he who had been shown the irons to encourage him to deny his truth. Was there not a denial of God in the words he spoke and in those who forced such words onto his lips? Knowledge may seem a sin; but the soft skin is a kind of knowledge which will never come to those who would deny its authority. For those who believed in witchcraft's rule to deny the power of such possession was to offend both God and state alike. That was real which they did declare to be such and many a soul had to bend the knee and confess to a sin which never existed under God and confirm a truth which was never truth but which power made such and fear of the unknown made regnant. Thus was men's weakness displaced on to those who summoned it forth and guilt at women's suppression given a night-time shadow when they reclaimed that power at men's expense.

To break the taboo is to force through into another world, to become a traveller in time and space, to find a new sun round which to orbit. For sin, it seems, is malleable. You have but to move a thousand miles, or less, much less, to journey forward or back, and it becomes no sin at all, while others are born on a winter's morning. There have been sins in the past without which we could not be, rules which if not broken would have left us savage on a distant shore. In like manner, the journey may perhaps not be continued unless we should contrive to sin again, so that there is no sin unless we chose to make it so. But for

Hester and Dimmesdale such thoughts would be sins themselves and to acknowledge their relationship for what, unbeknown to them, it had surely become was to necessitate its end and to sink them in their private sea of guilt. They sought one another out, as they thought, for companionship, if think they did, as they travelled together on a journey to a new land which they had in truth found long before they should set foot on the unforgiving soil of New England.

The *Hope* had one more storm to weather before she would reach her destination but it was a storm which quickly left the word itself behind. It began with a cloud like a beached whale lying heavy and inert on the far horizon; but within an hour this had raised itself up and dissolved into a black and yellow liquid which seemed to boil on some cosmic stove. Lightning lit the sky without cease as the heavens seemed to turn about the ship. Where but an hour before a churchlike silence, thick and humid, had hung about them, the air itself seeming to congeal, now the thunder sounded as though all the battles of humankind were being replayed about their heads. The wind hit the ship, an invisible yet solid fist of air. The sails were quickly down or they would have pulled them immediately to their fate, but the masts bent under the force like the bows of English archers. The sea which had been like beaten lead now rose above them, then fell away beneath their keel, one moment a solid wall of liquid glass, the next a chasm of purest black which sucked them down.

A sea storm is as like one on land as a bull is like a mouse. You have only to look it in the eye to know that it seeks your life. On land a storm will lose its power as it tears through valley and dale. Each tree it snaps, each roof it strips, drains its power away. Like a bee it wins its victories with its life. The sea is another universe where the wind draws its energy from its own progress, circling like some monster bird of prey which touches down only to tear the life of that on which it feeds. On ground the air may be tangled like the sheets of a fever patient but the ground itself will not deviate and turn. You may hug it to you as a child will grip its toy or cling to the tangled shreds of the blanket on which it has travelled through the terrors of the night, but on the sea there is no fixed point, no still and quiet retreat.

Take a journey in your mind upon a train which plunges through the darkness of a tunnel lit only by lanterns spaced some hundred yards apart and set beside small alcoves in the red-black bricks which form its side. These cusps of safety are for those who work upon the line. As the wall of cold and fetid air advances before the train and the single eye of the advancing engine or the orange glow of her fires lights up the black circle of this avenue to hell, the men will lay aside shovel and pick and press themselves in these cell-like spaces until it should have passed. Imagine now that one such doorway to safety passes quickly by the grimed window of your carriage. Through the swirling smoke and sparks you see that it is quite boarded up, while across its front is a crudely written notice which spells a message of doom to he who would secure his life against the onward rush: NO REFUGE. The story requires no white-faced workman fleeing for his life or smashed against the tunnel side for what may not imagination supply if it but be prompted by a word. Imagination wrought its magic on Dimmesdale as he lay on his bunk. A storm at sea offers no refuge. There is no place as in a children's game where one may cross one's fingers and cry pax or barley. Journeys may require destinations but here survival replaces all such thoughts.

Nor was Hester immune as the ship seemed like a wild horse determined to unseat its rider; and you may be sure that no thoughts of Dimmesdale nor of anything but sheerest terror gripped her as she lay in her bed and listened to what must surely be the ship's dismantling. Likewise Dimmesdale, voiding himself into a sliding bowl. So much, you might think, for the power of love, though that word had entered neither his mind nor that of the woman who was herself now mimicking his actions.

The Captain's mind, though, was on other matters for he was no more captain of his fate than the youngest cabin-boy. There is little that the master of a sailing ship may do with his sails stored like squirming caterpillars on the deck and the masts flexing above his head. And beyond the ship, through a blinding rain which fell like a waterfall, he knew there was ice, driven, like them, through the waves; but where they were a leaf blown down the lane, the ice would be moving at its own steady pace so that should the *Hope* but cross its path, as well it might, there would be no hope for them.

The *Hope* was not crushed, though her main mast snapped close to the deck with a sound which shook the ship and which all on board felt as though a musket-ball had been fired into their own bodies. In a curious way the efforts to clear the rigging from the deck and cut the mast adrift were a welcome change to those who only a moment before had felt nothing but their helplessness. They were suddenly surgeons on the field of battle severing a limb to save a life.

The mast which fell was that from which Young Jack had plunged and there seemed a judgement in the fact that it should so soon have echoed his fall. Indeed, as it fell so the tearing sinews of the wood let out such a scream that the sailors felt must have rivalled that of their companion, while it now lay along the deck where all knew the wood was stained with the blood of their young shipmate. They were caught in a terrible rhythm as the *Hope* was taken by successive swells of what felt like liquid ice, shuddering with mock passion with each new violation. The holds were battened down but the falling mast had stoved through the deck to the forward cabins and though a rough repair of canvas and wood held back the worst, in the darkness below an inner sea surged through the arterial corridor like a paradigm of that beyond.

The ship which later sighted land seemed to Hester quite broken and destroyed. It had become her home and now it was in ruins. The deck-rail was no more than doubled rope where the mast had followed Jack over the side and the ordered deck seemed, like her self, to have been rendered into merest anarchy. It was true that grey-white sails now bent from the two remaining masts, and that the *Hope* once more seemed to throb with life, but she was not now what she had been before. But then neither was Hester, she might have thought, had she but allowed herself time for such introspection.

The land lay, a purple bar in the distance, and the ship nosed towards it like an injured hunting hound. It was not, she knew, their final destination but a place for temporary repair before a week or so which would see them, God willing, in Boston's harbour. None the less the sight of land after peril, or simply after so long in which the eye could focus on nothing but a homogeneous sea, was bound to lift the spirits, and so it did as she stood and watched the distant shape grow and change. The sky was cobalt blue while the flat, grey monotony of the sea was transformed into greens and blues and indigos. Once more white seagulls plunged out of a brilliant sun which now lay, a golden coin, off the starboard bow. Beside her stood both her cousin and Dimmesdale who stared ahead, his eyes, like hers, fixed on the approaching land.

'Don't raise thy hopes, Hester,' said her cousin, holding the doubled rope of the ship's rail.

'But the weather is beautiful.'

'That it is. And may it stay such. But this is no Boston ahead.'

'I shall be glad but to stand on something which does not move,' said Dimmesdale, himself holding that self-same rope, though with a studied fierceness as though he did not believe the tempest had quite left them.

'Ay, but thou wilt find it is not as steady as thou might think. Five weeks at sea does something to a man. It teaches a body that nothing is solid and still as it appears. Believe me, sir, it will move beneath thy feet as though it were another ocean, and there are those who are sick on land who never were while they stood upon a deck in the fiercest gale.'

Nothing, however, could have prepared them for the sight which greeted them as they moved towards the distant land. The first surprise was that, as they approached the grey-mauve line inscribed on the western sky, it seemed to glow with a kind of halo. Closer still and they could see it was surrounded by a low mist, brilliant white except where the feeble sun turned it russet red.

'Ice,' Hester's cousin explained.

'Ice? And shall we not be able to reach land?'

'We shall reach it. There will be channels still. The ice lies flat here. It will bear a man's weight and more but it is too early to prevent our passage.'

And so it proved. And so Hester wrote.

As we did near the outer edge so I could see a tracery of blue, as veins will stand out on a young girl's arm in the heat of summer. Open water lapped against the whiteness which sparkled so in the sun, as though scattered with the dust of diamonds. Above us a sailor shouted out and pointed with his arm. The wind, which but a day since had sought to tear us into shreds, now blew gently as we tacked backwards and forwards, a dog following a scent. The land stood out as low cliffs plunging to a foreshore, grey and treeless, yet softened by blue sky and winter sun. Then, while still a mile or more from shore, we came upon a sight which was a glimpse from hell.

For some minutes, as it seemed, I had watched what I took for an emblem of this beauty, a patch of scarlet against the purest white of sea ice. It seemed almost as though the sun had sought out some declivity or pinnacle in the frosted sheet to shine with all the wonder of the heavens. And though I confess I still looked to the shore for some sign of life it was to this crimson glory that my eye was drawn, as a single poppy in a field of wheat will compete with the golden fold of ripeness. It seemed a symbol of life after the dull sameness of the moving sea.

As we approached, obliquely, sometimes turning towards the sun, sometimes away, following the dark and narrow passage while feeling for the wind, so I lost sight of this deep red rose on the white breast of the ocean as a mist rose slowly from the narrow strip of sea. But, as the ship swung back again, its hull sighing like a sledge along the powdered edge of the ice, so I saw it again, lit by a sudden shaft of sunlight while softened by the cushion of the rising mist. And now I could make out dark shapes against the whiteness, shapes which moved amongst the red; and on the far edge, towards the land, was a low shape, a longboat as I soon realized, with oars like the limbs of some dead creature whose flesh has been stripped by the wind. I blush now to think that I felt a thrill of joy that we should encounter our fellow-men, creatures such as ourselves in this frozen wilderness.

The passage began to widen suddenly and we were in an inland sea. The water was quite still and the wind seemed like to drop away. Just beneath the surface, in water that was the palest green, as though it contained powdered chalk, I could make out pink creatures which seemed to twist and turn as one. The air was full of gulls but no longer did they trace their arabesques above the Hope. They flew towards the ice where red roses were in bloom. Nor were they alone, for, scarcely half a mile ahead, the longboat dipped its oars, drawn to the same destination. And as we neared so I could see that the men on board wore thickly padded jackets of fur and that their hands were in mittens so that I was amazed they could grasp the oars. One in the stern raised a hand of greeting, or so it seemed, and there was a flash of silver a short distance before him; but the boat continued on its way, intent, I thought, to run quite into the ice shelf itself. And so it did, but rather than splintering along its edge, as I had supposed, it rose up darkly in the air, then settled like the beached whale which one summer I saw on Yarmouth's beach and which eventually stank so that the whole town turned out to dig a pit and bury it.

The wind, which had been slight all day, now dropped entirely and we drifted on the gentle swell so that we became enforced observers of what happened but three hundred paces away, a scene with which I must now stain this journal. The men quickly disembarked their boat and moved as one to pull it on the ice, as though it and they were part of some single animal. Then they reached within for long sticks with which I supposed they would test the ground. But again that glint of silver. One ran ahead, holding in his hand a rope which stretched back to their boat; and then the horror of it came to me. For, as the Hope swung gently in the current we were brought hard up against the ice and I could see what I would wish not to have seen. The man had not raised his hand in greeting, nor were the poles for testing the safety of their footing, except, perhaps, as moral beings. They were no more than killers going about their trade. The mist began to thin and the rose withered before my eyes.

The ice was stained thickly with blood, which seemed to clot like a scab where dark carcasses were strewn. The fur-clad figures moved awkwardly amidst a moving sea of shapes, some dark and large, others so small and white that they almost disappeared, standing out with clarity only against the red-stained snow. Again and again the clubs were raised and I watched, who would not watch, as men knelt and ran a hand, with silver flashing, along the length of forms which suddenly bloomed red.

'Seals,' said cousin John, as though I had never seen them sleek off the Norfolk coast at Happisburgh or Cley.

'But how could they do so?' I asked, who knew no answer would suffice.

'Warmth. Food. Oil,' he replied. 'Life, here, leaves them clinging by their fingertips.'

So it does, I dare hazard, but as I watched them stumble and slide in the slush of blood and snow, here slitting a throat, there bending to peel the skin of an animal while it shivered and shook with death, I wondered what life might amount to if it required such a price. And what are we, who have such concern for our souls and yet could do such to one of God's creations?

I could watch no more and turned away to return to my cabin. I, who had survived the storm and much more besides, now sank to my knees, not in prayer but to purge myself of all that I had seen. I have watched pigs slaughtered, yes and lambs and chickens, too, with no more conscience than if I pulled a parsnip from the soil. But what I had seen here told me something I had thought not to know. We are dangerous creatures. I confess my hands shook as I wiped a cloth across my mouth. Was this, then, the world I was entering, a world far harsher than I had supposed? Was I, perhaps, travelling back in time to man's beginnings, a world before civility, compassion and belief?

They rested two days among the strange but not unfriendly hunters whose lives, it seems, turned around the creatures that they slaughtered. Broad-faced and narrow-eyed, they had skin the colour of waxed parchment. They fed themselves from the dark meat of the seals and clothed themselves in fur.

In the protection of the natural harbour, formed on two sides by the thickening sea ice and the third by the dark cliffs, the crew fell to sawing and hammering. A third mast was rigged, smaller than that which it replaced and thinner too, and the rigging spun filament by filament. They might, indeed, have rested longer had the temperature not begun to fall and the arteries to turn pale grey. As it was, the *Hope* had several times to ride up on to the ice, like a rutting bull, until sheer weight and the power of a stiffening breeze released her from the fast-forming prison.

After the first shock Hester had watched from the deck as the hunters completed their bloody work. She was indeed a daughter of the land and had been sufficiently trained in necessity to recognize the rights of those who struggled in this desolate place, though her heart grieved for those whose sacrifice was required to meet necessity's demands. But had she lived two centuries later she would have felt quite otherwise, as ingenuity and greed combined to transform survival into trade. So rewarding would it become that more than fifty vessels would be crushed by the ice as their crews hunted the seals whose lives were now forfeit to fashion and to profit.

It was terrible enough to Hester's eye but she had seen the sparrowhawk snatch up the mouse and the cat play with fluttering bird. There was a face to nature which she had long learned to accept. So, beauty itself may contain ugliness at its core just as freedom and slavery may be locked in an embrace; and had not God provided this bounty in such a lonely and inhospitable place for man's requirements? For those who must believe in providence and a divine plan nothing could be but that which had been imagined by the mind of God. What, then, of sin? It was a question which once had not bothered Hester, whose failings had seemed great to her but which were slight enough, she acknowledged, beside the evil which had been rumoured throughout the land. For these were dark and disturbing times when it was said that the elect of God was to be challenged in the very name of him from whom authority itself could be said to flow; and if the bond were broken might not brother do to brother what was done to creatures in this frozen land? Was not England in the grip of a terrible frost, and did not silver glint in the sun and blood stain ice and snow in fen and field? Where were the certainties at such a time? There were, indeed, those who learned a lesson from such affairs of state and wandered the countryside believing all things possible and themselves arbiters of good. This was the world in which Hester tried to find the northern star and Dimmesdale to cling to imperatives fast fading in the night.

Perhaps this was the soil which prepared for what must now follow, for which of us is separate from the society we inhabit? The fish is in the sea; the sea is in the fish. Perhaps we are never such a product of our times as when we imagine ourselves immune. So, as the *Hope* pulled clear of the ice and turned towards the south-west, a process, as natural and perhaps inevitable as the rise and fall of the sea, was about to work itself out. Hester was a believer. There were few who were not. The question was, what did she believe? She knew with total certainty that God lay at the centre of creation, that all exist and live their lives within his eyes. She acknowledged the responsibility which tied her to her God and hence her fellow-man; but a gap had opened up between statute and experience, much as the ice had opened under pressure from the *Hope*, creating a space within which she could freely sail. She no longer doubted the rightness of her action nor yet her right to take her fate into her hands. What she had feared as sin perhaps she might embrace as right in a changing world. But a greater change lay ahead where a lowering sky drew her on, uncertain yet but no longer quite alone.

Hester and Dimmesdale made no assignation. They had met each night, as travellers will, often with her cousin to make up a third, or they had listened, side by side, to the story-teller's art. But not on this evening. Their destination was near. The sharp, salt tang of the sea had given way to a dank breeze which seemed to carry the smell of earth and rotting leaves. As the last skull-cap of the sun disappeared they could make out a long, dark band of crêpe which was their destination. Above them, stars began to appear, one by one, but stars wrenched from their familiar positions.

Hester stood and stared above her, as though struggling to decode the meaning written there. By her side was another who on the morrow would be required to present himself in a role he was no longer certain he could perform, to announce as certainties what were no longer secure and absolute convictions. The altered stars were an image of his own shifting map.

As though by mutual agreement they turned from the newly crafted rail and withdrew into the darkness of the lower deck, she first, moving now with ease in the darkness, he behind, his step, as it seemed, more tentative.

'Goodnight, Hester. Tomorrow . . .' He paused, as that single word flooded his mind with a terrible regret.

'It is why we have journeyed here. I . . .' Then she, too, found her dictionary run quite through. They stood a second, unwilling to leave one another's presence, on the threshold of more than the cramped cabin of an insignificant ship on a distant sea. Nor did they do so for when Hester at last reached for the latch she felt him still beside her, as tangible as an embrace. And embrace there followed.

There are moments when all sense, all propriety, all will, all reservations dissolve and the world reorients itself around a different sun. There is no struggle. You pass an invisible line, as they had passed one with such doubtful ceremony but three weeks since. Time and place become as nothing. Nor is the self intact, for it, too, dissolves, along with prohibitions which have lost their true authority. The slightest touch has the power of the magician's rod. It can transform, redeem, render invisible those within the enchanted circle of desire. Neither was aware of opening the door nor yet of closing it once more. Neither registered the room, the chairs, the table or the bed. A candle was lit in the swaying lantern but they saw nothing but their own necessity as two dark shadows melded into one. Like blind people they ran their hands over features they had thought familiar, as though to imprint those features on the skin, to etch them on the mind. There must have been some part of them which watched appalled for both were breaking every edict and commandment which had shaped their lives. But we are made of more than precept, custom or decree, nor can these exert dominion on those enchanted. The stars have looked down on stranger couplings than that which now ensued, as in the darkness they possessed that which each desired and surrendered that which each would freely give. Love was asked; love was offered; love was inhabited as a place of refuge, embraced as a necessity of life, presented as a gift which in the giving was restored to the giver. In the swaying light of a single candle they spoke words which they had not known were there to be spoken to one they had not known would wish to hear them uttered. As the ship surged on so they travelled together on their private journey, struggling towards a destination which was as new to them as the land which even now they approached. They kissed who had never so kissed before, trailed hands over flesh which was silk or sand sifting through fingers. Then, at last, as the ship had been becalmed those many weeks before, they lay side by side and thought their separate thoughts, time was reborn and they were returned to that meagre cabin on a merchant ship carrying woollen cloth to a people desperately in need of warmth.

'Oh, Hester. What have we done?'

Hester lay silent, in need of no words. Nor did she move to cover herself as did he.

'I should not have . . .'

'Arthur. Say nothing. Rest still.'

But there was no rest, though he lay on the bed beside her, his arm still beneath her, as guilt, so lately driven out, began to find its way back into every crevice of his being.

As for Hester, she was not what she had been but there was a quiet contentment in her, nonetheless. She drifted in arcs of thoughtlessness. In her heart she knew that she had broken no injunction she would not wish to break. These weeks at sea had taught her nature's power. A sail might be trimmed, the helm turned subtly to search out the wind, but the ship sailed best when it ceased to fight creation's power. She had surrendered not to another but to necessity and such gentleness, she was sure, could be born of nothing but a harmony, a consonance, a symmetry engendered out of good. She raised a hand languidly and watched as a shadow rose to greet it, offering, as it seemed to her, a kind of blessing to their union.

They sighted Cape Cod at dawn, a low curve of land fringed with the white of Atlantic waves along its outer edge to the point where it turns in on itself like a beckoning finger. Certainly the *Hope* took the invitation, pulled forward by an on-shore breeze. The spit of land slipped past them to the south, its low dunes and tufted grass barely catching the morning light. But Hester saw none of this. She slept as deeply as she had ever done, a dreamless sleep. Her clothes lay strewn about and a pale arm rested on a crumpled pillow.

In the neighbouring cabin things were quite other for there a man knelt in the darkness, as he had knelt these four hours since. All feeling had left his legs. His hands were locked together in a pointless prayer as he sought forgiveness, light, punishment in equal measure. Above all he prayed that there might be no consequence to his sin. He did not doubt his love for Hester but was she not the temptation sent to test him? They had been brought together on this ship and could not but be companions in distress, but he had committed that which each night he had prayed to shun. The calm seas through which they now sailed were in ironic contrast to the state of his soul. He knew he had to break faith; the question was with whom and what.

The *Hope* edged forward over the furled foil of Massachusetts Bay, leaving, as it seemed, scarcely a ripple to mark its passing. The early mist had rolled back towards the open sea leaving a still and opalescent light. After the fury of their passage the silence seemed a kind of grace. Here and there a fish broke the film of the grey water with a sound clear and close, as only two nights before they had heard the rasping blow of whales, the sharp smack of fluke on sea.

Hester woke suddenly, the very silence, perhaps, summoning her to consciousness. She lay a moment, unsure of what she felt and why, and, as she did so, within that moment there came the realization that however free she might feel in her mind she was not free in fact nor could such a man as she had held to herself embrace her openly with the day's return.

And if these thoughts were in her mind what of the man who now rose to his feet to pace the cabin next to hers? With the approaching shore came duty and responsibility. Could they but reverse their journey . . .

There was a hammering on his door. 'We shall be ashore within the hour, sir. Captain's compliments.' The sailor repeated his message outside Hester's door.

Their last meeting on board lasted no more than a few

minutes. He knocked on her cabin door and when she opened it stepped inside. It can be imagined that Hester was not alone in her tears. Both offered to accept the blame; both repeated their love. Both began and ended their interview knowing it must be their last, as the *Hope* edged through a tangle of small boats into Boston harbour, even so early in its life the focus of a settlement which had grown from village into town. They stepped away from each other and with a last, long look surrendered each other to the day.

★

The city of Boston lies today enfolded in its provincial smugness. The lens of the great eye of Massachusetts Bay, it focuses the light on its own gentle privacies. To the left, the sea; to the right, the Charles river basin. Still further, Christ Church, Salem Street, shining white in the summer sun, and the golden breast of the State House.

It is a city state. From North Station, once the mill-pond, until a slice of Beacon Hill was dropped in it like mud pie in whipped cream, to Faneuil Hall, this is a town which elevated its status before log was piled on log or brick on brick. Century presses on century. The Mathers preached in North Square, where silversmith Paul Revere was to live (just possibly on the site of Increase Mather's house), he who was freedom's messenger yet still remembered to charge for the oats his horse consumed as he made through the night, warning of the approach of destiny.

Go back in time and Boston not only shrinks back into its seed, it halves in size. The Shawnut peninsula, renamed Boston by John Winthrop and his company, naming being a chief delight of those first eager years, was all but an island divided from the mainland to the north and east by the Charles river, with only a thin, emaciated arm of land linking it to the Roxbury mainland. Along it rose the Trimountain, now abbreviated into the simple rise of Beacon Hill. The very ground beneath our feet ebbs and flows like the tide. The Reverend John Cotton once lived on the slope of the eastern hill, imagining, no doubt, this to be the true city on a hill. If so, what would he make now of a hill which has been flattened and a city which embraces sin as close as virtue? And what of Mount Vernon, later known as Mount Whoredom, and now as detumescent as its eastern partner? Beacon Hill alone remains, so named for the beacon to be lit by sentries should ever danger approach.

None gleamed in the sky as Hester approached a town which clung for safety between the harbour and the Trimountain, a town set on a treeless plain, its frame houses covered with clapboard against the face-numbing, eye-smarting, bone-cutting winds.

This was the place where the world was to be reborn. Viewed from the sea Trimountain was a green hope, a curve of expectation, pregnant with a new truth and they the children hastening towards birth. Yet no child is born that does not bear the mark of parentage: a way of smiling, a disposition towards things sweet, a murderous temper or a broken lip. No fruit falls far from the tree, though the wind blow fiercely and the storm be strong. The land might be no more than grass and soil, an untimbered slope, but they would make it heaven's mirrored self and themselves its angels, winnowed by sin but burnished by faith. The land was without sin; not those who ventured there, though they did so in redemption's name. They sought to live a dream of perfection but the dream itself was perfection's flaw. For they thought to be what no man or woman ever was: the inheritors of heaven's grace with the right to judge and the destiny to prosper as though deeds alone must speak of their entitlement.

They presumed too much, these people, but presumption was what drew them here and who can say we would have it otherwise who are their inheritors. For though denial of history is our proudest boast yet we must acknowledge that the river was once a stream and the stream a spring surfacing from mysterious depths. What they did lives on in us so that this story is in part our own and guilt, if guilt there is, descends not only on the distaff side.

For Hester, this land was to have been pure escape. It was already shaping itself into a destiny, albeit one she could hardly see as such, tears being what they are and the loss of love seeming at times much like the loss of life.

Along the waterfront, merchants had built wharves which jutted into the harbour like so many carpenters' set-squares laid side by side. For this was no displaced village. In size, shape, significance and self-image it was already a metropolis. Those houses not made of wood were built of good brick and stone, with two-storey town houses for merchants and churches set by cobbled streets. The common was patrolled by constables, men whose acquaintance Hester would one day make.

Since it was a Thursday when the *Hope* nestled against a dark wharf, like the runt at a pig's belly at last allowed its turn, it found the town all but deserted. For Thursdays were appointed then, and long after, as the day businesses should close their doors so that all could attend a lecture at the First Church. It was as though the Last Day had come and all been gathered to their maker, as in a sense they had. For Hester, who had feared that she came to a desolate place where Indians and snakes coiled round each other in a land roamed by wolves, it was surprise indeed to see a world so prosperous and so established, though her heart was chilled at what she must now face, a world so absent of her kind. But, lecture or no, a ship's arrival still demands attendance and attendance there was.

The dockside was accordingly soon alive with movement, nor could the arrival of a ship from England pass without excitement. A bell sounded in the clear air and on the dock a line of carts was pushed towards them. Even so, Hester, who at first was struck by the greatness of this settlement, soon fell to comparing it amiss with what she had left behind. Was not Norwich the second city of England! As they entered the Great Cove and edged towards the quay she counted fewer vessels, so she thought, than she had seen at Yarmouth where it seemed to her she could have walked from one side of the harbour to the other across a parade of vessels large and small. Here, the greater ships were anchored in a rough crescent somewhat short of the wharves which reached out into the sea, while here and there small skiffs, piled high with cargo, rowed between them. The

Hope, however, edged past to a berth between two fishing-boats, high in the water and neat as the houses on the hill above.

Hester looked for strangers in this strange land. Had her cousin not told her, after all, of natives whose bodies were uncovered and animals which never roamed in Norfolk's gentle countryside. But what she saw before her was only a harbour, and those who moved towards the ship, though dressed, as it seemed to her, in uniformly sombre colours, were surely kin to those she had left behind. The stranger here was her for she had changed so that she scarcely knew herself. Her mind, her body, her soul had been transformed and never could be what they were. Nor were the tears which started to her eyes for that former self. They were for what could not be, yet for what she desired, now, with a passion she could barely comprehend.

The *Hope*, which had been rowed the last half mile, now ground along the wooden posts sunk deep into harbour mud and at last ceased all motion. With a hollow rattle and rough scraping a gangplank was slid over the side until it could be lowered to the dockside. Thus linked, they became part of the continent to which they travelled and, within the hour, Hester stood and breathed the air of a new land, watching, as she did so, a group of men, dressed all in black, close about the man she had held to her heart, like crows around a rabbit crushed beneath the wheels of a passing cart.

In the beginning all the world was America, said John Locke. Here the apple was returned to the tree. Here the hand ceased its concealment and shame itself was shamed. History retreated to its lair. A page was smoothed, white and clear, with no pen to hand. Here was built a city on the hill and he that would reach it about must and about must go. A thousand points of light shone out of a velvet sky.

In the beginning, America was its own future, legs drawn tight in the womb against the moment of delivery. Here was the dream of tomorrow which brought forth corruption. Nor was the past relinquished. Those who wiped the map of their birth clean no sooner landed among the sumac, the maple and the poison ivy than they named their new habitation for their old: Norwich, Ipswich, New London on its river Thames. And with this cartography, bred out of fear and longing, came a memory; so yesterday was reclaimed and in the space between yesterday and tomorrow a history was born. They carried more than smallpox with them on their sturdy ships, more than a hunger for gold and god, separated but by a single letter, that which doubled turns he into hell. They carried their own past wrapped in a sheet or folded in an oilskin packet.

So, Hester stepped into the past and future at one instant, believing it to be the present. History, however, had not done with her, as yet, nor the future begun to pull her to her fate, unless it might take the form of he who strides up the hill and forbears to look behind him where she stands.

Once on shore Hester's cousin proved his worth again. On previous visits he had lodged with a family who themselves had been only two years in the colony and laboured hard in the fields. Here, Hester, too, came to dwell, her room small and her duties many. She was mother to two children when their own mother was abroad in the day and would sew in the evenings to the sound of cricket and bullfrog and the shrieking owl. They treated her with kindness, especially when the *Hope* sailed out across the bay, her cousin waving to her as she stood upon the wharf.

She let it be known that she was come ahead of her husband who had affairs to settle and that she would have little by way of money until that should be done. And though it was unusual for a woman to risk such a journey on her own they accepted her account and gave her a modest wage along with a room scarcely larger than that which she had occupied on the *Hope*. The cottage was by the forest and looked out across the bay where ships huddled together in clusters.

She was a stranger but in a community where strangers were the common currency. Being but freshly come from England she found herself close questioned, for stories of dark deeds and the shifting tide of power reached them with every ship. For her part she was a blind woman on an unfamiliar road, seeking assistance from those whose eyes were bright and clear. The very food on the table was a mystery, as were the animals about the door. One day she saw a snake, then two, until by evening's end she had encountered half a dozen, each seemingly different; and so they catechized her on the dangers underfoot and in the woods.

One day, hanging clothes on a line which looped between the cottage and a hickory tree, she found herself confronted by a man, naked to the waist and streaked with colour. In his hand he held a bow and stared at her with eyes so fierce and brown she felt she had lost the power of movement as of speech. A kind of terror gripped her, as she stood holding in her hands a pair of dripping breeches. Then, with the slightest nod of the head, he turned away and, barefoot, seemed to glide like a water moccasin, back into the trees.

'He will have meant no harm,' the mistress of the house assured her.

'Nor I to him but I think we did both affright each other.'

'There are some who think them devils but they gave us the corn and last winter when we could not venture out of doors, laid a deer at our door. We give them cloth and trinkets. They are but men. John Eliot, the pastor at Roxbury, has learned their language and has brought many souls to Christ.'

There were nights aplenty when Hester lulled herself to sleep with tears. This was not her home nor never would be and for all the kindnesses of those she served she was alone who never had been such before. There was a severity here whose pressure she felt. For these were people whose kindness was bordered by commandments which bade them stare within their souls for the sign of sin; and sin was more general here, it seemed. For a man and woman to sit together under an apple tree on the sabbath was counted sin, as it was to take pleasure in a summer's day if there were work still to be done. Here neighbours watched for signs of falling off while a fruit tree sticky with blackfly might betoken the black heart of he who tended it. Hester counted herself a pious woman yet such piety could quite drive out joy and she was in need of joy whose heart was set on a man who no longer seemed to know she walked on God's good earth.

I am come into a new land and am determined that I shall live here with a free heart. The voyage is over and all that occurred must be as a dream. Nor shall I think of my distant home, save as a memory of happiness to be renewed amongst friends new found.

As we sailed our last mile I could see small houses on the northern shore, snug above a rocky beach and there were those that waved to see us end our journey, though I was not of a mood to wave to any, feeling in such despair.

The Captain gripped me by the hand as we parted and I fancy I saw a tear in his eye. He wished me good luck and then, for want of anything else to do, plunged his hand deep in his pocket only to withdraw it holding his pipe which he flourished in the air quite as though it had been lost a year and only just restored to light. I thought he might see fit to light it now that we had come to shore but he still stood with his scowling smile and made no move to put flame to tobacco.

There was another smile, too, with which I had to part, that of my living landscape man, my animated portrait. He stood before me as I went to climb the gangplank and with a flourish pulled off his shirt. There were doubtless those on shore who thought this strange indeed but none on board thought this any stranger than if a man should open his mouth to speak. Having thus divested himself he pointed to his body as a schoolteacher will tap a stick upon a board.

First he indicated a heart by which I took him to indicate the strength of his feeling, and then to a ship which sailed across a blue-red sea. Then he pointed not to himself but me and this did signify, as I thought, that which he had come to feel for me on our mutual journey as, about to part, I realized I felt for him and for all with whom I had shared these weeks. Then to his heart again before pointing behind me, so it seemed. I turned about and with a shock saw where he pointed for, standing behind but half a dozen paces away, was he whose face was etched as deeply and indelibly in my heart as were the images pricked into the skin of this dumb sailor who yet spoke as plain as any man. I blushed, as I am wont to do, and looked away, only to feel a tugging at my sleeve. He had not finished his monologue, it seemed, for he pointed now to the opposite side of his chest where another heart was drawn, this one, though, rent in two by a lightning bolt and edged in brightest scarlet. Then, bowing as though before a queen, he touched a finger to his head where a single eye stared back at me. He had seen what was and perhaps what was yet to *be.* Then, he straightened and turned away and, as a cloud passed *over a watery sun, the images on his receding back seemed to animate and flow, to go about their business as he went about his, bending to a bale of cloth which must be lowered over the side.*

And so I took my leave and ventured on to foreign soil with cousin John at my side. Arthur and I had said our goodbyes long since and neither had the stomach for a public farewell which must hurt us both. We would not be actors in some play and feign our truest feelings; but I tell thee, my diary, what must never be spoken aloud, that I did love this man and love him still. I am put in mind – and the thought comes from out of nowhere – of when I was but eight or nine. I kept a rabbit of my own. It was grey and warm and I alone had the keeping of him, feeding, watering and watching as he skipped about my bedroom floor. One morning I carried his water from the well and when I reached his cage he was laying flat, all stretched out. I touched him with my hands and he seemed both cold and stiff. I felt a sudden terror close my throat and watched for signs of movement: but he was gone. Some time in the night he had breathed his last and I had slept unknowing in my bed. I took his body, all rigid and unnatural, in my arms and sat in the sun for hope that it would breathe some life in him. Then there came a moment when the knowledge burst through, as winter rains will sweep away a summer dam. All my sorrow rushed from my mouth in one long cry of grief and in that cry, I well remember now, I uttered just four words: 'But I loved thee.' Love so strong cannot be deserted. Well, we learn otherwise and I must learn that that which was is no longer. What is and may be must now be my concern.

Though Boston be smaller than Norwich, it is a handsome place, more civilized than I had supposed. The houses are but new and boards not always weathered, yet there is a cleanness and an order here. It has the buildings which are supposed to be necessary to all communities: a church, a prison and a meeting house. Already in the churchyard are more graves than I had thought could have been tenanted in a town only twenty years from its first founding. Many, indeed, seem to have perished in those early years. Whole families here lie side by side in the land they had sought out with such hope. They are the compost, no doubt, from which stout trees will grow.

I write this but one week since landing here and even now my spirits recover with my balance, though there is scarcely a moment when I do not think of him and us, for here, at least, we may together make a single word. I know that I must free myself from such thoughts, and shall. I may not spend the rest of my life in regrets; and what better place to strip me of yesterday's self than this where the air has smells I know not and birds fly high above I never saw. The smell of baking bread may surely revive those who have greater sorrow than I. That, and the sight of the sea, for all that it is the colour of lead and a chill wind blows.

I am told the snow will come soon and we shall be locked away until spring. I met a Norfolk man, from Hingham, who did ask after his relatives, none of whom I knew, and he told me that the winters here are worse than anything at home. He nearly died, he told me, his first winter, for his roof was not on when the first snow fell and since it was a sabbath he could not remedy his situation.

There are many here from my own dear country and yet none whose path I had crossed before, though I did enquire. How strong the pull of the familiar. How strong the bonds which tie us to our past. Sometimes I think I would give anything to be with those I love. Then I recall the reason for my flight and the danger spreading everywhere in a land divided against itself. Yet would I have stayed but for him; and when I think of him I think also of another so different he seems a Gabriel to his Lucifer. Yet my Gabriel has made his visitation and has flown. I, being mortal, must remain. See how my mind comes full circle. Despite my resolution my lack of resolution compels me back to an absent centre.

Hester learned something of the fate of her husband in a letter which reached her four months after her arrival, as the ice of the Charles river began to thaw and jostle down its centre like so many church-goers passing through a narrow gate. Her father was no penman and the message he sent was brief, but it was enough to chill her heart. It spoke of Chillingworth's arrest on the Yarmouth road and of his detention, and that of his fellows, in Norwich gaol. They were suspected as royalists and his home had been searched and torn asunder by a gang who carried off his plate and threw his chemicals together until they caused a fire which burned all night. But the letter also spoke of his escape and of his taking ship first to Amsterdam and then the Virginia colony.

Thus, for the next six months, as that first spring turned into the shimmering heat of a New England summer, so hot that it seemed to clot the air, she lived in dread of his arrival. She calculated the time it would take to make the crossing and then proceed by land. To have broken with that life only to find herself pursued! To have forsaken family, friends and a familiar world for one in which she was such a stranger to herself and others only to discover that she carried the canker within her was more than she could bear. She had no one to turn to here, least of all he who had chosen to distance himself so from her: and so she waited. But no figure with a sloping shoulder walked down a Boston street. No shouted accusation sounded in the heavy air. Like her fellow-townsmen and women she suffered through the airless heat, brushed aside the droning mosquitoes and the small, black flecks of flies which plagued the colony that summer. With each day that passed her fear began to lessen. Why, after all, she began to ask herself, should he pursue her here. He had a life to live and perhaps secrets to keep and she had learned, surely, that she was only a tangent to the circle of his life. Day followed day and with each day a conviction grew that a page had turned. A narrative had run its course. The play was done. A weight was lifted from her as one condemned to death by pressing stones might be reprieved.

Now he seemed no threat she could think of him again as she had once before and see her own confederacy in their mutual error. But, oh Hester, how quickly does your mind turn to another, to a man who had so swiftly moved to the centre of the society in which she still felt such a stranger.

Since their time together on the ship they passed one another as two distant acquaintances. They had made no pact to remain apart but the moment he had been claimed on the quay she had recognized that they belonged in two quite different stories. Yet, was she alone in thinking that each sabbath, as he called them to repentance for their sins, his eyes would seek her out in the dimness of the church or was it simply that her own eyes could not leave a face which she had cradled in her arms and drawn to her own? There was a passion in his sermons which moved those used to drier stuff, those, indeed, who might have distrusted as a wayward enthusiasm, itself tainted with sin, such sentiments and such energy in another. She knew another passion which she alone could unlock. Where they heard a voice which exhorted them to prayer, to honest toil and discipline of manner, she heard a gentleness which pulled her back to a night whose memories she fought to keep alive as you would blow on the embers of a fire to see it glow.

Yet, of course, a memory is soon lost or loses its precision. We remember not the thing itself but our remembering and even passion may become a fact to be recited by rote, an image in a tarnished mirror, a fading echo. As the pain of childbirth must be wiped away so the sharp edge of passion is blunted so that it may be sharpened once again. For Hester, though, the edge was as keen as ever so that the slightest touch could bring forth blood.

These were not times, though, when a woman felt free to act. So she watched him as one might watch a sunset, astonished by its beauty at once so close and yet so far away. She performed her daily chores and slowly became a part of the community she had joined; but there was only one centre to her life and, like many a woman, both before and since, she prepared to live a life rooted in nothing more secure than denial.

But, if that were all, there would be no story to tell. For can we imagine that the man she watched, the man with whom she had shared the dangers and terrors of the voyage and much more besides, would be able to drive her from his mind? There are shipboard romances which die with the first sight of land. Inhibitions, stowed safely for the voyage, are taken out again, as blackbird replaces gull about the rigging. Their relationship was not one such. They were forged together by sin. To break such a commandment was to become isolated in some private sphere, and a sin once committed makes further sin more possible. A guilt which at first incapacitates and bewilders will lose its power with time. The mind becomes more generous, the conscience more accommodating, as a lawyer eagerly seeks out precedent and arcane statute to excuse what he knows to be a crime.

This time was not as other times; this place had customs of its own; this action justified itself. I am I and she is she and never before were such as we. Something of this kind, perhaps, was in their minds, for who is there that cannot find a justification for living the life they lead. There are some things which may never be but there are others which may not be denied. Nonetheless, they were children of their times and, if truth were told, they took a perverse pleasure in their mutual denial of one another's company as one in thrall to strong drink will feel a surge of pride with every glass turned aside. Yet this very pride generates its own vulnerability. For such a supposed strength will one day feel the need to test its own implacability. A single drink will underline resolve. A word passed between lovers, a hand rested for a second on another's hand. We have such a capacity to deceive ourselves that it is our despair and yet perhaps also our redemption. If we were no more than we believe there would be no urge to discovery. For what is life but constant revelation. Always travel, never arrive. Always be falling in love, never love's fool. The very distance between Hester and Dimmesdale is perhaps what necessitated its closing. Certainly, believing themselves to be resisting, they were slowly being drawn back to a common centre, at first in dream and then in the dream which we choose to call reality.

Yet Hester would have rested less securely than she did had she known that the man she feared most was not three thousand miles away nor yet so many whitened bones in an ocean's depths but indeed on the same continent as her and were he free to be so would be at her side. Where she believed that he had lost all interest in her and traded vengeance for remorse, he was delayed by other forces than she supposed.

He had indeed been arrested and accompanied to Norwich where he was taken before a grand jury. For though he himself had no politics, beyond those of science, there were those among his number who did. Documents were produced, letters and, from the eves, it was said, of the Tombland attic where they had met with such regularity, ten muskets and a quantity of ball and powder. At such a time few were who they seemed. And so to Norwich gaol and thence perhaps to somewhere more final had not his fellow-supposed-conspirators been part of a genuine conspiracy which sent assistance to them so that one night their gaoler breathed his last face-down in a bowl of carrot soup.

On horseback through the night they followed Hester's path, though she had long since been driven from his mind by all that had befallen. A little down the coast from Yarmouth, whose loyalties, like that of most of Norfolk and its surrounding counties, lay with Parliament, they scrambled down a crumbling cliff which crumbled rather more as they fell until one of them was nearly buried in the slide. Thence, splashing through the icy water, they boarded a skiff and were rowed out to a fishing-boat and thus, smeared with silver scales and blood, reached Amsterdam, across a choppy sea.

Then their paths separated, for he was indeed not of their number nor interested in their plots. For three weeks he lived in some penury while a trusted friend travelled back to England only to find his house a partial ruin with little to be saved. But he carried letters with him and when he returned Chillingworth was once again the master of his fate with gold to pave his way.

Why, then, should he set sail for the New World? His anger against Hester must have stilled as a pot moved from the stove will cool. Yet he had no home and no country to return to and though Holland might be his second home he was not alone in seeing new possibilities beyond the western sea. The bitterness had quite drained away. Blind to the secrets of his companions, he came to realize that he was blind to much else besides. So it was not with vengeance in his heart that he left the gabled city behind and, in early spring, committed his future to the waves.

His journey passed without any of the storms which had beset the *Hope*, until a bare ten miles from the Virginia coast a squall seemed to rise from the surface of the sea, turning about in a tight circle. The sky went from grey to yellow to deepest black until suddenly the air seemed sucked back into the heavens. The ship heeled over and was driven in a circle so tight that those on board were made dizzy with the movement. No sooner did they brace themselves against this movement, though, than the wind changed quite about and, from being at risk of taking water from the starboard, heeled over to the port. There was no question either of pulling in the sails, for they streamed like tattered banners first in one direction, then the other. A shudder went through the vessel like that which afflicts the body on the point of death and then, a greyhound released from confinement, it leapt forward and rushed before a chasing wind, seeming scarcely to touch the surface. For a full hour they clung to each other as to anything else which might save them from the waves. Ropes flew horizontally like the tresses of Medusa while splintered wood showered all about them as if the ship were reducing itself to fragments as they sped. Yet the force of wind and sea alone seemed to keep them on their course, for certainly the rudder no longer served its purpose, until it seemed that they might yet reach their destination, for it was towards the invisible coast that they made their progress. But, even as the tortured screaming of the storm seemed somewhat to lessen, their hopes were all destroyed. A sailor in the bow shouted a warning which none could hear as the ship rose up as though to heaven then settled on the hidden rocks.

Chillingworth returned to consciousness with no other feeling than a numbing cold. For a second he was back on the banks of a Norfolk river, as snow blew about him. Then he had proof that he was nowhere such, for on looking up he saw beside him a figure stately and calm but with features such as he had never looked upon before. Thus he met a man whose face he would see daily for many a month and more ahead. For this was a warrior from the Tidewater tribe which, little more than a decade before, had killed nearly three hundred and fifty of those who had settled along the James river and were to strike again.

Discovery is mutual. One stared in the mirror and saw the past, the other the future, and each recoiled in horror as in a dream. Each weighed the meaning of meaning. One man's exultance, another's tears. A myth of new beginnings and a myth of eternal recurrence collide amidst tall trees. The sound of arrows was but a sigh at loss and loss had only begun as two men looked into each other's eyes and one had to decide

whether to kill the thing there, to stop it even as it rose from the ground. Was it pity or fear? What stayed the hand that could send death quivering through the air above a hundred paces or sliding through the ice-cold ribs? Was it weakness or strength? And was either aware that they were but minor figures in another story which they would neither know nor comprehend?

Cold and terror now had their effect and Chillingworth remembered nothing more until he came to his senses in a darkened space. He started into consciousness with the acrid smell of smoke in his nostrils and his eyes smarting in the gloom. There were other smells, too. That of sweat and a kind of sour greasiness. It was to be a smell he would come to know too well.

Few men would have thought to survive such a capture. Women and children might serve well and there were those that did, escaping or not, embracing a new life or opening veins in cold river-water. Men were otherwise and so it proved with the one companion who had survived the storm with Chillingworth. He saw nothing of him but heard his screams one night, though those about him showed no signs of doing such themselves. But he, himself, had what others did not. He had a knowledge of plants and of the powders in the earth. He could sprinkle some in fire so that it glittered and grind both leaves and berries so they broke a fever. Though they kept him close they were in awe of his powers, save one among them who was himself the possessor of such knowledge; but Chillingworth was careful to share some portion of his skills with him and thus to stay his hand. He had what many others in his plight could not sustain, a patience which meant that they began to trust him until at last they should let him gather herbs and tree-barks some distance from the lodge; and so he watched and waited and kept his counsel.

It is one of the wonders of the human spirit, and yet perhaps also the source of some dismay, that we can so easily learn to live with absence: absence of love, absence of hope, absence of

that excitement born of a day's new dawn. As a cut finger fades to white scar so a damaged heart may function quite as well as though it were never struck a near-fatal blow.

Hester was not so feeble that her life must turn about another, even if that other was seldom from her mind. Not a day passes but that two people part for love's surcease or for the necessity of social or religious fact. Death likewise, which cuts so deep there seems no repair, fades with the ticking of the clock. Within a twelvemonth the soil is settled and a marker put in place. Lips once turned downwards in despair may smile again. How could we live were this not so when at this time a baby's cry could turn so quickly to a mourner's keening. There are those, of course, who will not have this so or, if believing, find it more than they can bear. Young girls have walked into rivers, pockets loaded down with pebbles, rather than live to find such resilience in themselves. One such, indeed, had walked into Hester's river when she was but eight, only to be fished up like some monstrous pike, lips drawn back and limbs so twisted and stiff they had to be broken before she could be made to fit her coffin. Hester had watched and Hester had perhaps remembered. Certainly she searched out no deep water nor looked for pebbles on the beach. She had loved and lost, not once but twice, and resolved no longer to build her life on such foundation.

Though modest in her actions and quiet by nature yet she was noticed at the Thursday lectures and the sabbath church. There were not so many young women in Boston at that time that it should be otherwise. She had never been a great beauty, she who had lived her life in summer field and winter barn. Yet there was a quality to her which drew the eye for there was a beauty there, simple, clean and honest. She moved with a natural grace and had a smile with nothing of guile or craft. She was open and serene, or so it seemed, so that when she passed there were those who nodded to themselves as though recognizing some balance, some harmony that made things just so, exactly right, in tune. Nor, since there was a husband to follow, was there that anxiety, that subtle shiver which seems to emanate from a woman who has as yet not bound herself in nature's perfect circle.

The settlement was fringed at this time by a broad sweep of forest and though its approaches were flooded with the colour of wild roses and lavender, yet it was always thought of as a place of darkness. There the Indian moved with ease, blending with the shadows, flowing through the trees; there, at night, hollow sounds, the insucked breath of terror, the shriek of tortured spirits echoed through the air. Parents would frighten their children, as parents will, with tales of its terrors. People would venture there to gather wood, dead trees shivering under the blow of axes, while women gathered blueberries and boysenberries from the tangle of briars along its edge. But for the most part this was a place to be shunned. Yet there were those who took the narrow paths trodden down by animals which lived there like creatures in a nether world. For there was a wild beauty here which stirred the soul, a sense of danger, mystery even, which lured those tired with the blandness of the settlement and the tightness of its discipline. For the community's writ did not extend to this world where the ground was soft underfoot and the branches blotted out the sky.

On the settlement paths, in the quiet houses and even in the solitary places of the soul, there was no privacy in Boston town. All acts required an accounting. But on this woodland sea you could sail upon your own, quite isolate, for here there was no social space, and no judgements were to be made. Here was no boundary, nor edge, nor limit, nor circumference, and there is a pleasure, even, in being lost for then you may set out to find yourself anew. On the other side of fear you may encounter an unknown self. This was a testing ground and those who ventured to the heart of its darkness did so for many reasons. It was a place of escape, a place of refuge, a place of encounter. Lovers would thread their way, like the stitchwork on a sampler, through upright oaks and swelling limbs to touch a hand that must be denied them in the light. Mad souls and children would be drawn there, until they were led away by those who hunted for them in fear of what they might find. If the minister should speak of the darkness of sin there were many who thought of this place where darkness had its sway.

141

Yet to Hester the forest was a home. She had a taste for wildness, as she had confessed on board the *Hope*. She liked the dank smells and cool softness of the trails and still more the sudden cold and sense of abandonment which came when she edged her way between the trees which closed about her. As she moved away from the sea-fringed town so she became more fully herself.

But it was not regarded as legitimate to venture on such walks, for metaphors have a way of being misread as fact. So she would often carry a rush basket on her arm to gather berries as she went; but as she penetrated deeper into the forest so the dull green light made even the most familiar fruit seem to glow with different colours and, indeed, there were berries there which could not be found anywhere save in this place where she could hear her own heart beating in the gloom.

Hester did not possess, could not imagine, the words with which we locate ourselves. Even the language of Shakespeare had not as yet soaked into the earth, while of Schopenhauer and Locke, Carlyle and Emerson, she could know nothing at all. But her age had its own science, its superstitions, its crafts and its cosmology. There are things invisible to us that to them shone with the brightness of sunlight on river. These were a people who lived symbolically, their lives an expression of God's purpose. A snake was a snake but it wrote other meanings in the sandy soil, unlocked a whole series and system of coherences. No anarchy here, no drifting without faith or purpose, yet mystery was respected. For us there is no question without answer and if no answer now, why, then, tomorrow will bring reply. Then, faith performed this function and faith is a mystery, a sea on whose shore we can only stand in awe. All questions and all answers were contained in He who saw each sparrow fall to earth. He was the flake of mica on the river's bed, the money spider, invisible on the wind. Even as today the very elegance of the spiral staircase to our beginnings leaves us in awe, then something in the rightness of the shape, the beauty of the form, compelled assent. It is not a matter of understanding nor yet of language. What we feel most strongly we speak least articulately or speak not at all. We slough off words as a snake sheds its skin. They become a prison we must escape. Hester's challenge was to free herself from a vocabulary of sin, transgression and damnation. This she could do most easily in the forest.

Dimmesdale, too, walked in the forest gloom, pressing towards those clearings at its heart which seemed to shine in the darkness. For he, also, sought refuge from a public world of duty and civility. He longed for a place where truths need not be spoken aloud. He was drawn, some would say, had some but known who did not, by sin, though whether to challenge such or to succumb is question indeed.

Thus in the spring of her second year, when she had begun to adjust to her new life, living now with a family in a sturdy house near what today is the common and working as a seamstress, governess and help about the home, Hester sought out her favourite spot in a distant clearing. Spring had come early and the sharp-edged smell of new growth was already giving way to the deeper smells of early summer. Indeed it was a Boston May like a Boston August. By noon the heat was all but unbearable, except here in the forest, and the air was heavy and humid. Released from her chores she made her way to this small green patch of grass like an echo of the meadow back in Norfolk; and there she lay, beside a fallen oak whose decaying length was mottled with fungus, as though a painter had run his finger over the bristles of a brush filled first with orange, then red, then earth-brown tinged with black. Termites moved along what must have seemed its hills and valleys, pausing to test the air from time to time, antennae like a blind man's stick.

Only in the centre of the clearing did the sun bear down with a relentless pressure, the sharp edge of the shadows attracting a cloud of small insects which drifted in and out like pollen, flickering to and fro as fish fry in a stream. Hester sat in the shade with her embroidery, passing the needle back and forth through the cloth stretched tight on a small circle of wood. Had you been there and able to stare over her shoulder you would, I suspect, have been unable to make out the design, for Hester was no systematic worker. She was, in that respect at least, already one of the breed that would become Americans, improvising, inventing on the spot. But pattern there was for those with eyes to see.

Within the hour, however, she had succumbed to the heat and lay back in the grass, her work beside her, its needle gleaming silver even in the shadow. She drifted into the sleep which seems reserved for those who lie under an azure sky and hear about them nothing but the song of birds and in the distance the barking of dogs so remote you can hardly be sure it is there at all. That is to say she drifted into a half world of consciousness in which images flowed at random through her mind.

As the day advanced so the shadows which had seemed fixed began to move and there came a moment when only a slender finger of the bright sunlight cut across the darkening clearing like a wound. This thin finger crept slowly up her dress, flowing over fold and pleat until it pointed at her breast, a crimson dagger of warmth. It was not until it reached her face, however, its vermilion light glowing in her hair, that she suddenly woke. Blinded by the light she saw nothing at first. Her mouth was dry, her body aching from the hardness of the ground. Yet that same light seemed to lift her up, to leave her floating free in space. She eased herself on to one elbow and as she did so moved her head into the shade. The light now fell on another, illuminating him like an angel come to beckon her to heaven. It was Dimmesdale. How long he had been there she could not say and even now, as their eyes met, he did not move. His clothes were starkly black. But for the beam of light, down which a thousand specks of dust floated like fireflies, he would have blended into the darkness. For a second, though, he stood in a glow of flickering light which made her wonder if she were still asleep and this only another image drawn out by the heat of the sun.

In fact he had stood beside her for ten full minutes, looking down on the woman who lay on the crumpled grass, her hand still clutching an embroidery in whose design he half thought he detected a form familiar and yet not quite within his conscious grasp. He sought to continue on his way but could no more move than he could turn his eyes from the woman he had struggled so hard to drive from his mind. He had watched as the light had moved over her body, flowing like liquid gold over her breasts until it illuminated her face. When she opened her eyes he thought to step back into the shadows but could not stir. Two stories which had separated were about to rejoin and become one.

Yet it is at this point that language sinks into the soil. There are no words which speak the truth of such moments. Certainly they looked into one another's eyes, as though trees and shadows and sun had no existence. Certainly he spoke her name, or so it seemed, for, if he did, he spoke it so softly that none but she could have heard. But how to supply the absences in this text, the silences so full, the stillness replete with energy? Certainly, too, he knelt beside her and placed a gentle restraining hand on her shoulder as she made to rise, just as she reached up a hand towards his face. If it touched him, though, it was with a softness which can have been no more than the suspicion of a breeze. Did she reproach him for his inattention or he her for failing to summon him to her side? I cannot tell. The shadows began to lengthen. High above, the white flash of a gull as it turned in the heavy air.

Love may be denied in words but it inscribes its own necessities. Body had shaped to body once before, when the sea rolled beneath them and they felt the gentle rise and fall of life. So it seemed to move now as pale arm entwined with paler arm and hand reached out and down and round. A soft cry, which might have come from some distant creature in the forest, escaped her lips. There came a gentle rustle of leaves, as the cooling land started a current of air towards the sea. Then there was no space, no separation, no denial, only the endless need to blend and be. No hesitation, only a rhythm of breathing, eyes softening, hair damp, pressing, heart racing. Giving. Taking. Nor knowing which was which. Here, at a certain time, in a certain place, which was no time and no place but a now which all should know should they inhabit it.

And so, as the last glow of sunset passed from crimson to palest pink before fading into a grey-edged black, in the very heart of a forest which shivered with an evening breeze, a life was started. In the momentary shudder of two lovers, who spoke nothing but one another's names, and paid no heed to the gathering night nor yet the yellow-green eyes which shone amidst the trees, was engendered the world that was to come.

The journey from ecstasy to despair is a long one but may be accomplished in the merest moment. As they lay together so the man, who only moments before had been so urgent, so gentle and yet so demanding, beat his fist on the cool, damp grass.

'Hester! Hester!'

She reached out her hand, seeking his.

'We have sinned.'

'We have done no such,' she replied, withdrawing the hand. 'I had no husband then. I have none now.'

'It is not that, Hester. When we were on the *Hope* it were but us two. We were our own world. There were none to mind. None to harm. Here, I have duties. It is not thou that is married. It is I. The Church.'

'Is it so? Is it even so? And can I not be one of those duties, Arthur?'

Could he really wish to break what they had just mended? She had married one man with a hard will but no trace of gentleness or love. Now she had found another who would burn with passion's light but was disfigured with guilt. There was scarce a woman, ever, though, who did not believe that she could bend the iron of a man's soul, even one who pained her as he pained her now. Had she not, after all, broken the bonds of her own upbringing?

He looked up to the sky in which a first silver point of light had appeared, beautiful, untouchable and cold. 'It may not be.' He spoke it with the finality of a judge, yet within him there was no certainty. There is a terrible clarity which follows love and he was caught in its beam. He felt quite empty of warmth and pity so that he had become as distant and unreachable as the stars he watched.

'May it not? Then why . . .' She left the question in the air, itself cool now as the dew began to bead the flattened grass.

He shook his head as though in debate with himself. 'I cannot tell. There is in thee, Hester, that which I cannot . . . Thou and I . . .'

'Thou and I?'

'The body is weak, Hester.'

'So it is, Arthur. And soft. And forgiving. And true, I think. For there is no deceit. Yet when thou speak thou would deny what a moment since thou told me plain without the benefit of speech. Dost thou think so little of me that thou imagine I would have . . .'

Neither, it seems, was capable of completing sentences.

'Thou knowest I have no thought for any other. Believe me, Hester, thou art in my thoughts from morning's break until I pinch the night's last candle; and as I lie awake with but the smell of those candles in the air there is light still. It is the image of thy face, and it doth torture me.'

'Then, Arthur . . .'

'There should be other things in my head and there are none.'

'I don't ask for that.'

At last a smile. 'I know. I had not thought thou dwelt on me. I see thee in the church but thou givest no sign.'

'And what sign should I give?'

'I preach the soul redeemed and yet find no redemption save in thy face. This is a kind of sacrilege, I think, and yet it could never be. Hester, what have we done? What have I done?'

'That which thou would do, and I also. But if thou wish it had not been . . .'

He turned away from her, feeling, indeed, that he would blot out this last hour and yet exalting in it, for what was it but what he had wished for? Of all our emotions, though, guilt must be the one with the strongest grip and at this moment there was nothing he wished so much as forgiveness.

Let us leave them now as together they make their way along the forest track, he ahead, she behind in the fast-dwindling light. Later, as the moon rises, anyone passing that way would have seen silver-edged footprints on the dew-laden ground, separating as they approached the town. If that passing soul had chosen

147

to follow those dark signs he would have seen one falter and retrace a step or two before resuming, while the other laid a trail of shadowy steps on a sea of silver, heading towards a cottage where a light burned long into the night, the solitary eye of some wild creature, blinded but watchful and alone.

I danced on the sabbath
And I cured the lame,
The holy people
Said it was a shame;
They whipped and they stripped
And they hung me high,
They left me there
On a cross to die.

Dance, then, wherever you may be,
I am the Lord of the dance, said he,
And I'll lead you all, wherever you may be,
And I'll lead you all in the dance, said he.

It was in July, in a close and airless heat, that Hester realized she
was with child; September, with the smell of fruit on the stove
and the cracked parchment of corn, brittle yellow in the field,
before she fancied she felt the stir of life within. The terror and
the joy which had haunted every day were dulled now and she
was launched on a voyage whose destination she could not
control. Since that night in the forest she had met only once with
the father of the child who grew with the season. It was a tearful
meeting, not least because she found a man so torn within that
her love was tinged with pity rather than contempt when she saw
the terror her news inspired. Where she looked for strength, she
found weakness. Where she had hoped for support, she found
fear. Where she had wished for companionship she found a deep
unfathomable privacy. Yet in the strange detachment which had
come since first she realized her condition, she acknowledged the
truth of her position. This was an unforgiving place. The church
was their consolation and their master; and at its heart there was a

man whose face she may not see or, seeing, must deny.

Hester, though, had not been driven here by faith, nor, like those others, by a hope of profit. For her, these men and women had paid a price beyond their labour in the field, beyond the sickness and the death which took so many in the first winter time. They had become joyless, afraid even of themselves. They sought the light but extinguished that in their own hearts the better to see that which beckoned from another world. They punished those who left the stony path of their narrow truth. Each sabbath day they gathered to hear the dark cadences of their own condemnation and scarcely raised their eyes towards the heaven they invoked, staring rather at the earthen floor or the clogged soles of upturned shoes, like pairs of tiny tombstones in the dim light of the church.

She listened to his explanation, watched his tortured face, and finally left his side. She could feel within him the love which she would claim but he was a defeated king on a battlefield, torn between conflicting duties and aware of nothing so much as defeat itself. For her part, she felt a new strength which grew within as sturdily as the child and was ready to face whatever might yet come. Should she have need to stand alone she would stand thus, though it be in the full light of the noon.

Hester was found out. It could scarcely have been otherwise. There were ways to lay aside a child, to tear it from the womb. Even here there were potions to drink and sharp instruments to pry away a life thought inconvenient. But Hester would have none of these. Shall the soil refuse the seed? It were denial of herself and more besides. A gentle peace seemed to have settled on her and she walked the byways of the town and while there was little cause to smile she did so a hundred times a day, though never realized such. And by degrees another self was formed which heard the surging of her blood, as her body turned its energies to nurture a life which ached for birth.

This was a time when a fierce light was shone into the darkest corner. There was no need of informers, though such there were, for here each soul was placed within the keeping of another and the social good linked to the moral self. So there were those who read the signs and having read them constructed their own narrative which was missing only one particular – the hero or the villain. For though by now Boston was a domestic place there were single men aplenty, and why restrict the possibilities to these. Yet the mystery was that Hester was a solitary. None had seen her consort with any who might fulfil the role, and though they thought her absent husband surely dead, nonetheless indignation spread through the town like summer fever. Her crime seemed magnified, as though her fault were a blemish on their venture. Rumour connected her with everyone but the Governor, but not even the most scrupulous could render any evidence, save perhaps her habit, now abandoned, of walking in the forest on her own.

Fast as a grass fire, word reached the minister, who prayed within the humid darkness of his church, for who but he could wrestle with her soul and win the name which all now longed to hear. It can be imagined with what mixture of astonishment, guilt and fear he heard his fatherhood thus confirmed who still hoped, Hester's words aside, that a single night of folly might be atoned for in private on his knees and in public in the assiduity with which he laboured on God's work. Indeed, had the officious merchant, whose still more officious wife had driven him to consult the young minister, felt anything but his own importance he must have been struck by the look of horror which passed across that young man's face and the trembling hand which seemed to reach out for some invisible shield before dropping to his side.

'Thou know thy duty, I hope, Mr Dimmesdale.'

'My duty?' Dimmesdale half thought that he was being called on to confess and confession was as near his lips as anything else.

'Thou must summon her, man, wrestle with her soul. Seek out the name. Thou must demand the name. Then she must answer to another.'

'As must we all,' replied the fearful minister, staring into the vortex of his own soul. Suddenly the heat of the clapboard church seemed to suffocate him and he sank into a sweating pew. 'There is no doubt?'

'No, man, she does flaunt it. There be those who would stay

151

close to home and stir forth only in the night. Not she. She walks the length of King Street, and has been seen everywhere about the town. It seems she would spread news of her sin as widely as she might. There be those who never saw her since the day she came who now must look upon her lewdness.'

Again, the half-raised hand, warding off an invisible force.

'And her husband! We must stand in his stead, I think.'

'But he be dead.'

'So she says.'

'There was word a year since, was there not?'

'I know nothing of such but are we obliged to take for gospel such convenience? Besides, the sin is clear and it is for such the law provides.'

'The law?'

'Why, yes, man. Thou art new here, still, minister, as new as she. There have been times when the price demanded for such sin was to swing on the gallows, and may be still. We are on the very lip of hell here, sir. In England Crown and Parliament do divide the kingdom, denying God's clear law. Here, beyond the town, dark anarchy stalks abroad. With such an act as this the anarchy is within, nor may it be denied. Man, this is a mockery of God. Think but, sir, how this sin was engendered.'

And think he did, as did they all, for these severe men and women were but ourselves, in another time, with passions no less keen and desires as powerful as our own. What they condemned in public they were drawn to as any might be in another age. They warmed their hands at the fire of their own indignation, sought out the very details of the lust they chose to decry. It is not that they were hypocrites and we untainted by such contradiction. It is that sin lay at the very centre of their minds, while guilt was a daily companion often only to be accommodated by discovering it in others. How else to keep a pure heart but to seek another who would bear the burden? There is a comfort in confederacy.

We think of those times and that place as eternally cold: black clothes wrapped tight against the wind, black souls pinched close against humanity. We see a sharp frost of the spirit and a lowering sky, and it may be that such images may penetrate where the harvest mouse may not, that there is a truth which lies not in fact but in fact touched by poetry's staff. But there is no doubt that love flourished there, that there were men and women honest as the day, that the sky was often blue, that laughter could be gathered in like wheat and that there were times when ruffles graced a sleeve. We must imagine happiness and pain blended then as at any other time nor were they the first to try to govern the human spirit as a piano teacher strikes the knuckles of a child to bring forth harmony. There is that in us which seeks submission, that welcomes the law's restraint.

Yet was this a strenuous time. A single truth, a single voice, a single text prevailed and there were those who swung by their necks on Boston's common for supposing that it might be otherwise. Conscience was in other hands and he who spoke of hearing only an inner voice offered himself thereby for judgement by his peers. They read the world as a professor in his study might read a text, with not a word redundant, not an action that did not feed into the main. So a citizen, no more foolish than we be, no more or less seduced by myths, would stir in terror and self-doubt when a pulse of lightning rent the fabric of the night or cool milk curdled on a winter's day: and should a child but die then look within for the sin which took it from you and repent in misery your blame. It is a just God who reads your heart, the story of your life. No wonder they should forswear the theatre, where voices contend and people seem what they are not. For there we are taught that we may be other than we are and the mouth shapes words with such seductiveness that they may enter our souls unbid.

There are times when the world seems to enter a spiritual ice age. A single idea so dominates that life becomes provisional. Meaning is presumed to lie ahead in some distant future and all we do is only a preparation, good or ill, for the wonder of that day when governance shall fade away and we shall step into a new grace should we but have humbled ourselves enough and never left the one true path. And one of the sacrifices required to bring that day to pass is that of private pleasure, for the body writes its own meaning straight and that writing, too, may need to be constrained as surely as words upon a page. What is it about the naked form which so threatens the state? The answer, I presume, is clear. It reshapes the world around it, and in that world are others who must live their lives, while its natural warmth gives a lie to those constraints which would bid us surrender all that is good to another world and find grace awaiting only beyond the grave.

These people read their Bible with an eye to the Old Testament, not the new. Grace for the fallen and a gentle love fitted ill the world they chose to see. In the early years of the colony young women were dispatched from this world to another when once their child was delivered, there to seek a forgiveness not available on earth. Nor should we forget that these were times around the world when punishments were sharp and life often ended with no more thought than a candle was snuffed out between thumb and finger. Firm paths between dark swamps were narrow indeed and those who strayed from them quickly swallowed in the mire. Though we live in brighter times yet mother and babe may still be forced away from hearth and home and perish on some country lane for want of human charity.

Alone, at last, Dimmesdale sat in the semi-darkness and though the heat was oppressive shook as in the last stage of a fever. Had he been confronted in the full light of day he must have betrayed himself. Here in the gloom his confusion was concealed. But what should follow now? He would scarcely be human were his first thought not for himself. Had he travelled so far only to destroy himself? Yet should not Hester turn to him in her distress? The memory of that spring evening, which he celebrated in the guilty privacy of his being, seemed now transformed by the public gaze. It was sin. It was crime. It was conspiracy against the public weal. Yet Hester, so beautiful and so alone.

Do not judge him. He bore a burden far greater than did she whose condition required of her no confession. Her act, whose consequences were now open and plain to see, was concluded. The damage she did to a community built on the idea not of

154

paradise restored but of purity pursued was clear enough, if scarcely yet unique. She was but a minor part of the building which they raised. He, though, was the stone itself. To confess his guilt was perhaps to purge his own conscience at too great a price to those he served. May the building stand when its foundation is removed? In the days which followed he asked himself this question many a time.

There was a public platform from which sinners were required to speak their foulness and thereby begin the process of their redemption, and, more importantly, the healing of the state they had damaged so. There were moments when he saw himself mounting this confessional, but the damage he might do made him feel this to be the easier path. So, by degrees, and with a sense of horror, he came to realize that he might have to bear the greater burden of silence, that he must, indeed, deny himself the forgiveness and relief which would follow such confession. It may be that there was self-deceit in this. Who can be sure of their own motives: we are, perhaps, most suspect when we believe ourselves to act for the well-being of others, but there is no doubting that the silence which he came to feel he owed was one which struck a terror into his being. Or was it weakness? His was a subtle enough mind to be aware that one pain may merely conceal another, and so, from moment to moment, he swayed, one minute duty, another private need predominating, until he could no longer tell which might be which. A kind of moral paralysis began to afflict him and the passing days brought neither clarity of mind nor relief from his dilemma.

There came a day when Hester was summoned by the magistrates and brought to stand before a long oak table while grey-faced men stared unabashed at her swelling form. They sought contrition and humility, confession and abasement, for authority will always seek its validation so. Beyond all, however, they wished a name so that they might reach out and bring such evil to its knees. Nor did they think to make such a demand in vain, for Hester was not the first woman to be called to name her co-conspirator and it can be imagined what fear must have driven those who stood alone against such power made manifest. Their lives hung in the balance and these were to be her judges. Nor did she doubt that they had much support beyond this room to justify their acts, though she had found nothing but generosity of spirit in the family which gave her shelter.

'What corruption, mistress, dost thou imagine thou bring to thy charges? Art thou fit to have such innocents in thy care?'

'I am bid to stay by those who gave them life nor do I teach them aught but what is writ in Jesu's name.'

'Can thou say such who have torn up the book of God to write thine own in thy flesh?'

'I have done none such.'

'And dost thou not have a husband, then? And is he not far from this place having placed his faith in thee?'

'I do believe him dead or I should have heard of him ere now. Nor was ours a marriage such as any would say was sanctified.'

'Is it theology thou would teach us, mistress? Take care. We are scrupulous nor will we allow the tempter in this place. Let me tell thee this: there is one here who does not stand before us and if thou keep his name it means thou would see sin conquer good and give the devil victory.'

'I am what thou seest and no more. I bear the burden all myself. There is no other thou need seek to question. He has regretted deeply and has no more converse with me. Nor shall I bring him to this place who has a better destiny.'

Though they tested her hard and long and uttered threats which embarrassed some of their number yet Hester would not recant and when she fainted after many hours of further examination they were forced to desist.

Dimmesdale himself was urged to speak to her, to probe into her soul and read there the truth which she concealed, for in the time he had been with them he had acquired such a reputation that it was believed he could succeed where others must have failed. There was something in the man that made men and women feel he understood their secret fears and trangressions. Those who stood in judgement of others knew well their own weakness and felt in him a comfort and a guide, yet one who would lead them back to truth. When he declined he did so with such an inward shudder that those who asked took it for a sign of his revulsion from the crime. Though there were those who urged it as his duty there were others who took this for the delicacy of one who fled corruption and erred on compassion's side. Certainly when severe punishment was mooted he became distracted, even asking of those who believed themselves the elect which of them might be without sin.

Though those who stood across the table from this woman were severe, yet we must judge them by their own standards, not our own. Who, after all, are we, who so readily kill those who are our foes and watch the poor slip to their graves? Indeed, even these dark figures who confronted her across an oaken table were not unaffected by her subtle beauty or her dignity and though her answers seemed to challenge them yet she spoke with such composure and in the quietest voice that there were none that took offence. They were mindful, too, of the probable death of a husband who, it was rumoured, had been on board the ship which had foundered, not long since, off the coast of Jamestown. Yet there had to be some indication of displeasure, of the breach she had made in the contract which binds husband to wife and which had laid the foundation for their settlement. Thus it was that they turned to alphabet. How else to tell a devil from a saint? How else to break the proud spirit? How else to speak disapprobation to the world?

Who, though, should have proposed this badge of dishonour but the man whose waywardness had led to her iniquity, the minister into whose hands her soul was placed. Desperate to save her from those who would place a noose around her neck – to save her soul by sacrificing life – and thus, perhaps, himself from a guilt which he could not sustain, he raised his hand in the gloom of the townhouse, where the magistrates had summoned him, and when they turned towards him recalled a custom they had quite forgot. The woman, he proposed, should wear, embroidered on her clothes, a sign which should spell out her sin. And just as later there would be those who read quite other meanings into the scarlet letter she would wear so we can be sure that for him, too, the 'A' which he traced with his finger in the air meant not adulteress but first and only, the alpha of his being, the angel whose wings had brushed his soul and bruised it in the passing. To him it would be no more than the merest birthmark, the imperfection by which perfection may be known and rendered thereby more complete. To be sure his proposal was made out of fear and desperation, out of a kind of panic which reached deep into his being, but in that confusion and despair, which was not untainted with cowardice, there was, beyond all, a desire to reach a hand out to the woman who had so stirred his being and who now stared her tormentors in the face with a calmness which amazed those who thought their civic dignity must humble a mere woman whose sin was manifest.

The months passed slowly for Hester until that day when she should bring forth the child she bore. Nor did they incarcerate her until the birth was near. She was enjoined to stay within doors and did so while the sun shone high above. The family, with whose children she still played, had proved their strength, nor were they ready to surrender her to prison cell until that should prove necessary. But of the night she would still go out of doors, walking down the forest lane in the light of a moon whose changing form was a silver echo of her own. Nor did she feel alone, for, though the father of her child could never hold her hand and walk beside her there, she now had another to soothe away her loneliness and quiet her mind. She would talk to that companion still in the womb and the better so to do gave her a name. Perhaps the silver moonlight was her clue, perhaps the precious nature of what she bore within, but, unaware even of the moment of decision, she began to call her Pearl: and Pearl she was, long before her lungs drew air.

When Hester gave birth, a month before her time, two women gripped her hands and a length of cloth was clamped between her teeth so that her cries should not remind the community of her sin. Beyond the door an officer of the court awaited, though why he could not say for she could scarcely steal away. The birth was far from simple and the pain quite took her by surprise. Wave on wave flowed through her until she seemed the pain itself, and there was nothing more than this.

Those who attended were rough in manner but gentle with their charge. Many a fingernail had left its mark on their arms before nor was this the first child brought into the world without benefit of a father's name. Yet they were not above storing what they saw for retelling later in the street, for there were those who took pleasure in the fall of this stately young woman whose dark hair and black eyes had turned the heads of those whose own eyes should have been fixed on other things.

Then, at last, scarcely an hour after the candles had been lit and the windows closed against the night, the trying time was done. Smooth-limbed and flecked with blood, there slipped into this world a young girl-child, her whiteness slicked with red. Nor had Hester's instincts failed to prove her true, for she had never thought it would be anything but one such as she, a soulmate, flesh of flesh, to keep her company.

You might have thought that she would long to teach her child the waywardness of men, for she had suffered both from disdain and love alike, but there was nothing of this about a woman who wedded strength to understanding. She blamed herself for her folly and, though she scarcely understood her first mistake, would still not deny the feeling which had led her to her second nor yet the one who shared her love but would not share in her distress.

Then, as she lay back, submerged alike in tiredness and a kind of ecstasy, she heard first the choking cry of young life protesting to be born, and then a sharper cry from one of those who tended her.

'What is it? What is amiss?' She raised herself on an elbow, feeling a lifting surge of pain where she was torn.

'Nothing, mistress. Nothing.'

'Nothing? Why dost thou cry out?'

'It is nothing. I have seen it often times before.'

There is a greater pain than pain itself, a terror which lurks somewhere within to seize our hearts. That terror now emerged to claim its soul. There can be few mothers who will not understand the sudden rush of fears, like circus tumblers flying all about, which sprang and somersaulted through her mind.

'It is but a covering on the eyes. It will doubtless drop away.'

'A covering?'

'Ay, and there are those who say that be the mark of second sight and who would not wish to have such to guide them through this life.'

Her companion, though, could not conceal the look she gave, for these were times when nature's errors were seen as but the devil's touch while second sight came far too close to witchcraft for content.

'Let me see,' cried Hester, opening her arms for the babe.

'She is not cleaned, mistress. Thou must bide awhile.'

'Let me see. Give me the child.' Nor can such imperative be denied.

Again exchanged glances, and the baby, wrapped tight about with muslin, was placed in Hester's arms. She saw at once the film of pink skin. Beneath, the eyes moved as though seeing through the veil, a kind of double shadow beneath a curtain of spun silk.

'Don't touch it, mistress. Never fear. I have seen such before, and more than once. It will be gone by morning and, if not, by week's end. Think of it as but a protection against the light.'

So Hester tried to do, fearful to touch a membrane which divided her from one she loved not for actions done nor yet for dependency's demand, but for being there, for being hers, for being's simple sake. She hugged her close, her own eyes bright, until a sudden tiredness caught her in a fitful sleep, a grace to still her terror.

With the dawn Hester took young Pearl in her arms once more and felt a surge of joy as two clear eyes, bluebell blue and yet with a touch of violet besides, stared up at her, unfocused but plainly bright as summer's sky. The covering had quite dropped away and there she lay so perfect and complete that were she a song and not a child she would sound out in clearest harmony, though, as she was put to the breast, she pressed so hard that there seemed a demon locked within. Indeed she was born both with a sharp

160

white tooth and with fingernails which, however soft and pliant to the touch, could yet score their marks on Hester's soft white flesh. When once she had drunk her fill there was thus a tear of blood on Hester's breast and a subtle mark where a hand had grasped and scored.

From the moment of the birth Hester was held in the prison with her child by her side. Pearl's world was thus defined by brick and mortar and her window crossed with bars and, though she could know nothing of this, are we yet so sure that we do not bear the marks of memory's memory? When in later life she ran so wild, and would be constrained neither by place nor etiquette, could it be that she remembered this first dark and secluded place? Could a spirit later so strong and proud have been forged in this crucible where men had chosen to place her out of sight? If she cried little she still seemed intent to punish her mother for this strange nursery, so that at times Hester wondered at her strength and winced at the pain as tooth bit down and fingernail scratched its signature.

From time to time one or another visited her to instruct her in her duty or to demand the name the law required. She held the babe tight to herself and listened closely before a subtle shaking of her head sent them on their way. Then, when Pearl was but a mere month old and the two of them had learned a routine which passed for life, he came at last. Entreated by his fellows and no longer with excuse, Dimmesdale stood in the doorway, his shadow falling across the floor before him. Pearl, who a moment before had been at the breast, seemed to turn towards him, her violet eyes struggling, it seemed, to fix his face. But what would she have seen except a dark shape, in dark clothes, standing in the light of the door? For there he stood a second, as though unsure of his welcome, and then closed the door behind him. Light became dark.

'Hester.'

'Arthur.'

The familiarity alone seemed to stop him and it was some moments before he could continue. 'Is the child well?'

'The child is Pearl. I trust thou like the name.'

He nodded. 'I would have come earlier but . . .' he paused, 'could not.'

She nodded in return.

'Shall I sit beside thee?'

'So it please thee, Arthur.'

Again, a hesitation, for hesitation was his very being. He carried a Bible in his hand and clutched it with a double fierceness when she claimed his name.

'They have asked me to come but I should have come ere now.'

'Sit beside me. There are none here but Pearl and I. Nor needst thou have any fear that I shall . . .'

'I am not afeared . . .'

'That I may speak thy name.'

'But I am come to ask that thou shouldst do as such. I have no strength to speak what I should speak. Thou must be my voice. Hester, I would speak my sin, yet cannot do so. I no longer understand what is the best. I would stand in a public place and confess my sin and yet may not that yet pull the temple down? But should it stand which rests on such poor soil?' He turned the Bible roughly back and forth, as though he would tear it quite in two. 'It be hard, Hester.'

Was Dimmesdale, then, a hypocrite who could not speak in public what he knew in private, who would allow Hester to stand in the light of the day and he in the shadow? There were none more subtle in interrogating their consciences than these men and women who stood before their God, on one side the ocean, on the other a wilderness without limit. But they were as you or I, and who shall know himself? There are some who know their limitations while others draw a line and live within its limits never knowing, therefore, what those limits might be. They fear the edge, though whether he was one of these there is none can say. Hester had turned his life about, or he had willed it so, but that life was turned about by other forces, too. He who, in Cambridge, had doubted faith and much more besides, as the authority of Parliament and King were debated until authority itself was void, was here the fount and origin of faith. There are some who bear such burdens easily. With others, anxiety of mind may, by degrees, eat at them from within. He had found himself out in blasphemy, for when he climbed the pulpit stair to preach God's truth his mind was fixed not on the radiance of Christ but on a woman who even in the gloom of meeting house or church compelled his eye and drew his very soul. Was this not blasphemy and he not kin to Lucifer?

He and Hester had met as though in Eden, knowing nothing of love's power. How should one know the apple for temptation who has never tasted fruit before? Yet did not the warning stand out clear in text and lore? At Cambridge, where no woman passed the college gate, womankind was known as temptation's paradigm, and though there were of his number who lay in sin, as they said, to know the iniquity they must abjure, yet he had stayed within the college bounds to wrestle there with devils in his mind.

Nor did Hester feel contempt for his vacillating ways. Though it was love which brought her to this pass, love's denial would do no more than unmake that which she had made. And what of Pearl? Was she, then, nothing more than sin incarnate? Nor was Hester unaware of the burden that he bore and love will forgive and understand what others never will. He was the mast which must carry the canvas as the storm winds blew; she the willow beside a stream. And she had seen mast break and willow bend before.

'Thou must do as thou must. But tell me this. Dost thou love me still?'

How many times has that question been asked by woman of man and man of woman? We are no sooner fed than we must feed again; but what may love be which withdraws to safety's harbour? Hester had proved to herself that she could forgo his presence and though it pained her that he should not have come to her when his child was born had reconciled herself to this desertion, too. She clung still, though, to the reason and justification for her present condition and despite her strength needed this one staff to lean upon. Nor could he deny her this, for though his future was clouded with doubt and indecision yet he, too, needed to believe in some constancy.

'I do love thee, Hester, and there's the heart of what does torment me so.'

'Do not say such, for thou and I broke but the law of men.

There is forgiveness in Christ, I think. We did but acknowledge that which was true and truth will have its day.'

Dimmesdale shook his head and looked up to the heavens; but all he saw was the steep-gabled roof.

'If that be true then help me to speak that truth in the square beyond, when thou art summoned there.'

'And it please thee that thou shouldst do so, let it even be so. But it will be at no urging of mine for I have no need to share with others what I do know in my heart and what thou knowest as well. Nor will I speak thy name. Come, hold thy child in thy arms, Arthur. Here, at least, there are none to see and turn our love to sin.'

He seemed to pull away from her even as she spoke but then allowed Hester to lead him to the crib. Pearl slept on her back, one hand partly raised as though inviting him to place his own around hers.

'Is she not beautiful?'

'She is, indeed. And I see thee there.'

'And I had thought I saw something of thee.'

He shook his head, though whether in doubt or trepidation who can say.

Hester bent forward and lifted the baby free of the thin cloth which was tucked about her lying form. Still she slept, still her hand reached out.

'See, Arthur, where she reaches for thee even in her sleep. Hold her. She is as much thine as mine.'

Like a sleepwalker, he held his hands in front of him until Hester placed the sleeping child within them. Instinctively, he pulled her to him; but whether it be the roughness of a man's grasp or a sleep interrupted by such movement, she let out a cry so sudden and so piercing that he would have dropped her had not Hester seized her in her arms. Immediately she returned to sleep, the outstretched hand now grasping at her mother's breast.

'Can one so young detect a sinner's grasp?'

'Arthur, she is but a child woken from her sleep. Thou seest the world too much from within. The sun may rise and fall without thy agency. These days are narrow and this place is too.

But there will be other days as there are other places. The writ of Boston is but circumscribed.'

'But the writ of God embraces all.'

'And if it does there are those aplenty who would not interpret it to spell our doom. Arthur, let us leave this place. I will pay my debt, if debt they believe there is to pay, but we may live our lives where there is no talk of debt. The sun sets to the west and there are those who have gone before us. We have travelled far; perhaps there is further still for us to go before we may rest ourselves at last.'

Nor was this a thought that Dimmesdale himself had not entertained. There were indeed those who found the ways of Boston more than they could take. Some had gone south to seek the lighter ways of Virginia, while others still had travelled through the forest and beyond. There the burden would surely be lifted so that he and Hester could walk together towards the sun. For a moment they both stood separately imagining the future which might be theirs. To claim the future, though, we must first free ourselves of the past and though Dimmesdale had travelled so far from home yet he, like those before him, had travelled only to reclaim the past, to live where today's corruptions might be purged. Tomorrow was perhaps beyond the imagining of one so shaped and formed by what had been. Hester was another kind. She came not seeking to be purified but to escape the threat of danger. She was tomorrow's woman. She wished to breathe the air of freedom and though her mind was set on God that God was not constructed of men's fears, for there was that in nature which breathed his purpose nor did she feel that she had stepped outside his realm.

Yet Hester, too, was not without a dragging anchor. She would not go alone where she would joyously depart were he but by her side. She knew her will to be the stronger but she knew, too, that it was not his will which detained him here: and so she waited for his answer, with their child pressed at her breast, while beyond the iron barred door a bell was tolling the time of Thursday meeting.

Beyond that oaken door, indeed, was more than a tolling bell, for Hester's was but one of many stories which overlap each moment of the day. Down by the harbour's edge cold fish spill into woven baskets as, in a tall brick building, not unlike a church, horses' entrails slither across a stone-flagged floor. A lawyer enquires of his client whether he can afford his fee while shaking a hand at a passing fly. His mind, though, is elsewhere, with a young woman who smiles when he passes and bows her head so slightly you would not believe she had moved at all. A child squats in the road and watches astonished as a dark puddle spreads around her in the dust. A shopkeeper stands in his doorway, arms crossed, with apron stained with molasses, and reckons up the profits of that day's trade. A cow, tethered to a peg, slowly circles as the shadows move. A man shaves flowers of wood from the edge of a small child's coffin without shedding a tear.

From all of these and many more are stitched the sampler which is our lives yet none may see the pattern save God above for we are but the needles which draw the threads nor do we see what each stitch contributes to the whole. We stand at the centre of our universe quite unaware that other planets circle other suns nor that those suns in turn are but the scattered dust of galaxies.

There are those who would draw conclusions from such thoughts, see us as but tangents to a circumference we may not know. Yet we write ourselves across the sky and sing our songs with each brave new day. We may be the word shaped by another's lips but we speak out in confident expectation that we are heard. Listen! Do you not hear? And if you do not, is it silence or simple deafness which is the cause? This has been Hester's story, but it could not be such were it not the story of others, too. When we brush against another's soul it is easy to believe that it springs into existence with our passing. But, seen from that centre, we are ourselves but a moment's happening, a tiny pulse of light lost in another's sun.

Hester sits now with a silver needle pulling a thread through scarlet cloth, and if the figure which she sews seems clear enough in its form its meaning escapes true understanding. For, with careful fingers, and a fine gold thread, she has fixed to her gown an heraldic 'A'. She holds it from her for a second before taking the thread between her teeth and biting it through. She replaces the needle in a small wooden box before turning back to the cloth and smoothing it with her hand. Pearl watches with delight as the gold catches the moving light of the candle. She reaches out a stubby hand and laughs, quite as though this were some game contrived for her amusement, and after a second or so that is how Hester, too, sees it, for she holds the glitter towards her daughter's hand, only to whisk it away once more. Again and again they play this game, the gold thread seeming to light up the outline of a letter meant as a burden, meant to spell out infamy, meant as a reproach and as a punishment. Yet when she tries to stop and lay the robe aside Pearl begins to cry out in distress so that the game must continue until weariness or sleep may call an end.

As Hester holds the cloth once more towards her daughter the red is reflected in her eyes so that you might think a demon infant played here in New England's second Eden. At last, however, sleep does claim even this most recalcitrant of babies and Hester can lay aside the robe and take up, in its place, her diary to make her last entry before the torment of the morning which lies ahead.

If there were a life that it were better I should lead I should endeavour to set my feet on a different path. If I should be what others bid me be and say what others bid me say then I would be and say what they demand. But there is that in me that cannot regret that I am as I am. For though I sit and await the morrow when I must declare my sin before the world yet I am content for I have a pearl greater than price. Yet would I more for I am lacking he who is my partner not in sin but in the making of this wonder. Would he but come with me we should indeed become some other thing and walk a road which is not laid out by those who have no heart for gentleness.

I have stitched my penance. They thought, no doubt, that I should stitch it small and seek to hide the brand they wished to burn into my soul. That would betoken shame, and shame is not my name. I know that pride be a sin and there is pride in me, I think. Yet I am not haughty in spirit. It is that I will not deny what I never can regret.

My sin was not committed here, no, nor not on board the Hope. *It were when I consented to join myself to he who cared for nothing but his* books and saw in me no more than another mystery to be solved. Am I to be tied to him who by now may be with his maker? I feel a freedom, here; yet I sit in a prison cell. Nor is it made of wood and iron but of another construction. For I am held by the iron in men's hearts and that is forged by fear. They speak of my rebellion as though I were back in England with a musket in my hand to turn the world awry and yet I think it is their own authority they seek to keep intact. What authority, pray, can it be which quails before a baby's cry and needs a woman's voice to set it back in place? I am content in my discontent. I would that this world were different and yet were it so should I be here with one whom I do love beside my chair and another close to hand, though he may not hold me as I wish or set his course by a star which to me shines bright above.

I have sewed my scarlet cloth with a golden thread because the letter that they bid me write may stand for him I love. He who is the beginning of my alphabet, who is the author of my fate, the one earthly authority to whom I long to bow my knee, is thus pronounced aloud for those with eyes to see and ears to hear, shining at my breast where he should be. I bear his mark as he, I know, bears mine. I ride to battle with his favour thus emblazoned and will not remove it though they do bid me to. So, I fancy, with the world. What one will see is not what others see. We find what we seek and not what may be there. I came on a journey of escape but to find that it were one of discovery. Nor did I find but this colony, nor yet he who I would have now at my side. I found one I thought to know so well, yet, as now I see, knew not at all. Myself. What should I have been had I stayed by my father's fire, and not ventured with my one-time husband, but a country girl counting out my days with hen's eggs and barley and a harvest feast? What should I have been had I stayed with that husband who never was such to me, but a timid soul like a deer who fears the air itself? Here I am isolate and yet never so. For I have Pearl, and in my heart, locked safe away, another treasure which others may not see. I have courage, perhaps, which I never knew I had, no, nor never knew I should need neither. And tomorrow I may stand in the sun and hold my child for all to see nor shall I do so with aught but pride and this pride be no sin. For I am become myself and myself is what I shall be.

cheronta movebo (if I cannot bend the higher powers, I shall move the infernal regions). He befriended Dimmesdale and so worked upon him that guilt became lethargy and lethargy ease and as the years went by a young man seemed to age and look towards the grave, until, driven by remorse, he found himself, some seven summers on, standing, at midnight, on the scaffold in the market square where Hester had stood before, a mockery of the public confession he believed himself to seek. There were none to see him, though, excepting Hester and her daughter Pearl, but before they could grasp his hand another time, her husband and his nemesis, to claim him for his own.

*

What Chillingworth's motives were who can say? Not jealousy in a simple sense, surely, for he acknowledged his own hand in Hester's flight, responsibility for a marriage which yoked naivety to self-deceit. Pride, then, perhaps. Had he not failed to see in her a rebel's spirit? He was a man who set himself to uncover secrets, to read texts opaque to others, to understand if necessity drives by dissecting living tissue. Yet he had failed to see what lay before his eyes. Now here was a secret which bore on himself. Another man had unlocked a door he had not ventured to try. And whence Hester's new found strength to challenge authority when he had seen the ease with which he plucked her from her village scene? A transformation had been wrought and transformation was his avocation. Whatever the cause, whatever the motive, his silence on that first day was but the setting of the stage for a drama of his own devising.

How did he find his quarry? He perceived what others did not. They saw the minister, he the man. They dreamed a dream of Jerusalem reborn; he saw but a new constructed town inhabited by the old Adam and the old Adam has the virtue of consistency. Those in love will betray themselves if not by looking towards each other then by looking away, if not by what is spoken then by what is not. Though he had read her awry those years before yet he knew enough to see beyond mother and child to a trinity and the third stood revealed by the tone of a voice, a name not spoken, a face so studiously unacknowledged. He built his

I danced on a Friday
When the sky turned black
It's hard to dance
With the devil on your back,
They buried my body
And they thought I'd gone,
But I am the dance
And I still go on.

Dance, then, wherever you may be
I am the Lord of the dance, said he
And I'll lead you all, wherever you may be,
And I'll lead you all in the dance, said he.

The day dawned as other days dawn. Darkness thinned and birdsong pierced the gloom. Hester was visited early. Still, it seemed, the public shame might be deferred. A name would suffice, an acknowledgement of authority's right to demand and her duty to obey. But she was far beyond this. She had the child. Had they but threatened to remove her she would perhaps have found her tongue. Loyalties will collide. But none suggested such so that she was quite content. They thought her a sinner; she saw no sin that could result in life. Their solemn voices were as nothing beside the cry of a child whose necessities were the sole commandments she obeyed. At length they desisted. Even the tide retreats from the rock, and if it come again still it meets resistance.

So, as she prepares for the humiliation they have prepared, consider this woman who must face the censure of her kind. Who can but admire her in her solitariness and in her silence, too. The one set against the many; a woman they would trick out in an actor's role, were actors allowed to corrupt the heart with greasepaint and lies. She has a part prepared for her, must enter on cue, costumed at their behest, to speak the lines they would hear her say. But she will have none of it. She breaks the bounds of the frame, a baroque figure who will not be contained by art. She has a story of her own and will tell it in good time, be it only to a child when she should be old enough to understand.

★

The door of the jaol being flung open from within, there appeared, in the first place, like a black shadow emerging into sunshine, the grim and gristly presence of the town-beadle, with a sword by his side, and his staff of office in his hand. This personage prefigured and represented in his aspect the whole dismal severity of the Puritanic code of law, which it was his business to administer in its final and closest application to the offender. Stretching forth the official staff in his left hand, he laid his right upon the shoulder of a young woman, whom he thus drew forward, until, on the threshold of the prison-door, she repelled him, by an action marked with natural dignity and force of character, and stepped into the open air, as if by her own free will. She bore in her arms a child, a baby of some three months old, who winked and turned aside its little face from the too vivid light of day; because its existence, heretofore, had brought it acquainted only with the grey twilight of a dungeon, or other darksome apartment of the prison.

When the young woman – the mother of this child – stood fully revealed before the crowd, it seemed to be her first impulse to clasp the infant closely to her bosom; not so much by an impulse of motherly affection, as that she might thereby conceal a certain token, which was wrought or fastened into her dress. In a moment, however, wisely judging that one token of her shame would but poorly serve to hide another, she took the baby on her arm, and with a burning blush, and yet a haughty smile, and a glance that would not be abashed, looked around at her townspeople and neighbours. On the breast of her gown, in fine red cloth, surrounded with an elaborate embroidery and fantastic flourishes of gold thread, appeared the letter A. It was so artistically done, and with so much fertility and gorgeous luxuriance of fancy, that it had all the effect of a last and fitting decoration to the apparel which she wore, and which was of a splendour in accordance with the taste of the age, but greatly beyond what was allowed by the sumptuary regulations of the colony . . .

From this intense consciousness of being the object of severe and universal

observation, the wearer of the scarlet letter was at length reliev on the outskirts of the crowd, a figure which irresistibly took thoughts. An Indian in his native garb was standing there; but not so infrequent visitors of the English settlements that on have attracted any notice from Hester Prynne at such a time; m have excluded all other objects and ideas from her mind. By the evidently sustaining a companionship with him, stood a whit strange disarray of civilized and savage costume.

He was small in stature, with a furrowed visage, which as be termed aged. There was a remarkable intelligence in his person who had so cultivated his mental part that it could n the physical to itself, and become manifest by unmistakable to by a seemingly careless arrangement of his heterogeneou endeavoured to conceal or abate the peculiarity, it was sufficie Hester Prynne that one of this man's shoulders rose higher th

The misformed physic, escaped from captivity to such fortuity on the day of Hester's shame, now bega homeopathy, draining health from the healthy and heaven's plan. He had not stepped forth before the named himself. He did not claim his wife nor she h they stared at one another, each waiting for the oth Like the two clocks which had struck different ho distant hall in a distant country, they seemed separat than space. The moment passed. Her public penanc she stepped down from the scaffold to begin a lif shame would have no part. He stood a while commenced one last experiment to test the limits of though now he had little need of retorts or crucibles o he had discovered the power locked up in certain wor himself to see what their effects might be.

He sought no revenge on Hester, nor raised his ha her, but that other who had stolen, as it seemed, his soon found out. Yet there was no anger here but in its cold and soulless trying of the spirit, as though he wou limit of life's need. In his diary he wrote the words o Juno which he had once read as a student: *flectere si neque*

picture from small fragments of colour until at last a face emerged.

The man once intuited, discovered, exposed, revealed, he set himself a task. He forbore to act at once. It would have been simple, indeed, to whisper a name, point a finger or intimate a knowledge which could not be spoken. He did none of these and in return Hester kept her own secret close, nor did she reveal his name or identity. They were thus now in a confederacy as they had never been before. But what Hester did not know was that he was a patient man, that he went about his experiments with a kind of tireless care. If not this approach, then that; if not these berries and herbs, why, then, others. He sought to destroy this man not by anything so crude and direct and immediate as physical assault or simple betrayal. He wished, instead, to disassemble him element by element until he should be fully exposed and inert before him, voided of all truth, all mystery, all life.

So the steady drip of water will slowly wear away the strongest stone and Dimmesdale was no granite, no, nor nothing like it either. The truth is that guilt corrodes as fast as salt spray a copper rivet. In time must come collapse. He that awaits the shipwreck has but to bide his time and the sea will commit the crime for him leaving him beneficiary. Chillingworth had to do little more. The salt spray had already begun to turn bright copper into verdigris.

And where was Hester the while? She was building her life from the materials to hand. Like her fellow settlers she was about the business of invention, writing a new song to sing, contributing her mite to the common weal.

It was as though she inhabited a fable. Reality was the place she had left, four square and irresistible, except through flight. Here, reality was extended until it became its opposite: the summer too hot for belief, the winter more than could be borne by some. She had seen winters enough, to be sure, and snow half a dozen times or more, and as one who had laboured in the field knew that what is pleasant to the eye may prove painful to the limbs, and perhaps even to the soul. But here snow fell that seemed as if it sought to make an ocean fathoms deep. Wind stung the face until it was possible to doubt there was a face at all. To keep one's feet in walking from house to wood store was a kind of victory.

If this was Eden then Adam and Eve would scarcely have survived the day. No wonder, she might have thought, but did not, they sought each other out. Warmth alone was sufficient reason for eating from the tree of knowledge. Hester had known that warmth and longed to know it more. The interdict was not God's alone.

She had seen death her first winter, she who had never known such save that of her mother, when she was too young to know, and that of the animals who served their purpose, as she supposed, in the ordering of the world. There came a day when a young child of the neighbouring family, a boy of seven who combined angel and devil as all such do, slipped into the barn at night to see a favourite horse which shivered in its stall, taking with him a shrivelled apple and a light. In the morning he was found with candle and life quite out and with one of his legs so frozen to the ground that it took a man dressed all in black, and his assistant besides, some hours and a little fire to ease him from his frozen bed.

Hester followed him to his grave and stood in the freezing air as the new minister spoke his words of comfort and despair under a sun so pale and watery that it looked the colour of a sickly chicken's egg broken in the pan. His voice was clear and melancholy and spoke of loss with such power that though it were a sin to think he spoke of ought but the departed child she must believe he spoke to her. His breath hung in the still air as though the words themselves would reach out to her, envelop her in a soft cloud of sadness and regret. He spoke of dust and ashes and of a life ended, and what could he mean but the end of a story which had once held them fast in its truth.

And yet he offered hope and redemption, for death, he said, had lost its sting. The very words reached up to heaven in a gentle mist. They hung above her, against the icy blue-white sky. The mother of the child looked towards him and Hester could see her face soften. The child, then, who had clung so fast to this earth that it took two men to loose his grasp, was now raised up and warmed by God's own love. And she, Hester, who cried for a child not her own, must she stay frozen to this world and be re-united only when she had passed through heaven's door? She could not believe it would be so, for to stand so close to a man who spoke of heaven's love was to understand that love is all of a piece, that the sacred and profane might yet be one to those who choose to call them so.

She knew that such thoughts were wickedness to those who clung to the unforgiving land, but to deny the truth of what she had known was to deny herself. She and he had made a compact first by yielding of themselves to nature's law and second by offering what was theirs alone to sacrifice. Yet even now she saw no necessity. Truth is truth no matter the day, no matter the place. And love must have its own authority. But all things have their season. They grow, they blossom, they wither and they die. Even such a child as this is gathered in. So must she reconcile herself to nature's rhythm. But as this small band of mourners turned about and dragged their feet back through the snow, writing their sorrow in the lack of care with which they trod, she looked back once and saw him standing there beside the fresh wound in the ground. He was as she remembered him aboard the ship, standing amidst nature's bleak and glorious dawn. And as she looked so his eyes met hers, as she knew they must, for promises once made may not be broken, only placed in a box and hidden below stairs. She turned again and smiled but in doing so found that her tears had frozen to her face.

What were these people who had ventured so much for so little? She had been drawn across the ocean by necessity's command. They journeyed to rediscover what was lost and build a city from the ruins of the past. Others like them, even now, were sighting along a sword before seeking to cut disease from a body they judged far gone. These, too, wielded a sword but they turned its blade against themselves. Each soul must be struck like a bell to see if it ring true. And should it not, the crucible awaited to render them anew. She prayed they would not sound her for she knew herself to be flawed nor would they understand that she celebrated the flaw; for who would seek perfection if the price be to be placed in a solitary tower, there to strike the knell of their humanity?

The Papists say that seven is the age of reason, by which they mean that it be the age of faith. Whether or no they are right who can say, but in seven years we may see a deal of the world and choose to believe what we see or no.

It was seven years since Hester had stood in the light of a New England day and showed her daughter to those who saw not a baby but a living sin. Since then they had asked for no other company than their own and for the most part received none or none that they would care to welcome. Pearl's education was in her mother's hands and she had lessons to teach should she but wish to do so. But there is gardening appropriate to the moment: first the snowdrops, then the roses, then the lilies. For the moment she contented herself with words and embroidery and perhaps a little of philosophy besides.

This is to say that she sat her daughter to sew a sampler with which to count her blessings and spell out her grace. And this Pearl set herself to do, working with a silver needle which glinted in the sun and in the candle flame alike. Her brow wrinkled with concentration as she threaded the needle through the cloth and made each letter form, as though summoned from the air itself. The first, though, once her numbers were complete and approved, she looked at with a special delight, holding it up to compare it with that self-same sign which adorned her mother's breast. Hester took a pride in such accomplishment but the sight of that symbol, so carefully wrought, could not help but leave her less than peaceful in her mind.

'Now let me see how thou wilt form the next,' she said, looking down into her daughter's thoughtful face.

'Indeed not. For a sampler requires I form each letter twice or thrice.'

'There is no need.'

'I have seen others. It is right, I think, and we must do what is right, must we not?' She spoke so earnestly that Hester could do no less than nod and watch her as she returned to sit by the lamp.

Her shadow, meanwhile, grew as she advanced towards the light making her look less like a child than a woman, she who in truth knew nothing of life but what she had seen in her mother's eyes.

Hester was not shown the work again until it was complete at which time it was placed in her hands with great solemnity. It was the work of many days and nights and had served its other function which was to still a voice which otherwise was full of questions and some questions must needs be answered. The letters were carefully shaped, each line with a different stitch and of a differing height, the skills of needlework being taught along with such other knowledge as must deliver the world into her hands or the other way about. In places a letter had indeed been doubled but the letter A was repeated six separate times as though the one who spoke this picture had stuttered somewhat at the start.

'And why is the first letter writ so often, Pearl,' enquired her mother gently.

'Why, because it is the first. It is the foundation on which the whole house of letters is built. Like the beam beside yonder door. Is it not so?'

'But can the foundation be at the top?'

'Is heaven not above?'

'It is, indeed, or so we are told by those who should know which way we are set to walk. But the beam of the house is at the bottom.'

'Why, of course. It be made of oak. But letters and words may fly. I have heard them in the air.'

'Thy stitchwork is much improved,' said Hester, not anxious to add to such flying words herself.

'My fingers are not. Why do girls stitch and boys do not?'

'Because we be the ones who must hold this life together. They be the ones who do tear it apart.'

Pearl laughed. 'And do we do such?'

Hester looked at the black eye of the window and had it not wanted glass would have seen in it a reflection of herself, the scarlet letter on her breast shining dully in the gloom.

'Perchance. But what is this?'

She pointed below the rows of letters and numbers stitched so carefully and at such expense to one who would far rather have run free along the forest edge. There, between two patterned rows, one cross-stitched, another chain-stitched, a thought to carry the reader through a day and on through life, affecting because written by one whose expression outstripped her knowledge. Hester read it aloud.

' "The days that are past are gone for ever. Those that are to come may not come to us. The present time only is ours. Let us therefore take the moment for our own." Is this right, Pearl? I had thought the last line were, "Let us therefore improve it as much as possible." '

'No. I have it right.'

'But should we do no more than take the moment for our own?'

'I do not know. I had thought it were so.'

'How should thou think it such?'

'I know nothing but what I have seen. Say I am not wrong. I cannot unstitch what I have stitched.'

'Thou speak true. And I should know. It is a good saying, and I think on it, for in making it our own we do improve it as I believe.'

'And does that mean I may leave it and not undo the words?'

'Indeed. But what of thy name? It is not finished. "This sampler was finished in the seventh year of her age by Pearl . . ." And then a space. Didst thou run out of thread, my child?'

'No. I did run out of knowledge for I do not know my father's name.'

Mother looked at daughter and daughter at mother. 'Thou must stitch Prynne.'

'And am I then without a father?'

There were times when Hester thought Pearl not so innocent as she seemed, for behind her words she could sense something else which the words alone would not disclose.

'No. Thou art thine own person nor ever should be less. Hang thy sampler on the wall when thou hast done. I would have those who call know whose house they enter in and what pretty skills my daughter has besides.'

'But none do enter here. Those with sewing do but hand their garments to thee at the door.'

'They have no need to enter.'

'Save one.'

'Save one?'

'My father, for surely he will come. And on that day I shall unstitch my name and write another.'

'Do not look for him, child?'

'Will he not come?'

'The days that are to come may not come to us.'

'And is the past truly gone for ever as it says?'

'The past is never dead. Look at thyself. Thou art the past for thou art what the past has made of thee. Yet art thou here. Thou art the future, too. What thou hast writ with thy needle be prettily done but these are but words and as thou wilt find, as years go by, words do oft prove false and those that use them no less so.'

The next encounter of Hester and her minister was a chaste and sad affair, at which she broke the vow of silence which she had made to the man who had promised in return to keep her secret. She exposed the man who looked to take the life of he she knew to be her true husband. Nor could this be done without confessing, too, that he still lived who made their love a sin, but for such a one as Dimmesdale, whose conscience was already overthrown, there was little room for further pain. Indeed, like a fever patient who experiences remission, he seemed to recover his old spirits and plan escape with the woman who still drew him to her side.

An old bond was renewed and passion's light relit. The merest glimpse of freedom melted the winter ice and that which was fixed began to flow. Who knows, perhaps he believed that two acts made but one sin, as in a sense they do, and a third would not multiply. Let us grant it then: one act, one sin. Yet who may drink but twice from the well and never return once more? Like a fire which burns beneath the ground and smoulders through the years, to burst the surface with its flames in winter's cold, so did these two light the darkness with their love one distant summer's eve.

For all her youth Pearl was wise beyond her years, though Hester took great care not to load her with a burden of too great knowledge of their plight. So all she knew was that she and her mother walked alone down the forest track, that no blueberry pie came hot to their door, nor rattling harness announced the arrival of friends or of the father she believed lost and whose return she looked for with a confidence as vain as it was mostly unexpressed. Their cottage was on the edge of the town, on the very margin of the forest which harboured the Indian and the evil spirit and where the bruised leaf floated to the ground to rot into a mulch in which strange seeds might propagate and flower unseen by human eye.

Now, when secrets were at last whispered in the night, one did come to their door. She heard the soft, unconfident tread of feet on the birchwood and loam of their path as she lay in bed in a room lit only by the cool silver of starlight and a crescent moon which bore the thumbprint, so they said, of God. She heard whoever it might be approach and withdraw and then repeat the motion quite as though he were a nervous guard outside some palace gates. Next came a double tap, not on the door but on the shutter of the room where mother and daughter slept. The sound repeated and her mother stirred to wakefulness. A third time, and then a voice so low it could almost have been the wind stirring the leaves.

'Hester!'

Even from across the room the child could see her mother start as though a burning ember had fallen from the fire into her hand.

Hester woke, aware of nothing but her racing heart. She was at sea again, though this was no blue water on which she sailed but a mass of sargasso which seemed to breathe as though it lived. The green weed, stretching far away, seemed like New England hills and indeed became such as though the whole world were liquid and unsure. Then, as the sky began to tilt and turn, perhaps with the rhythm of her beating heart, so she woke, listening for a sound. When it came it was so soft that it seemed no more than a memory, but a memory with the power to move, for she trembled and felt the sudden abrasion of nightclothes on skin. She crossed the room, drawn less by the word, her name, than by a tone, an inflection, which seemed to live within her. A glance at the child, asleep in a sea of silver, and she was at the window's edge or would have been but for a shadow image which stopped her breath. It was only her reflection in a tarnished mirror, half turned towards the wall, its surface blotched with age like the marbled skin of a widow, but it halted her a second. In the moon's clear light what she saw there was not the dark sheen of her hair, which seemed to stream with stars in the soft white beams, nor yet the cool beauty of her face, marred only by the glistening line of a night-time tear, but a sudden absence. Where an embroidered letter should have been, spelling out her sin in golden thread, there was nothing to be seen but a silver shine. Not a blood red mark but the white of cotton which shone the whiter in purified light. It was as though nature had restored what man and nature too had taken from her: innocence.

At first she saw nothing but the clear-edged shadows cast by a night in which the sky seemed full of stars. Then a movement drew her eye as the one she knew best but least thought to see stepped from the trees, no more than a shadow's shadow as a single cloud passed over the moon and the figure faded to gloom. A second passed. An owl's screech sent feather and fur scuttling. Nature trembled at the wind's behest before the cloud's departing filled the world again with milk-white light and silver dazzle. Now she felt a second shock for so accustomed had she become to seeing him in the sullen black of repentance that he seemed another being. He stood before her now in a ruffled white shirt which seemed to glow in the crystal light, his hair wild, his hand half raised as though in greeting or absolution. He seemed, indeed, part fallen angel, and part mad prophet of the kind she had met with more than once on Mousehold Heath. For a second they froze to tableau: he, on the very edge of the forest, with, spiralling about his head, the yellow-green lights of bugs tracing their subtle hieroglyphs; she, within a house which kept its secrets close. Were this scene to have been captured by the soft striations of a painter's brush it would be clear that there was locked within this arrested moment a story in which attraction, need and space were dominant. Thus, perhaps, would Romeo have met his Juliet should they have met far from family and city street.

What had brought him here except a sudden hope that the implacable may be dissolved, that we may be as we wish and not as we are bid? For certain, earlier that evening he had had no thought of such a visit as he sat at a low oak table, his Bible before him. In the light of a spermaceti candle he watched as the words seemed to jump and shake. To the left a steep hill of pages compacted with stories in which he had read of the origin of sin, of spilt seed, forbidden love, the sacrifice of children; to the right a gentler slope where were to be found other stories of the sick made whole, the hungry fed, of a fallen woman raised to grace, of a thief saved with his last breath, of repeated denial become the rock of Christ. But he had read, too, from Revelations' prophecies and found there a man on horseback who rode the sky and, as it seemed to him, had one shoulder higher than the other.

Yet there was another text he followed, another figure who filled his mind and commanded his attention, so that words on a page, bending and distorting in the candlelight, faded, finally, as he saw again a face which had never left him from the moment he first saw it in the dim light of a ship's cabin. For a living being had already written something there that would never be erased.

Slowly, button by button, he undid his heavy tunic, finally pulling it roughly over his head and hurling it into the far corner of the room. Staring deep into the blue-orange centre of the candle he pressed his hands to his head as though determined to drive out one image with another. So he remained until the candle flared for a second, then flared again before dying in its saucer of water. His room now flooded with silver light and he rose at last and strode out into the night.

A light breeze had sprung up, sifting through the trees. It tugged at his sleeve as he walked along the dark road which took him through the empty streets of Boston, empty, that is, except for one who leaned out of her window and watched as he strode past. Mistress Hibbins, sister to the Governor, a shrewish woman with hooked nose and deep-set eyes, nodded sagely and whispered to herself: 'Gone to meet thy witch wife, are we, to see what thou may conjure?' But he saw none of this, seeking out the track which would lead him to the forest's edge.

As Hester opened the door a ragged train of geese, escaped from some distant enclosure, progressed solemnly between them, like a parade of spectral judges, nodding as they walked. Neither man nor woman noticed. Their eyes were for each other. Hester, forgetful of her nightdress, stood in the cool night air and stared at the man so transformed by the loss of a coat, by hair blown in the breeze and dusted silver, and by a stance which suggested release from burden and constraint. He saw less a woman than the shadow of his desire. The geese disappeared into the forest, so many wraiths dissolving in the night. Still they stood. Still they stared. There was a cold fire burning in each heart, and when at last he turned she followed him until they disappeared together into the heart of the forest, the door to her cottage left open wide nor no longer any thought for the sleeping child.

It is said that there is no darkness which is complete but there were times, within the forest, when the world itself seemed turned blind. It was through such a darkness that they walked now, the trees above them shutting out the light, not touching but together, one before the other, until at last, at the very heart of this darkness, a pellucid pool of light formed a sudden stage. And thus they stood. And thus they knelt. And thus they lay. Nor did they see what there were no others there to see: a young girl, dressed in white, who sat cross-legged among the ferns, and watched a silent ballet danced on a silver sea.

We dream a world and believe it for the truth but with the dawn such fancies fade away. The escape, for which they planned, was not to be, at least neither by ship nor forest track. Chillingworth made certain of that, arranging passage on the self-same vessel that was to carry them thence and shadowing their steps until Dimmesdale came to feel that he was wedded to this man more fully than Hester had ever been. The only escape, the only redemption, the only absolution now was to be gained by climbing where he had climbed in darkness once before and there acknowledge his guilt before the world. And this at last he did.

On the morning of the day on which the new Governor was to receive his office the fallen minister preached a sermon such as none had heard before. Guilt and pain and resignation, too, perhaps, had brought him finally to declare himself. He stood in the pulpit, his hands pressed hard against the wood, and, as he thought, poured out his heart to the unforgiving congregation. He spoke words which had been locked away, laid bare his soul that they should know how deep betrayal may go, how great the divide between what is and what appears to be. Yet, though he spoke quite plain, or so he thought, those who listened heard another tale. For his words unlocked their own secret guilts and there were few who did not feel he spoke to them. They were winnowed on the threshing floor and there was little grain and much chaff. A holy wind had come to scatter them.

And yet they heard understanding in the voice, the grace of revelation and absolution, and there were few who did not fall upon their knees to pray forgiveness for their sins and offer thanks for he who led them through confession to redemption. He beat his breast; they felt the blows. Tears filled his eyes but scalded down their cheeks.

Beyond the church walls, in the dust of the square, Hester and Pearl stood and listened. No single word could penetrate the ordered bricks and grey glass windows but she heard the rhythm and the timbre, the muffled keening of his voice and her heart opened to him. She knew in that instant that she had won him back, even though the winning would mean a losing.

When at last he reappeared, weak with effort and faint with the disease which for so long had eaten away at his body or mind, she stood beside him before all the congregation. He took her hand, and that of the young Pearl, too, for once quiet and composed as she looked into the eyes of one who had at last kept an appointment with his daughter and, yes, wife, too, as with his conscience and his fate. Together they mounted the scaffold and stood, a trinity. Only then did Pearl kiss a father lost and found and Hester kneel before him, as he fell, to hear his last farewell.

And there the story ends, and yet not so. There is no more end to story than to life. A candle lit some distant day will blaze into a flame when memory of candle has decayed. So, Hester walked towards her grave, down forest path and city street. No longer held as emblem of man's fall, she was a heart to Boston's cold and theocratic body.

Each day she visited a grave and stood a moment there, but never let regret become her life. What she might have been had she not left her shore we may not know but here she brought a gentle understanding to her neighbours' homes. As one who let her heart deny the law, who stood her ground nor would betray her love, she understood the secret flaws which make us what we are. And when at last she stepped beyond our grasp there yet were many who thought an angel may have left their sides.

Nor is the grave the end, for whether heaven rules or no the earth which falls on oaken cask may yield a mass of violets some day. But the flowers which last the longest do not root in soil or clay but linger in the heart of those we send upon their way with love.

So, though the circle closes and a last page seems to turn, yet there are other mysteries still to tell, for long before Hester lay in death she sent a daughter into the world who crossed an ocean of her own to find a home she never knew. There, perhaps, a true fire burned whose heat she felt; there a man reached for her life. But there are stories for today and there are stories for tomorrow and this is tomorrow's tale.

Warm hands were parted, which once never could be so; tears fell aplenty where tears had been denied. But it was ever thus, as generation gives to generation freedom's key and waves away a love it would hold close. So, when at last the day did come for Hester to take her sleep at last, they laid beside her in the grave, at her request, a ragged piece of scarlet cloth. Nor was the letter there inscribed a simple A, as it had been before. But, stitched instead, in golden thread, the name which made her life stand justified, child of her love and future of her hopes: Pearl.

And as they laid her to her rest there stood round about many who in years gone by had thought to cast her out. Nor had they come out of charity, for Hester had won their hearts with more than kind deeds and simple goodness. In her they found a forgiving heart in this cheerless company of sinners who would be saints. She would not condemn who had herself been condemned. In her they found the first light of a new dawn, neither perfect nor yet repelled by imperfection's scar. They knew that she had suffered loss, saw her tend a simple grave and stare across the bay for sight of sail which never caught the summer sun. Yet she had made this place her home and turned her face against regret. She had stood alone. She had written her life. She was the author of more than her fate. In this new found land she had inscribed her name and in doing so turned the first page of a book whose narrative has yet to reach its end.

But an ending of sorts was at hand and, as the minister read from the *Domine Refugium*, so a gentle rain swept in from the sea and mingled with the tears of those who once had seen her on a sinner's scaffold but who now wished her on her way to redemption's golden city.

'Lord, thou hast been our refuge: from one generation to another. Thou has set our misdeeds before thee: and our secret sins in the light of thy countenance. For when thou art angry, all our days are gone: we bring our years to an end, as it were a tale that is told.'

The years have passed. Decades have become centuries. Now only a blind man's subtle fingers could trace out the name of Hester Prynne on a gravestone which itself seems stooped with age. Yet there are those who on a certain day still lay blood-red roses in the tangled grass, as they were taught to do by those who came before, and tell the story of a woman's love and of man's capacity for good and ill.

They cut me down
And I leapt up high
I am the life
That'll never, never die,
I'll live in you
If you'll live in me,
I am the Lord of the dance, said he.

Dance, then, wherever you may be,
I am the Lord of the dance, said he,
And I'll lead you all, wherever you may be,
And I'll lead you all in the dance, said he.

A NOTE ON NATHANIEL
HAWTHORNE

Arthur Dimmesdale fell in love with another man's wife. Not so unusual, I suppose, though it took him many years to admit his crime. But I, too, must acknowledge a fault, or at least confess to a debt I owe.

Several years ago, in the basement of a Salzburg bookseller, I made a discovery. Alongside editions of Longfellow and Poe, James Russell Lowell and Oliver Wendell Holmes, wedged securely on a shelf and coated with Austrian dust, I found the biography of a man I had long admired, a biography written by his daughter. There was nothing distinctive about the cover, a dull green with gold lettering which threw back no glitter. I bought it because it was cheap, because I wished to use up my schillings and because it was there.

When I unpacked my case some days later I noticed something which had escaped my attention before. It was signed, in black ink, by the author herself, a woman by the name of Rose. That is all. Signed editions were rarer then than now but even so there was nothing perhaps so very remarkable about a name written on the title page of a book more than a century before. But it was then, I think, that *Hester* was born, for in looking at one book I recalled another which began with a woman emerging into the sudden light of a New England day. That book was *The Scarlet Letter*; its author was Nathaniel Hawthorne. And I repeated Dimmesdale's sin: I fell in love with her.

Hester is not designed merely as pastiche, though I have set myself to create a narrative which could have been written during Hawthorne's lifetime. The fact is that there is another voice there as well. It could hardly be otherwise. Nor can I say that it is my own for the truth is that I doubt that we have a single voice and perhaps it is one of the functions of fiction to remind us of that. But in so far as Hester was born in the mind of another author let me introduce you to him briefly and if the reading of *Hester* takes you back to *The Scarlet Letter*, or leads you to it for the first time, then I shall be content.

A word of advice: the novel begins with 'The Custom House' sketch. It is different in tone from the rest of the book and has its pleasures but, if it should pall, stay with it for ahead lies a remarkable story of a woman who was born, in England, to one fate but who grew up to discover another, and to realize that a better word for fate may be destiny as a better word for sin may yet be love.

In an old burial ground on Charter Street, in Salem, Massachusetts, a slate gravestone records the death of Colonel John Hathorne, Esq., in 1717. The stone lies at an angle in a tangle of tall grasses. The name is all but obscured by moss and by the dimpling of the surface by wind and rain. There was a time, though, when that name cut deep into the soul, for he was the witch-judge who wrote names in black ink on a white page and made the world subject to his cosmology. He announced fantasy as truth and God protect those who would not subscribe to his writ.

These were days of depositions and warrants and certificates of execution. What was written had authority and the imagination had more power than fact once its phantoms had been inscribed for all to read. There were lists, then, jotted accusations, formal complaints. It was as well to see that your name never found its way into print for those who perfected this science of persecution and claimed an expertise in demonology found their sanction in books. Great tomes identified the ways of the devil's children, while the Bible itself sanctioned the pursuit of those who denied authority to Scripture. When they crushed their victims by laying stones on their chests until it became impossible to breathe, they placed the Bible there to teach them what a weighty piece of work it was and how it held the power of life and death within its covers. If they had been able to stand apart from their own rigour, if they could have heard other voices than their own, they would perhaps have seen the irony. No authority ever, though, could tolerate such irony nor allow ambivalence to obscure the pure light of certainty.

Nathaniel Hawthorne had a secret, which was no secret at all. In his blood there were slivers of ice. He was the descendant of hangmen. Not one but two ancestors had laid a heavy hand on the scales of justice and watched as victims were led away to death. They hunted women they suspected of possessing power they could not control. They hunted men who succumbed to Eve's temptations. This was his inheritance.

Hawthorne hid behind a letter, though this one not sewn with golden thread. They were Hathornes then. He stood one letter removed from the infamy of history, from responsibility for time's revenge. Nor could he fail to understand the blood power of texts, he who also sought to give fantasy the ring of truth.

His redemption lay in irony, in ambivalence, ambiguity and doubt. They believed in certainty, he in indeterminacy. They dealt in allegory, he in symbols. He even shunned verse for fear of metaphor, for metaphor carries its own fatality.

Nathaniel Hawthorne was born in Salem, on Union Street, on Independence Day, 1804. Every fact in that sentence identifies a key fragment of the helical spiral of his identity. Salem was where his family stained its name with guilt. The still-new country was to be his central subject, while independence was a main concern.

Grandfather and father were sea captains, the latter, scarcely Christlike, dying at the age of thirty-three. Grandfather Daniel Hathorne commanded a privateer called the *True American* in the Revolutionary War and was wounded for his country. There were those who sang 'The Ballad of Bold Hathorne', though not too many, I suspect, and hardly tunefully. In 1756 he had married a blacksmith's daughter and, a year before his brief musical footnote to independence, she gave birth to Nathaniel who in turn became a ship's master and sailed on the *America*. They waved flags no less then than now. Whoever would mistake an American? They are so unsure of themselves they have to announce their identity each day for fear that it might have dissolved during the hours of darkness.

Hawthorne knew Latin. Along with Harry Wadsworth Longfellow he delivered an oration in that dead language at Bowdoin College where he studied; but, then, his knowledge extended in unlikely directions. Beyond an intimate familiarity with the local taverns, which led to a dollar fine, he attended lectures on anatomy and physiology in the medical school. Perhaps this was the origin of Chillingworth's experiments and the physical effects of spiritual disease that he was to explore in *The Scarlet Letter*.

As he later wrote in his notebook: 'symbolize moral or spiritual disease by disease of the body; – thus, when a person committed any sin, it might cause a sore to appear on the body; – this to be wrought out.' Those last words have their fascination. Here he is again: 'A person to catch fireflies, and try to kindle his household fire with them. It would be symbolical of something.' First the symbol, then the meaning. Here was a man who worked backwards. Select a destination then identify how it might be reached and why. And if that seems to concede that meaning is arbitrary he had other evidence to hand that randomness may subsequently be seen as order in the making.

While at Bowdoin Hawthorne was a private in a military company commanded by a student one year ahead of him. A quarter of a century later that student ran for the presidency of the United States and Hawthorne wrote his old friend's campaign biography. The election of Franklin Pierce led to his sharing in the spoils, just as the election of another president led to the loss of his job in the Salem Custom House which in turn created the economic necessity from which *The Scarlet Letter* was born.

Nathaniel Hawthorne, not our Nathaniel but his father, kept a journal when he was at sea and in that journal are the scribbled writings of another Nathaniel already practising his skills. This Nathaniel, our Nathaniel, was born when his father was absent and since his death followed so swiftly on, perhaps the desertion of woman by man, wife by husband, was a theme laid down in his consciousness at an early age.

He began his fiction at Bowdoin. *Fanshawe* was a gothic romance which later caused him such embarrassment that he tried to gather back all copies, like Rachel searching for her children, though, unlike Rachel, he burned them all, along with stories of a similar gothic cast. Ashes to ashes. There was a yearning for the forms of the Europe which the family had left behind. The first Hawthorne, bereft of the 'w', left the family seat at Wigcastle in Wigton, Wiltshire, where Ws were in oversupply and as alliterative an origin as any writer could ever wish, and sailed for Massachusetts colony in 1635. Others said their home was Bray in Berkshire but whatever the truth he abandoned more than alliteration, like all others who sailed towards the evening sun. He abandoned moral sense, later ordering Anne Coleman and four Quaker friends to be whipped, with knotted lash, through the streets of Salem, Boston and Dedham. As Hawthorne later confided to his notebook: 'On being transported to strange scenes, we feel as if all were unreal. This is but the perception of the true unreality of earthly things, made evident by the want of congruity between ourselves and them. By and by we become mutually adapted, and the perception is lost.' In his work he sought to rediscover that strangeness which was lost. Why else look backwards in a country dedicated to the future? And the agency to unlock this sense of unreality? Why, a young woman of independent mind inserted back into the very beginnings of a republic dedicated to male endeavour: first true heroine of American fiction, first true confession of a nation's error.

Despite the burnt offering of his stories Hawthorne loved the perverse no less than Edgar Poe, who searched in darker corners and found it too soon to understand its true menace. He spoke for imperfection in a country which pursued the perfect without self-doubt. He, whose forebears had sat in a Salem court and watched the innocent shrivel when touched with suspicion, knew too well the price of purity. For how could there be innocence without guilt and so the brightest and the best swayed in the breeze eclipsed by the bright light of an ideal. Hunger for Eden starves us of those who would feed the spirit and satisfy the soul. So he wrote of a man who seeks to cut the birthmark from the face of beauty only to find that beauty's heartbeat ceases with the loss of such a shadow. His stories speak of beauty which breathes forth poison and a man who carries the plague within his clothes. 'Rappaccini's Daughter', as he jotted in his notebook, was based on a story of 'an Indian King, that sent unto Alexander a fair woman, fed with aconites and other poisons, with this intent, either by converse or copulation complexionally to destroy him'. Sexual intercourse as death! And where should he have found this but in *Pseudodoxia Epidemica*, by the Sir Thomas Browne who walked the twisting streets of Norwich.

No wonder Melville, who lived close by, thought that they were co-partners in a pact which smacked of the blasphemous if not the diabolic: 'I feel that the Godhead is broken up,' said Melville in a letter, 'like the bread at the Supper, and that we are the pieces . . . You were archangel enough to despise the imperfect body, and embrace the soul. Once you hugged the ugly Socrates because you saw the flame in the mouth and heard the rushing of the demon, – the familiar, – and recognized the sound; for you have heard it in your own solitudes.'

Who is to say that he had not? His wife and daughter may have celebrated his 'sunny' disposition but he had demons of his own. There were graves in Salem beside John Hathorne's. Would Melville have written thus to him if he had not detected a fellow-soul in torment: 'My dear Hawthorne . . . I am not mad . . . But truth is ever incoherent, and when the big hearts strike together, the concussion is a little stunning . . . Lord, when shall we be done growing? As long as we have anything more to do, we have done nothing . . . Leviathan is not the biggest fish; – I have heard of Krakens.'

Hawthorne had a daughter. Her name was Rose – a scarlet name, perhaps. When he was dead she wrote the story of his life as he, in a sense, had written hers by fathering her. No hint of scandal in her narrative, no deep shadows. By her account he might be kin to a Concord neighbour of theirs, once they had moved from the Salem he abhorred: Louisa May Alcott. But Rose dealt with the blood guilt of the Hawthornes in another way, meeting her Puritan ancestors on another ground. She became a bride of Christ, a Catholic nun, a living white cross prostrating herself on the grey stone floor of a cathedral, a sign signifying sin expiated, sacrifice canonized, sexuality surrendered. How could she hope to understand Hester?

Concord was never over-populated with nuns. She must have stood out like a scarlet rose in a town where white paper blew out of study windows bearing the thoughts of transcendantalists, the adventures of little women, the exploits of contemplatives and philosophers of nature's mysteries. Cheery Ralph Waldo Emerson lived down the road where he kept open house to Hawthorne's youngest daughter, Una, so that she treated it as her own. But there was a darkness even to this high priest of self-reliance who one day cleared aside his other papers and wrote: 'How long before our masquerade will end its noise . . . and we shall find it was a solitary performance? . . . Our relations to each other are oblique and casual . . . Nothing is left us now but death. We look to that with a grim satisfaction, saying, there at least is reality that will not dodge us . . . It is very unhappy but too late to be helped, the discovery we have made that we exist.' They were deep people these New Englanders. Some of them drowned in their own inner seas. Hawthorne sat in a bright house, a proper man, a teller of children's tales, a walker of familiar paths, a husband, father, moral guide, and set himself to tell a story in which he sent his characters to the very edge of meaning, to the point at which their souls might be forfeit, as too their lives. Yet with Melville he could say: 'I have written a wicked book, and feel spotless as the lamb.'

There was a darkness to Nathaniel Hawthorne's mind. He felt it himself and confessed it, too. His notebooks are full of ideas which seem to come from a tainted well: 'A series of strange, mysterious, dreadful events to occur, wholly destructive of a person's happiness . . . All the dead that have ever drowned in a certain lake to arise . . . symbolize moral and spiritual disease by disease of the body.' Writing of *The Scarlet Letter* he confessed, 'I found it impossible to relieve the shadows of the story with so much light as I would gladly have thrown in.' When he read it to his wife, 'it broke her heart'. Melville thought he saw a greater darkness still: 'We think that into no recorded mind has the intense feeling of the visible truth entered more deeply than into this man's. By visible truth, we mean the apprehension of the absolute condition of present things as they strike the eye of the man who fears them not, though they do their worst to him . . . He may perish; but so long as he exists he insists upon treating with all Powers upon an equal basis. . . . There is the grand truth about Nathaniel Hawthorne. He says NO! in thunder; but the Devil himself cannot make him say *yes*.'

Melville looks in Hawthorne's eyes and sees his own reflection there, for he fished in deeper seas than ever Hawthorne did, and yet his power and his integrity did rest in his willingness to slide a scalpel beneath the skin, to reach a hand through to the still-beating heart.

Sophia Hawthorne saw nothing of this except in the books. When he married her he married another poetry to his own. Thus, in December, 1842, she writes to a friend of skating on the river below their house at 'the dolphin time of day' on ice become 'transparent gold' and 'so prismatic . . . that the snow takes opaline hues'. She speaks of sliding, like children, in Sleepy Hollow and believes the man she loves only 'faintly shadowed' in his books, for to her he is 'the flash of a sword in the sun'.

So he was. The name on the cover of the books is no more the man who slides in Sleepy Hollow than is Chillingworth the man he purports to be. In his notebook he writes of an incident in which a friend tells of a girl he wished to marry having confessed to the loss of her chastity. Guilt sought relief in confession; love placed its faith in forgiveness. Then the writer in him takes over: 'Much might be made of such a scene – the lover's astoundment, at discovering so much more than he expected.' There is a final sentence, though, which shows how much, beyond his books, he was a product of his times: 'Mr Leach spoke to me as if one deviation from chastity might not be an altogether insuperable objection to making a girl his wife!!' Consider those two exclamation marks. They stand like the bars on the window of a cell. Clearly a single moment of passion placed her in a prison from which Hawthorne was disinclined to release her. What, then, of Hester? Was it Dimmesdale or Hawthorne who was one day to condemn her to her fate?

Nathaniel Hawthorne began work as an inspector in the Boston Custom House in January, 1840. The railroad between Salem and Boston had opened the previous August. It stretched, two silver threads, binding together two homes, two people. Hawthorne had transferred his affections from one Peabody sister to another, from Elizabeth, whom they thought to be the one he cared for, to Sophia. She lived at the other end of that silver thread and in her heart, at least, wound in that silver as a length of wool is circled into a ball.

It would be a mistake to imagine that the straight-backed world of New England was unacquainted with passion. 'We *are* married,' he wrote to her. Indeed, he felt they needed no 'external rite' to join them. Hester and Dimmesdale felt no less. Afraid that the world might misjudge them, they kept their secret and wrote to one another of the day they would sleep together. Many years later when those letters were readied for publication such words were carefully inked out. Nor was Sophia less passionate as later she wrote of the 'miraculous form' of the body, and of what 'a wondrous instrument it is for the purposes of the heart.'

Hawthorne worked in the Custom House where his duties were many and various. One day he found himself quelling a rebellion amongst shovellers aboard a coal vessel; another he worked in the hold of a salt-ship: 'the salt is white and pure – there is something holy in salt.'

He was, for a time, a weigher and gauger, and there is something in that of the writer. He watched as coal was shovelled into Custom House tubs, to be craned out of the hold and then wheeled in barrows to waiting wagons. Everything, he noted, was 'sable with coal dust'. His was a world of colour and its absence.

Those with business to do on the wharf gathered before a salamander stove in the wharfinger's office, where the agents of packets sailing to and from Boston met with inspectors and an occasional ship's captain. Here, stories were told of a human skeleton found without a head, of the ghost of a young boy, staring through the blank window, while at the wharf's end an old man, dressed in parti-coloured and patched clothes, hauls his line with an occasional plaice or sculpin on the hook. Things move slowly. Cotton bales are piled on the wharfside, their shadows moving with the inconsequence of an abandoned sundial. Barrels of molasses, casks of linseed oil are pressed against iron bars laid crossways by the weigher's scales.

At the head of the Long Wharf is an old sloop selling wooden ware from Hingham, occasionally displaced by sloops called *Betsey*, *Emma-Jane* and *Sarah*, named after women who are the lodestones for wandering hearts. Why not *Hester*, for he who walked around such vessels and felt the want of a woman's touch, the blessings of a voice to gentle the storm's alarm and the heart's necessities, might have begun to imagine a figure emerging from the sable black of a prison cell into the salt-white light of a Boston day.

From here long flat-boats carry the salt up the Merrimack canal to Concord in New Hampshire, a Concord without the blessing of transcendentalists imagining an oversoul. Here, the brig *Tiberius*, out of an English port, landed factory girls, pale, with translucent skin and sunken eyes, to travel the Worcester railroad along the valley. On the wharf the cry of 'Tally, sir' sounds out with every sixth tub or bale of cotton, while others sweeten water with a ladle of molasses and still others drive iron nails home with a hammer.

It was not a trade which lent itself to literature. He kept his notes, as a squirrel stores nuts and berries, but found less time and energy for books than he would wish. He left the wharf. Ahead lay marriage and new worlds. They moved to Concord, the true Concord where the salt which savoured their life was provided by Emerson and Thoreau, by Margaret Fuller and Melville. They lived in the Old Manse, built by Emerson and his home when he was writing 'Nature', an essay which made Thoreau his follower and friend. They walked in Sleepy Hollow. Necessity, however, drove him back into the customs business and in April, 1846, with political patronage, he became Surveyor of the Salem Custom House and returned to a town whose shadows he still feared.

The job lasted a bare three years until a new administration in Washington swept him away. His friends came to his aid. Henry Wadsworth Longfellow and James Russell Lowell, among others, put their hands into their pockets and sent him cash. He was used to making do, having sold the grass round his home for thirty dollars and cut his own bean-poles in the woods. They knew how to look after themselves, these New Englanders, and, besides, he had Thoreau for a neighbour who knew how many beans make five and how to turn them into twenty-five by the season's end. But he needed to write. The mortgage must be paid.

He opened his notebook and hunted for the buried nut. There he found a sentence, written many years before: 'The life of a woman, who, by the old colony law, was condemned always to wear the letter A sewed on her garment, in token of having committed adultery.' Hester was born; Hester began her walk to Calvary.

The figure of the strong woman both fascinated and alarmed him. He had Margaret Fuller for a neighbour and admired and disliked her in almost equal amounts. She was educated by her father as though she were a boy and that left a kind of mark on her sensibility. She was one of the transcendentalists and founded their magazine, *The Dial*, with Emerson. Then, in 1846 she went to Europe where she became the mistress of the Marquis Ossolo and bore him a son. They returned to America in May, 1850, five months after the publication of *The Scarlet Letter*. They were shipwrecked off the coast of America. The body of the young boy was the only one to make the shore. Power and vulnerability, the mind made vulnerable by the body's need.

He found something of the same in the colony's beginnings. Anne Hutchinson, invoked as saint in *The Scarlet Letter*, had in an earlier work been guilty of a 'carnal pride' while the freedom of conscience which she wished to claim was there acknowledged as a danger to true unity of faith. He recognized the tenuous hold which the colonists had on their New Jerusalem which could be so threatened by a woman's voice and still more, perhaps, by her sexuality. So, woman became the moral fulcrum and a tale of dangerous love a tale of social danger, too.

The story came quickly. He wrote nine hours a day. Yet he distrusted words, which could be 'a thick and darksome veil of mystery' between the soul and 'the truth for which it hungers'. He was parsimonious with words himself, not a natural conversationalist, silent more often than loquacious. He was at his most articulate in his writings, but even here he let symbols do their work. There was a shadow thrown by language, within which he walked. It could be lit only by images, as he tried to break the code of experience with nothing more than imagination and respect for the human heart. Eventually he could write no more and fell into a kind of silence until at last silence sealed his life and he lay where once he had slid in the snow, at a place called Sleepy Hollow.